The Doctor's Two Lives

OTHER BOOKS BY ELIZABETH SEIFERT

Young Doctor Galahad
(*Winner of $10,000 Prize*)
A Great Day
Thus Doctor Mallory
Hillbilly Doctor
Bright Scalpel
Army Doctor
Surgeon in Charge
A Certain Doctor French
Bright Banners
Girl Intern
Doctor Ellison's Decision
Doctor Woodward's Ambition
Orchard Hill
Old Doc
Dusty Spring
So Young, So Fair
Take Three Doctors
The Glass and the Trumpet
The Strange Loyalty of
    Dr. Carlisle
Hospital Zone
The Bright Coin
Homecoming
The Story of Andrea Fields
Miss Doctor
Doctor of Mercy
The Doctor Takes a Wife
The Doctor Disagrees
Lucinda Marries the Doctor
Doctor at the Crossroads

Marriage for Three
A Doctor in the Family
Challenge for Dr. Mays
A Doctor for Blue Jay Cove
A Call for Dr. Barton
Substitute Doctor
The Doctor's Husband
The New Doctor
Love Calls the Doctor
Home-Town Doctor
Doctor on Trial
When Doctors Marry
The Doctor's Bride
The Doctor Makes a Choice
Dr. Jeremy's Wife
The Honor of Dr. Shelton
The Doctor's Strange Secret
Legacy for a Doctor
Dr. Scott, Surgeon on Call
Katie's Young Doctor
A Doctor Comes to Bayard
Doctor Samaritan
Ordeal of Three Doctors
Hegerty, M.D.
Pay the Doctor
The Rival Doctors
Doctor with a Mission
To Wed a Doctor
The Doctor's Confession
Bachelor Doctor
For Love of a Doctor

The Doctor's Two Lives

By ELIZABETH SEIFERT

DODD, MEAD & COMPANY · NEW YORK

Library of Congress Catalog Card Number: 78-108045

Printed in the United States of America
by Vail-Ballou Press, Inc., Binghamton, N.Y.

The Doctor's Two Lives

1

"Dr. Fowler?"

The question voiced in that particular tone made him know that he had been sitting in his chair, and still "away" from the office, from his desk. He smiled at the young woman who stood, her arms filled with big envelopes, and waited for him to "come back." His habit of mental departure was rather well known at the Foundation.

"Yes, Miss Bryan?" he said apologetically.

"I am collecting the 10-B reports."

He pursed his lips in a soundless whistle and pushed things around on the well-filled desktop. He knew that he had the envelope ready. . . . Yes. There it was. All neatly labeled, the flap firmly secured. He gave it to the girl, who nodded and went away, to collect more envelopes, to—

Sam Fowler tipped his chair back, folded his hands behind his neck, and stretched every muscle of his young body. *Dr. Fowler,* he thought, repeating the tone of Bryan's voice. He remembered the first time he had been called *Doctor.* He wasn't one, then. And he knew it. But he had known he would be a doctor. Still a third-year student, admitted to the hospital wards to watch, to do small, unsavory jobs—scut work—to learn. And a patient had called him "Doctor." Sheer magic, the name had wrought.

The leaden years of studying, memorizing, agonizing, were, in that minute, changed into something valuable, precious. At that moment, never to be forgotten, Sam Fowler became a man full grown, able to face the years still ahead of him, but knowing that he would be a doctor, ready and able to serve the public.

The years had passed. Four years, five. He was a doctor. And now . . .

His hand went to his throat; there was no stethoscope. His fingers stroked the cloth of his coat. Brown tweed, not white duck, nor linen. He was still called "Doctor." Miss Bryan had spoken to him as one.

But just as the medical student had known that he had no right to the shining term, Sam Fowler now suspected that he had no right to use it. Then, there had been the future, and the hope. Now— He tipped his chair down, and his hand rearranged the papers on his desk. He touched, and picked up, the three-sided bit of wood which said, in gold letters on walnut, DR. SAMUEL L. FOWLER. L for Lyle.

He looked about him, at his office—a space semi-enclosed within glass walls to which there was no door and which did not reach to the ceiling. Through the walls one could look out and see the receptionist at her desk, the people who waited on the couch and in the chairs. Sam could see into the other offices, luxuriously carpeted and furnished, with outside window walls and indirect lighting, and men behind desks like his own. He could hear voices, not loud ones, but they added to the muted hum of the Foundation as a whole. People moved about. Quietly, because of the carpeting. Telephones rang; there wasn't a lot one could do about telephone bells. Some posh offices had chimes, some buzzed. Here at the Harper Foundation, they rang.

In the next room there were typewriters and more activity,

more noise. In Lorraine Harper's private office there was a deathly hush, like the parlor of an undertaking establishment.

Sam preferred his place in the organization. At least it was alive. Not frantic, but alive, and he had better get to work to see that the life continued.

For five minutes he dictated into the machine. Then he touched a button on his desk, and welcomed the gentleman sent in by the receptionist. This man was well dressed, almost painfully so. Shoes polished, hair trimmed, linen immaculate, cheeks close-shaven. He would be asking help of some kind.

He was. Intently, Dr. Fowler listened to him and asked intelligent questions—that was where the M.D. proved its worth. He made notes and spoke on the processes by which the Harper Foundation allotted its grants and awards.

The caller repeated that he was not from a big research center; there was, he said, this small group of dedicated men working as best they could—they did need some financial support. The prestige of a Harper grant would mean a great deal to them.

Sam assured him that his project, and his request, would receive attention. There would be a careful investigation. "That's what we do," he explained, rising and walking with his caller between the glass partitions to the front door.

There his visitor turned and looked at the tall young man. Red-brown hair, a pleasant, alert face—brown suit, white shirt, a woolen tie of small checks in two tones of brown. He nodded. "Do you have any say?" he asked.

Sam smiled. "I have some. It becomes a joint project. I do the investigative work."

"I see." The gentleman held out his hand, and Sam took it. His own clasp was firm and strong.

"You'll be hearing from us, Dr. Hauser," he said, as the man went through the door.

Favorably, I hope, he told himself. He hated, in cases like this, to know that there had to be some refusals.

He glanced at the receptionist. "Give me fifteen minutes, Betty," he said quietly as he passed her desk.

Back in his own office, he looked at his notes, at the papers which his caller had left behind, and he talked again into the recorder's microphone. It was important to get a live impression of this case quickly on tape. Sam believed in using the personal angle. One of these days someone would find a cure for atherosclerosis, and it well might be a small group of dedicated doctors working on their own.

The Foundation did investigations—Sam was the one, mainly, who did this—to find ways of helping scientists and medical workers develop their ideas. And it preferred to give its help where it was needed. Dr. Hauser was right. A Harper Award always sent an investigative team up in the world of research.

Sam made his tape and played it back, his eyes on his notes. He was always surprised at the tone of his own voice. He hoped he did not, really, sound that way, a little reedy, sometimes even squeaky.

Next he turned his attention to the case of some mid-western doctors who wanted to convert two floors of a hospital to the specialization of throat surgery. These men had already developed their techniques, and certainly one could not argue the value of performing such surgery without affecting the ability of a patient to speak. In Sam's own background was knowledge of a woman who had developed throat cancer, who had undergone a laryngectomy, with damage to her tongue and loss of her vocal cords. A widow, for the past thirty years she had lived alone, and very brave, unable to talk over the telephone, to call out for help, to hail a friend.
. . .

If these doctors were now doing such surgery without this tragic aftermath—and they were—they needed, and wanted, additional space wherein to care for additional patients.

4

But—

The Foundation rarely gave funds to any individual for medical care. It never, to Sam's knowledge, had given aid to the enlargement of projects already researched and developed. He would present this case. His job was to investigate ways to help scientists and medical workers. These men could use assistance and funds, and perhaps the organization, and Lorraine Harper, would look favorably upon their request.

The Foundation felt that their money was best spent in the support of research toward detecting the causes of physical ills, and furthering cures of those ills. Sam, personally, was always interested in the plea of a man such as the one who had just visited him. He was inclined to be kind to a group of doctors who needed more space in which to demonstrate the effectiveness of their techniques in throat surgery. But he was only one cog in the machinery by which the Foundation selected and allotted its awards and grants. His personal feelings were noted, and perhaps the three supporting organizations would agree with him.

Perhaps Lorraine Harper would smile upon Dr. Fowler's enthusiasms. She put up the cash, but there was an established precedence of her not individually making the awards.

Still, it was with the hope of Lorraine's smile that Sam Fowler worked. He would look into the matter of the throat surgeons' needs. He would investigate Dr. Hauser, who thought he was on the road to a break-through in the field of arterial hardening. He checked on locations and considered his next month's schedule with the thought of clearing a time for travel. . . .

And he thought about himself. Going about with a thin-line dispatch case in his hand rather than a medical bag, talking to doctors knowledgeably, but not really one with them in their work. His days preoccupied with other men's work, his spare time spent in writing a book . . .

A book not about the Foundation, directly or indirectly. A

book, a novel, developed from the experiences, memories and beliefs of the man who was Dr. Sam Fowler. A man who was a doctor, a man who had grown up wanting to be a doctor, and who became one—but who now wrote about doctors, and investigated doctors. . . .

While the book . . .

He looked out through the partitions to the other offices and the people in them. At the girl in the striped knitted dress, at the slightly overweight personnel man, at the elderly man who was the accountant. Had they ever written, or considered writing, a book? They didn't know that Sam had done so, and he couldn't be sure but what one of them had, that same morning, mailed a neat, flat package to a literary agent. Eighteen months ago, with the book written for the first time, Sam had met with an agent, and discussed his book. The agent, Wynburn Clark, had been interested. "Type it up and send it to me. I'll see what I can do for you."

So—Sam had gone over the book, and typed it. He had talked to Lorraine about it, a little. And to Carole, his fiancée, of course. Not to anyone else. This Clark had been interested in Dr. Fowler's position with the Foundation, and was somewhat disappointed to be told that the book did not deal with the work which Sam did there, nor with the Foundation at all.

Lorraine, too, would be disappointed. Knowing that he was working on a book—she had come to his apartment, and found his desk covered with stacks of typewritten manuscript, a typewriter, folders, and carbon paper, and—

"What on earth are you doing?" she had asked him. "Writing a book?" Her laughter said that the idea was preposterous.

"I thought everyone wrote a book," Sam had answered.

"Well, they think they *could.* May I read some of it?"

"When finished. It's not yet presentable."

She had accepted that. She did not take the book too seriously, though now and then she would mention the project to him. And he knew that she believed he was writing about the Foundation, although once he had told her that the undertaking was a novel, fiction.

"With me as heroine," she had asserted. It was at the time when Sam was beginning to wonder about himself and Lorraine. About her feeling and plans for the young doctor in her employ.

He had assured her that the whole book was fiction. Characters, setting—plot.

But she still assumed that she was the heroine. She didn't think it ever would be published, but she liked to think that a young man would write a book about her.

Sam, however, wanted publication. He had thought he could write a book which would be published. He had worked hard toward that end—planning the novel, writing it, and rewriting, doing the necessary research.

He dropped in his chair and reached for the telephone. He was glad he had made this legitimate gesture before Lorraine Harper came into view, to be seen by him, and able herself to see him. "I feel like a damned office boy," Sam said, putting the telephone down with the number half dialed.

He pulled a large pad of paper forward, picked up a pencil and began to write. Lorraine had stopped at another desk, but she was on her way to see him. He wrote *Hauser* on the pad, and then several numbers down the side of the page. Once he swiftly glanced upward to locate his boss.

Lorraine Harper was perhaps ten years older than Sam. She was a very rich woman, a rich widow. She had, while her husband still lived, collected art, and her home was decorated with paintings by Dali, Matisse, Picasso. Knowing Lorraine was to receive an education in modern art. Though lately, for ten years, her main interest had been the Foundation and its work.

Lorraine was a good-looking woman. Dark-haired, fresh-skinned, she wore simple dresses, with small, flower hats on the back of her head. Today her dress was of navy blue, and the flowers of her hat were in shades of rose.

She came swiftly into Sam's office and glanced over his shoulder before going on to the chair which faced his desk. So swift was she that he could no more than half rise. He always felt that knee-bent stance was ridiculous, and now his cheeks flushed to reaffirm his feeling.

"Who's Hauser?" Lorraine asked him.

"A man—a doctor. I interviewed him this morning."

"I suppose he is a person on fire? Did you tape the interview?"

"You know I never tape an interview."

"And *you* know I wish you would."

"It's no good, sweetheart. They freeze."

"All right, all right. What mess of the world is your Hauser ready to clean up?"

"He and some colleagues are working on causes for hardening of the arteries, as well as possible cures."

Lorraine smiled.

"Somebody will make a break-through."

"I truly hope so." She was sincere. "And he doesn't want money?"

"I didn't say that. But you know, the amount we give is of much less value than the prestige, the . . ."

"You liked this chap?"

Sam frowned. She knew he would weigh his words, so she waited.

"He is definitely a man on fire," he said seriously. It was a favorite term of hers.

"And you think we might fan the flame a little?"

"If an award would fan that particular flame, if we should be behind any important discovery in that field . . ."

"We could then enclose these offices in Lucite and consider ourselves a milestone. Or something."

She was arch, she was flippant. Sam must guard his face, and his tongue.

Lorraine Harper carefully chose the people who worked for the Foundation; she had carefully chosen Sam. But she liked to think that she herself pulled the strings, that *she* discovered the worth of the people to whom the Harper Awards were made. She presided triumphantly at the annual dinners where the recipients were gathered and given twenty-five hundred dollars, a certificate, and a small gold statuette of the god Mercury. The prestige attached to the award was of much, much more significance than the money or the statuette. The Harper Foundation carefully researched their awards; anyone singled out to receive one of them was assured of support in his project. The Harper Awards were most important.

Sam knew this; he was satisfied to think that he had his part in helping scientists develop important projects—and he did not care if Lorraine took, and received, all the credit. She wanted that credit and she did not always act favorably upon the personal enthusiasms of anyone in the organization. So, if Sam wanted Dr. Hauser to be recognized, he had better be technical and impersonal in his presentation of the man's case.

"I have a tape of the notes of my interview with Dr. Hauser," he said now. "And of another interview I conducted this morning."

"Fine," said Lorraine brightly, standing up. "We can't talk here in the office. Suppose you bring your tapes—these two new ones and that one you made of the woman doctor who thinks she has something new in birth control procedures—and we'll put in the week end at my place thrashing the whole thing out."

Lorraine's "place" was a beautiful, large estate in the wooded mountains south of the city. It offered every means of relaxation, exercise, peace or amusement—whatever a guest should happen to want. And yes, there one could "thrash out" almost any problem. Seated on the wide deck overlooking the lake, toasty before the great fire in the manorial living room . .

"Are you planning this conference full-scale?" Sam asked, stacking papers and looking down at them rather than at Lorraine. "I mean, could you get all three of the Co-ops at such short notice?"

The Co-ops—Mental Hygiene, Public Health, Planned Parenthood.

At last he glanced at Lorraine, and her color was up. "We wouldn't need them!" she cried quickly. "I think you and I together could clear away the driftwood. . . ."

Cozy dinners together, walks in the woods, sitting on the deep couch— On one such week end they had danced to the soft music of the hi-fi. There would be excellent food, a good drink, some talk—a lot of companionship. . . .

"But we could ask your Co-ops," Lorraine was saying, the syllables clipping short and quick. "If you think you'll need a chaperon?" Her eyes lifted to his face.

"I do," he assured her gravely. And he was rewarded by a sunny smile.

She probably knew, as well as did Sam and the men from the three co-operative agencies, that whatever they recommended or decided had to please Lorraine. Of course there must be interviews and investigations, study, discussion, elimination and reconsideration. But in the end, the final decision was always hers. If Sam had a pet project, and was clever, things well might be decided on one of her week ends. All this was known, and never, never mentioned.

"You gather your stuff together," she said to him. "We'll get a lot of work done. We'll go down to the place on Friday, work all day Saturday, and maybe even on Sunday—"

"I don't really have that much material," Sam told her.

"Perhaps after I investigate the two things that came in today—"

"We can discuss the field, broad scope. You have a half dozen other leads, don't you?"

He did have. But those half dozen had been talked about, exhaustively, before this.

"And if there is time left over," said Lorraine archly, "you could get some work done on your book. How is it coming along? Are you ever going to finish it?"

"I doubt if an author ever finishes a book, Lorraine."

She smiled at him. "Who told you that?" she asked brightly.

He managed to evade a reply. To do that, he even suggested lunch, but she was to address a woman's organization, and he escaped—gratefully. Lunch would have afforded further ways for him to say more than he should, to reveal himself. He was getting increasingly nervous about the book. Having committed the finality of sending the manuscript away, he was aware of a swarm of second thoughts about the matter. Was the book any good? Why should he think he could write one? Why had he chosen his subject as he did? Why would he treat it as he had done?

And now, watching the rose-flowered hat go out through the maze of office partitions, he asked himself how Lorraine was going to feel when—if—he sold the book and she found that she was not the heroine.

Had he ever said anything to make her believe . . . ? He didn't need to have said one word. Lorraine was agile at jumping to conclusions. She had decided that she must be the subject of any book he would write. What other woman was so important in his life? And when she learned the truth —to face the matter squarely, and put the question bluntly, would Sam Fowler have a job? It could be as simple as that.

He went out to lunch thinking of himself as going, hat in

hand, to clinic and office and other places, asking for work. "I once was with the Harper Foundation," he would say.

Maybe he should make a good thing of her week end. Maybe he should ask to have his manuscript returned to him. Maybe he should rewrite the book and put her in it. Maybe he should go back and be the doctor he so often thought he wanted to be.

2

That afternoon Sam went to the medical school library and did some reading; he then talked to a vascular man, and he took a laryngologist for a cocktail. In these ways, Dr. Fowler kept up with his profession. Better, perhaps, than if he were practicing. He had to know what was being done, which of the ideas that came to his desk would be needed, feasible, and possibly effective. Lorraine liked to have their awards given to some startling project. It was not always possible to startle the laymen, but when Sam could turn up such a beneficiary, his employer was pleased.

At seven he had a date to meet Carole for dinner. He had time to go to his apartment, shower and put on fresh clothing. The day had been a long one; his feeling for Carole demanded that he appear at his best. He looked forward yearningly to her beauty, to her calm, cool manner, her comforting response to him, as well as the excitement he always felt in being with her.

Carole, he often thought, was a side-by-side person. She wanted the man in her plans to have a life of his own, his own ideas and opinions. She herself wanted to have those things. If they—if she and Sam—could build a future together, with each contributing his, and her, share, that fu-

ture would please and hold Carole. He thought that she neither wanted to dominate nor to be dominated. He believed
that she would take her husband's hand, and walk with him,
proudly, joyously, two strong young people . . .

Since the woman was Carole, tall, blonde and beautiful—
volatile, clever and impatient—green-jealous of Lorraine—
Chuckling, Sam knew that he wanted everything Carole Tebeau wanted. He—

Putting on his watch, he noted the time and whistled. He
would be late if he missed one traffic signal.

He was late, and Carole was smiling about it when she
came toward him across the terrace of the roof-top restaurant. There were white flowers still blooming in the boxes
that marked the stone railing.

"They are to warn drunks and impetuous lovers," Carole
had once told Sam. "Not for beauty."

"I wouldn't have your analytical mind for anything!" he
had assured her.

"It goes with the package," she had answered.

Tonight—

Carole worked downtown, in a brokerage firm; it would
have been silly for her to go home just so Sam could pick her
up and bring her downtown again. So they met at the restaurant. Carole's smooth blonde hair, dressed in a small
chignon, her skin, her suit and accessories, were as fresh and
crisp as if she, too, had just showered and changed.

"I don't know how you do it," Sam told her, kissing her
cheek. Her jacket dress was of blue wool, plaided in a light
brown that exactly matched her gloves and round purse. Her
jewelry was a single strand of creamy pearls and a silver
bracelet. She must have looked well coming to work that
morning, performing her office duties all day; she looked
wonderful as she walked beside Sam into the restaurant, as-
suring him that she was starved. "I do hope they have
chops."

Sam ordered a drink for her, and clam juice for himself,

confessing that he had had a business cocktail after five. "I'll get some wine with your pork chops," he promised.

"I didn't say . . ." she protested, then laughed and wrinkled her small, perfect nose at him.

The city lights were blooming through the mists of evening; the river curled its tarnished ribbon below them; an incoming plane roared past the tower, its lights blinking red and green. . . .

For twenty minutes they talked about little or nothing. About a friend, about some amusing happening at Carole's office, about the new parking facilities at the recently enlarged airport. "They are going to have helicopters to take you to and from the main building," Sam said seriously.

Acquaintances came in and talked to Sam and Carole for ten minutes; the gypsy musicians approached their table, and went away again.

They ordered dinner—there were chops available—mutton chops. "Be sure they are well done," Carole told the waiter. "I am not fond of pink sheep."

"Mutton, madame," he corrected her reprovingly, and departed on their ripple of laughter.

Sam stretched his hand across the small table, and took Carole's fingers into its warmth. They gazed out of the window and said nothing for minutes.

"What happened today?" Carole asked then.

Sam's grasp tightened. "I had bean soup for lunch," he began.

"Who came in?" In the glow of the candle, her smile was gentle.

"Well, as a matter of fact, two applicators." This was an inside joke at the Foundation; Carole knew about it.

"Possible?"

"One man was. I hope."

"He must have a good thing, or be a persuasive personality."

Sam smiled and nodded. "He has a good thing," he said.

"He is earnest and proud. He brushed up his old coat, polished his shoes, and met me with dignity."

Carole leaned toward him. "I love you, Sam," she said softly.

He could feel the glow spread, warming him. "I'll answer that later," he told her. "Now, your sheep chops would get cold."

"And that's the last thing I want!" she agreed, laughing merrily. "Tell me more about your applicator."

So he told her about Dr. Hauser. "I'll handle this with kid gloves," he concluded.

"Can't you make Harper feel it's one of her enthusiasms?"

She seldom had met Lorraine, but she knew her quite well. "I'll handle it," Sam said again.

"Will this mean travel?"

"Most investigations do. Maybe you would come along?"

She nodded, smiling. "That would really be handling it," she agreed. "Besides, we can't afford non-expense-account trips."

"I'm doing all right. And you'd ride half-fare."

"The airlines have expansive policies?"

"I'm proposing, sweetheart. Again."

She flipped her hand. "Not at all necessary."

"I'm proposing that we conclude the contract."

"Get married," she interpreted. "That would deflect Harper's attention from your applicator, all right."

"You worry too much about Lorraine."

Carole considered the charge. "Do I?" she asked with simple curiosity. "Should I consider why?"

"Perhaps you are going to be jealous of all my bosses." He watched her face.

"A lot of bosses," she said musingly. "That doesn't sound too much like stability."

"But if . . ."

She lifted her eyes to his face. "I know what you will say next," she assured him. "That I had better decide you have a good job, that you seem to be earning enough—all of which is true. But I don't like your boss, Sam. As for not liking any of your bosses, I would agree to your moving about, if you would better yourself. As of course you should do. And in doing that, perhaps you won't have another boss who is rich, a stunning dresser, and clever."

Sam leaned back and pursed his lips. "I've known some men who would fall under those headings, and I don't believe you would be jealous of them."

She laughed, somewhat ruefully.

"I claim a woman's rights," she admitted. "But it's true. Your boss's being a woman does make a difference in the way I feel."

"I sometimes wonder if I should be jealous of *your* boss."

"Mr. Syberg?" Carole asked in surprise. "He never *bosses,* as such, you know. And the only vehement opinion I can remember his ever expressing had—has—to do with people who say 'bye-bye' on the telephone."

Sam laughed. "Eat your sheep bone," he told her. "And tell me what happened on your day."

She regarded the remains of her chop. "The market closed . . ." she began, glancing at him mischievously.

"Sometime," he promised, "I am going to let you tell me how the market closed, the Dow Jones thing, the Standard and Poor thing—the works. Then I am going to check on you in the next morning's newspaper."

"I'm safe enough there," she told him. "Sam, darling, I want chocolate ice cream with mint sauce for dessert, and do you think, this week end, we could spend both Saturday and Sunday leisurely . . . ?"

When she glanced at him, he was shaking his head.

"No?" she asked. "But I haven't told you—"

"And *I* haven't told *you,* but the truth is, Lorraine has tied me up for this week end."

"Oh, no!" she whispered the protest.

"I'm afraid so, my darling."

"At her place? I wish it would slide into its precious lake. I wish—"

"Not this week end, darling. I'd go with it."

"Today is only Wednesday. Things could happen tomorrow. What does she have in mind?"

"Reevaluation of our prospects, I think she would say."

"I'll bet she would. I hear our salesmen make the same sort of arrangement. They talk about 'going over your list.' "

Sam laughed.

But Carole was not inclined to be amused. "Don't order me any dessert," she said coldly.

"Oh, now, let's not spoil this evening."

She nodded. "I suppose I shouldn't. But that woman—"

"That woman, as I have quite recently explained to you, is my boss. And it is my job, sweetheart, to work with her as well as for her. If she wants me to work overtime, and to do that work in the beam-ceilinged living room of her mountain retreat, if she wants to send me to the wilds of Maine, or Florida, or Utah, or California, I have to do that work where she wants me to do it."

"And enjoy it?" Her tone was cool, her face was cool, but her eyes were distressed and anxious.

"Sometimes I enjoy it," Sam said quietly. "Oh, my dear, I know this is hard on you, and will be. But marrying any doctor is always a hazard. He—"

She stretched out her hand to him. "I know all that, dear," she told him. "I am prepared to make noble sacrifices. But, just now, I would like one thing. And that is to be told what part I play in your life."

Sam smiled at her. "It is a very big part," he assured her. "You come first, always. And will do so. This week end—If you'd really ask me not to go with Lorraine to the mountains, I would not go."

"And be out of a job by special messenger on Monday morning," said Carole wryly.

"I could be," Sam agreed. "And a job is an essential part of a man's life. For me it is essential to the part I want to play in your life. As well as the part I want you to play. I cannot ask you to marry me, I cannot establish a home . . ."

"You are talking to me like a child," Carole told him. "I know that you must work, and I want to help you do that work. But just now—"

"Just now you don't want me to spend this week end working."

She nodded, and laughed a little. "I am not really convinced it will be work," she said. "As things are set up."

"I'll tell you what," he offered. "Marry me, and you can go, too."

She stared at him. Then she leaned toward him. "We could do it," she agreed. "Maybe not by this week end, but certainly before the next. And the minute we were married, if we were married, you, dear Dr. Samuel Fowler, would no longer have a job to support your blushing bride. You would no longer be working for La Lorraine."

"Nonsense!"

"I am not going to put it to the test, my dear."

"Oh, now, look . . ." He broke off to order their dessert. The chocolate ice cream for Carole, pot cheese and crackers for himself. Then, his eyes on the waiter's departing back, he returned to his argument. "You are being foolish," he told her. "You are beautiful tonight, and most unreasonable. You are . . ."

"And you know I also am dead right," she challenged.

He laughed. "Well," he conceded, "I suspect you may be right."

"What are you going to do about it?"

"What do you do when some guy in your firm decides he wants to see more of you?"

She stared at him. "Do you want a serious answer to that?"

"Of course. In case I need help in handling my situation."

"Well— And you do need help, my boy. You do need it. Lorraine . . . But you asked me what I do. And I can tell you that I play things cool, Buster. I play them *very* cool!"

"But, Carole . . ."

"I am well aware of the differences." She spoke tensely. "A woman on the prowl presents a different problem. She . . ."

He put both of his hands on hers. "Stop it," he said. "You're verging on hysteria."

"Oh, I am not!"

His eyebrow lifted.

"I had plans for our week end," she told him.

"And I am sorry we cannot follow them. I know I would like doing the things you had planned better than I shall . . ."

"You may not have enjoyed them more," she said reasonably, welcoming the silver dish of chocolate ice cream, its mound rising richly above the green sea of mint sauce. She tasted the confection. "Mmmmmn, good."

"First score I've made all evening."

"Oh, no, dear. I liked my sheep chop. That's hard to say, you know?"

He chuckled.

"And even if you wouldn't want to do the things I had planned for us," she continued, "you should be spending your free time on your book. You have a right to your freedom, to expend your leisure on your own interests."

Sam listened. He ate a toasted cracker spread with cheese and decided he would not tell Carole that he had submitted the book. Once she knew that, she would give him no rest. He knew that he would not get a report on the book for days, that even if it pleased the agent, it would take time to let a publisher read it. Publishers.

Carole was a fine person; she worked hard and intelligently at her job. She liked that job, too, and the independence it gave her. But lately her main passion, her main ambition, had turned to a concentration on her life and Sam's, the life they would lead together. She wanted Sam to feel that concentration, too. And of course he did, but . . .

She was telling him, "I thought this week end we would explore the suburbs and try to find a possible house. Maybe two or three of them. At least we could select neighborhoods. Maybe we could even have looked at the new apartments they are building here downtown. I understand they are marvels of comfort and beauty."

"It sounds wonderful," he told her.

"But this week end belongs to Lorraine."

"I'm afraid so. And I suspect you are right. My job well may depend on my doing what Mrs. Harper wants me to do."

"You don't like that, do you, Sam?"

"No. No, I don't."

"Then, do you know what I think? I think you need a new job. That's what I would decide if I'd turn up a boss bent on seduction."

Sam laughed. "There's that hysteria again."

"It's time somebody got hysterical. And I think a new job could be the answer for you, Sam. For us." She was apparently taken with her idea. "Yes!" she cried. "You're to look for a new job, a better job, and one without a Lorraine Harper attached to it. That is exactly what you need, Sam."

"You're sure."

"Of course I'm sure. You think about it, and act upon it. You'll see. You'll like it better."

"You make it sound so easy."

"Not easy, maybe, but I know you could do it. Will you try?"

"I always try to please you, Carole. But for the present, there's this job, and the week end down at the place . . ."

"You'll be back in time, won't you, for our usual Sunday evening at Don and JoAnn's?"

"Oh, I surely will be. I take it, you want to go out there?"

"Well, of course. Don't we always go?"

Yes, they did. Or almost always.

"They are nice people. I envy them."

So did Sam. He took out his wallet for money. He was thinking about their friends, Don and JoAnn Chaffine. Their home—Don's work as a busy pediatrician. Their children. The Chaffines' life was one he would like to live. A house, kids—medicine.

3

Sam made it to the Chaffines' on Sunday in time to help Don solve the problem of a smoking fireplace, to help Peter, eight, build a bridge with his Erector set, and for Carole to announce to their friends that Sam was going to get himself another job.

They looked surprised.

"It's her wishful thinking," Sam told them "Carole doesn't like the environment of my present employment."

So they all considered the matter as a joke. Don made offers. He could use a really good yardman, he said. And the technician in the offices and lab he shared with four other men simply did not know how to clean pipettes. As for test tubes . . .

They joked, but over the week end Sam had thought seriously about Carole's suggestion—he even began calling it a solution. On Tuesday morning Don called him for lunch.

"I've a line on that new job," he said over the phone.

"Carole's new job?"

"Yes."

"I don't think she'd make a really good yardman."

"Can't we talk about it over liver and onions?"

"I can talk about anything over liver and onions."

"Good! Twelve-thirty?"

Sam and Don had attended medical school together; together they had sweated through internship and their first residency, short of funds, overloaded with work. When they could afford it, they had promised each other, they would belong to the Professional Club, and eat lunch there together in luxury.

Among other dreams and ambitions, this one had been realized by the two young doctors; there had been times when neither could really afford to belong, or use the Club, but they persisted. And today they need not say where they would meet. Don came into the Club, a little breathless, the collar of his raincoat awry.

"Get measles and squeezles all morning," he told Sam. "And at eleven fifty-five, what comes in?"

"Let me guess."

"You wouldn't in a million years. Who else has a patient who would swallow a string of pearls?"

"Good Lord, Don!"

"Yes. I used His help, too."

"What did you do?"

"Looked at the kid. I took X-rays, I sent him to the hospital for further observation. I'll go over there from here."

"Is he . . . ?"

"The mother's in distress. The kid was a bit choked up at first, but the thing went on down. Of course the mother can't wear the beads for a day or two."

"Now, really!" Sam protested.

"You think that didn't come into discussion?"

They ordered their lunch, and talked a little about the weather, which was rainy. Their soup came, and they began to eat, hungrily. For two minutes they talked to a friend. When he went on to his own table, Don squared around and leaned toward Sam.

"How serious were you on Sunday night about wanting another job?" he asked.

Sam shook his head a little. "Lorraine Harper sometimes complicates things for Carole and me. This past week I had to go down to her place and talk business."

"And your girl thinks you should get out from under the Big Thumb."

Sam smiled. "Something like that. And occasionally I feel she's right."

"She is. Though you've done a good job at Harper's."

"And liked it."

"Have you, Sam? Really?"

"Well, sure. I take a lot of personal credit for any research project we have encouraged."

"Fair enough. But do you like bird-dogging these projects better than practicing medicine?"

Sam considered this question. He frowned about it, and squinted his red-brown eyes. "I have to think back . . ."

"You're a good doctor, son."

"Medicine has become a rather complicated field, old man."

"Yes, it has."

Their plates of fragrant liver and onions arrived sizzling hot, and were given immediate attention. This was a Tuesday specialty at the Club, and popular. "Think of all the cloves, Clorets and Listerine due to be consumed," Don chuckled.

"And the patients smell the disguise and decide the doctor's been at the bottle again."

"A lot of doctors and a lot of bottles," Don agreed, looking around the well-filled room. "Now listen, Sam—"

"What do you think I'm doing? Three feet away from your horn—if I lean back."

"All right, all right. And I have to get over to the hospital. But I ran across this lead yesterday, and if you are serious about making a change, this well might be a better job for you."

"What have you got?"

"A better job. These people want a doctor—or at least someone who knows his way about the profession, hospitals and stuff—and they want someone who can write. So I tell myself, that has to be you, Sam."

Sam grinned. "Did you get any back talk on that?"

"Now, listen. . . ."

"You're repeating yourself. So let's hear about your job."

"I think Carole has a point, you know."

"She's jealous."

"Of course she's jealous. With a dame like Lorraine Harper in love with you?"

"I'd better not talk about that, Don. Lorraine isn't ever going to take Carole's place."

"But she is in love with you?"

Sam said nothing. Yes, Lorraine was in love with him. She had said so, this past Saturday night. Pretending to be whimsical, rueful—but she was in love with him. And a different job was the best next step Sam could think of.

"I'm not a devastating man," he told Dr. Chaffine.

"No, you're not," Don agreed readily, with the frankness of old friendship, tried and true. "But you're a good guy, honest and dependable. They don't make many of them no more, Sammy boy. And we can count on Lorraine to know that."

"Mhmmmn. Tell me about the job opening. Details, please, doctor? Pertinent ones, by choice."

Don grinned. He was a good friend, a tall, rangy man; his hair line was beginning to slide back on his head. . . . "You've heard of Hospital Administrators, Inc.?" he asked.

Sam's eyes widened, then narrowed. He pursed his lips. "Robins, huh?"

"The man's a living wizard, Fowler."

"So I've heard. A one-man corporation. A big one, with all the personnel his stooges. That's what I hear."

"Oh, now, wait up, Sam!" Don protested. "That's no way

to approach this thing. Anyone as successful as Robins is bound to have his detractors. He's a genius, perhaps. He works very hard, and he works his staff that way, too. Do you have any objection to work?"

"Not if the purpose and pay is good."

"I think it could be. I think this could be a very good thing for you."

"A Robins puppet instead of a Harper one. That the idea?"

"Are you a Harper puppet?"

"A lot of people probably think so."

"I know you better."

"Thanks." Sam poured fresh coffee into their cups, and glanced at his watch. "Is there really an opening?" he asked.

"I understand there is. Lately there's been a still-underground swell of asking and feeling about. The thing first came to my notice last week. Yesterday I looked into the matter particularly. Because, you remember, you came to our house on Sunday sounding a little more than sour on Harper."

"I was late, too." Sam had been, and he had not wanted to be.

"Yes, you came in late. Carole was in a fume about it."

"She was," Sam agreed.

He had called Carole before he left Lorraine's mountain retreat. He would be late, he said; Carole had better go on to the Chaffines', help cook supper—he would go directly there, saving him the drive into the city and back.

She had protested. They would have two cars to contend with—unless of course Mrs. Harper was driving him?

He had suggested that he not go to the Chaffines' at all. "If you are going to be cross . . ."

"I shall be. I am now, and it doesn't seem that the mood would wear off."

But of course he had gone, and he had tried to conciliate

Carole. He agreed that his "free time" should be his. He agreed that Carole's demands on him were legitimate. He thought they would be much more pleasant to fulfill.

"Tell me more about this Robins job," he now said gruffly. "Do you know the man?"

"Who? Me?" asked young Dr. Chaffine. "I'm just barely on a couple of hospital staffs."

"I think I could be an administrator," said Sam thoughtfully.

"You could be one hell of a practicing doctor, too. But at least you know what Robins does. Organizes, administrates . . ."

"That's no word."

"It is for me. I'm not a writer."

Sam laughed. "You said they wanted one . . ."

"Someone who knows the medical field and can write. Yes."

"Public relations?"

"Perhaps. You know what the firm does. Everything from setting up new hospitals to getting old ones into modern running order. They are trouble-shooters for hospitals; they are specialists in the administrative organization of the same— You must have read about Robins. Have you ever seen him?"

"I think I have. I know he lectures and makes appearances at medical convocations."

"He does. He's a good speaker."

"Would he want me to write his speeches?"

"I don't know what he wants. I'm just trying to fill in the picture. Do you want hot gingerbread or lemon pie?"

"Okay," said Sam.

Don threw him an exasperated glance and ordered the gingerbread.

"Robins does all sorts of things," he continued. "His name

crops up everywhere. He lectures to medical students on hospital administration. He plans hospitals, big, little, and in between. Architects consult him, and when he is given a hospital to organize, I understand he does a bit more than consult with the architects. One of his pet peeves seems to be the serving of cold meals to patients. He sets up new organizations in old hospitals, and corrects faults. He heads a big business, Sam, and he has been successful."

"I know it," Sam agreed.

"And if you are ready to make a change . . ."

"I'll have to think about that, too," Sam said, eating his gingerbread.

Don pushed a card across the table. "This is the man to ask for if you go to Robins," he said softly.

"Have you spoken about me?" Sam asked in some alarm. Medicine was a gossipy business. Should Lorraine guess . . .

"I told you there was some recruiting. I said I was interested. I was given this card. In case I—not you—wanted to look into the matter."

Sam put the card into his wallet. "Thank you, Don," he said warmly. "But please don't talk about this to Carole."

"I haven't even mentioned it to JoAnn." Women had their place in a doctor's life. That place was not, ideally, professional.

Walking back to the Foundation offices, Sam did some heavy thinking. About Don, his good friend. About Carole, and the opportunity which seemed to be open for someone with Robins. This led him to think about the job which he had with the Harper Foundation, and so, inevitably, he must think about Lorraine.

A clever woman; she had done great things for the medical profession. And Sam had done good work for her. His own ability and reputation had built up to his credit while he had been with the Foundation. He was paid a good salary for the work which he did; he lived well, and easily could plan a good future.

Not that his plans for that future were the same as Lorraine's. The past week end had been more than a little sticky. Now, against his will, he thought again about that experience. He thought about his arrival at her mountain home on Friday night—the hospitality, the comfort. . . . Heck, it was pure luxury!

Saturday morning he had taken a walk around the lake. That afternoon he had done some real work with Lorraine, discussing projects in hand, planning the investigations which he would make, even the presentation of the projects that might be given awards.

By dinnertime he was tired and he would have thought Lorraine would be. He asked if guests were expected.

No, they would dine alone. He need not dress. . . .

Dinner was served, intimately, before the fire in the huge living room. Shadows danced on the linenfold paneling, touched the colors of the paintings on the walls. He remembered the glow of the fire upon the curve of a certain great amethyst glass jar.

The meal was delicious, the wine excellent, as was the brandy served with the coffee. He had said something whimsical about being able to grow accustomed to beef tenderloin and "brandy like this."

And, given the small opening, Lorraine had moved in. He could become accustomed to many things, she said. He fitted graciously into that way of life. His fine mind, his attractive person were assets to him, and would be to the woman whom he allowed to share his life.

She spoke of her own wealth, about the "few years" she had to count above his own. She felt like the Queen, she said, forced to speak herself and not wait on the male creature's instinct to woo, and win.

She had made a good job of her own proposition and Sam Fowler had found himself faced with a real problem. He was not a conceited man; he must feel that Lorraine had not succumbed to overwhelming passion, but rather was selecting a male companion whom she felt would be an asset. A pleasure, too, perhaps, but—

She was not suggesting an affair, either. Not that the difference was of great importance. Affair, or marriage, Sam wanted to pick his own woman, to marry her, and not be married by one. Anyone.

Besides, he loved Carole Tebeau. He had picked her, courted her, and wanted to marry her. He had given her a ring which she had accepted, and wore.

He supposed she was still wearing it. She had had it on Sunday. But she had not been pleased with him on Sunday, and for less reason, before this, she had taken off the ring, and suggested that they call quits on their relationship. She could do that again. Sam could not entirely blame her. He should try to please her. What he really wanted in his life were the things which Carole could give him, and pleasing her should be of first importance to him.

As for Lorraine—there, too, he must make, or take, a definitive stand. He had given her no answer on Saturday night, nor on Sunday when, again, they had done some work. Friends had come in at noon; there had been no further opportunity to talk of personal matters. But soon—very soon—he must say yea, or nay. And to say nay . . .

He went into the building, and up to his office and desk. He drew his typewriter toward him, selected plain stationery, and on impulse he wrote a letter to Hospital Administrators, using the name on the card which Don had given him.

In his letter he asked for an interview concerning the position which he had been told was open. Briefly he stated his qualifications, his M.D., and the position which he now held.

He addressed the envelope, stamped it, carried it to the elevator, then down to the lobby and deposited it in the mailbox beside the doors. He turned away and went back toward the elevators, feeling a load dropped from his shoulders, the lift of hope in his heart.

He had not guessed how unhappy and uneasy he had become at the Foundation.

Now he could leave, now he would leave. . . .

Provided Hospital Administrators did want a man, provided they wanted a man who would ask for a job, not wait to be sought out and interviewed.

He spent the afternoon vacillating between hope and no hope. He had made no carbon of his letter, so he began to wonder what he had said in it, what words he had used, how he had phrased things.

He spent the next day waiting, and wondering.

On Wednesday, Lorraine came back to the office, and Sam was relieved that such contact as he had with her could be on a friendly, businesslike basis. He debated whether he should tell her what he had done. And decided that he would wait until he got a reply to his letter, or at least until he returned from the trip which he had to make to look into Dr. Hauser and his affairs.

On Wednesday night he took Carole to dinner, as had become rather a custom with them; she was her usual cool, and lovely, self, good company, ready to talk on any subject he chose, ready to dance if he liked, or go back to her apartment for a restful, happy hour. He mentioned the trip, saying that he would leave the next afternoon.

And he debated whether he should tell Carole of his application. He decided against it, because, as with the book's submission, she would become entirely too fired-up. Time enough to talk about those things when he had something definite to report. In the case of the job, that time might never come.

No mention was made of Lorraine, and he was grateful

for Carole's restraint. Things would be easier for her if he did get the new job. Robins as a boss might have his angles, but the occasion for feminine jealousy would scarcely be one of them.

The next day Sam started on his trip and put in a busy two days, able to lose himself and his self-concern in his exploration of this other man's work, his environment, his colleagues, the man himself. On Saturday he started home, convinced that he liked Dr. Hauser personally, that his work had great promise, and that Sam wished he had traveled paths such as these, of work, intense research, and now possible fulfillment of his dreams.

Sam was in a position to help this worthy man, and that made good the work which he did for the Foundation. He could wish that the work were all of it.

He wished Lorraine had not presented him with problems which she must recognize, which he certainly did, and which, he felt sure, the organization itself recognized. Others probably awaited the solution of those problems as eagerly as did Sam.

Really, the woman had put him—or he had put himself—into an untenable position. Now his only chance for advancement would be on a basis which he could not contemplate with any calm. He wished he could have returned to the city on Friday when he might have gone to the office, made his oral report, promising a detailed one, and able to tell Lorraine. . . .

He sat up straight in the plane seat. But he couldn't do that! He could not tell Lorraine before he told Carole. Even if he never got the job with Hospital Administrators. . . .

Carole was going to meet him, and he was glad because he could tell her what he had done, and they could talk about it, and make new plans. She would be relieved to think he was ready to leave the Foundation, though she probably would not mention Lorraine's name.

Carole did meet him, bundled into a woolly gray coat, its

collar pulled up behind her head. The wind was cold, she told him, accepting his kiss, and patting his arm. His car was parked; she had come to the airport in a cab so that they could go back together. Could they go straight to her apartment? she asked. She had plans to cook dinner.

He smiled at her. "It sounds fine."

"I'm not a very good cook."

"I'll take my chances."

"And if the meal is a complete fiasco, we can go out."

"I'll see that the fiasco isn't on the menu. . . ."

Sam was a good cook; the tiny kitchen in Carole's apartment would scarcely admit them both, but they had fun. And the meal turned out well enough. "I think there is more smooch than sauce," she told him pertly, her color rising.

"If there is one thing I enjoy it is smooched ribs," Sam assured her.

"We should be too mature . . ."

"Look. *You* may be mature. *I* am still a very young doctor. My man Hauser told me as much when I was in Detroit."

"Did things go well?"

"Very well indeed. I think I can be sure he will get some Foundation money, if not an award. That is, he will if I don't blow the bit when I make my report."

"Oh, I can't imagine your doing that."

"It is going to take planning." He paused, thoughtful, holding a rib bone between his hands. "You see . . ." His eyes searched her face. And he went on to tell her of his application to Hospital Administrators. "I knew you were not happy with the environment of my present employment," he said wryly.

"Oh, Sam, I'm sorry!"

"I thought you'd be pleased."

She shook her head, and waved her hand as if to rid the air of any suggestion . . ." I *am* pleased," she said warmly. "But I don't want to be a bossy woman."

"You won't be. I'd take steps."

She laughed. "What kind?"

"I'd take 'em. Want some more biscuits?"

"Yes. Then tell me all about this business, concern, or whatever it is. What does it do? And what will you do?"

He fetched the hot biscuits. One for her, two for himself, and a jar of strawberry jam.

"With candles, don't you think we need a dish for that?" Carole asked him.

"With biscuits, I want jam."

"We are being silly."

"It is Saturday. And I am happy to be home, where I can eat jam out of a jar, take off my coat—"

"And tell me about your new job."

"Oh, Carole, Carole."

"You'll get it. So tell me about it."

He leaned back, and he told her about Hospital Administrators in general. In doing that he also gave her a thumbnail sketch of Patric Robins. Dr. Patric Robins, with no *k* and only one *b*. A trouble-shooter of the first magnitude.

"You'll be wonderful working with a man of that sort!" Carole told him

"I'd work *for* him, sweet nut."

"Oh, I know you, Dr. Fowler. Just what would you do? Where are the offices? Would you stay in them and direct, or go out in the field? Would you—?"

"Hey, hey!" he cried. "Hold it. I don't know what I'd do. I gave you a picture of the firm and its activities. I heard they needed a man who could write. . . ."

"Which you can do."

"We don't know about that, either. And certainly I've never administered anything. In fact, I don't believe I have any qualifications. I don't think I'd hire me."

She would not listen to that sort of talk. Clearing the table, washing up the dishes, she talked excitedly about this promised change, about Sam's prospects—as Sam had known she would do. Carole had an exaggerated idea of him and his talents, which was flattering, of course, but—

When everything was shipshape in the kitchen, they went back to the living room and the couch which faced the big window. Only a lamp in the far corner was lighted and in the shadowy room they could sit, watch the lights of the city, and talk.

"I think you have every qualification," Carole decided.

"I'll refer Robins to you for that information," Sam teased.

"But, Sam, you have! Look." She turned to face him, drawing her pretty legs up under her. He leaned against the cushions and smiled at her. "You've done plenty of investigations," Carole reminded him. "All sorts. People, medical work—"

"But not hospitals."

"You could extend your activities. You know about hospitals."

He shrugged. "A little," he conceded.

"All right. You could investigate them, and make your reports. Write. That's the important thing! You can write, whether it's a report, or—Look! You've even written a book!"

Sam sat thoughtful. "An unpublished book," he agreed, speaking slowly. "Which may be more of a liability than an asset."

She put her hand to his lips, to silence him. He took her fingers into his own hand and sat holding them, stroking them with his thumb. "I do believe," he told her, "that we should wait to see if my book sells, or not, to endeavor to make my writing an asset. We'll know more about the situation then. . . ."

"But you write things for the Foundation, don't you? Reports and stuff?"

"Stuff," he agreed, chuckling. "Yes, I do write that sort of thing. And in venturing to make an application . . ."

"When did you make it?" she asked keenly.

"Oh—Wednesday, I think. No, Tuesday. Because that's the day for liver and onions, and—"

She moved closer and laid her head on his shoulder. "You're tired," she comforted him. "You're not making sense. But you'll be hearing from them, very soon."

He did hear, and very soon. When he went to his office on Monday, thinking about the reports which he must assemble and get set down on the Hauser case, he almost indifferently sifted through the mail on his desk. And there it was. The long envelope with the return address—embossed—his name very correctly done in crisp, handsome type. He sat staring at it. He held it in one hand while he sorted through the rest of the mail. First class, pamphlets, clipping service, magazines. Nothing directly addressed to him was ever opened. It had better not be! There were a couple of opened envelopes, marked with memos, "Attention Dr. Fowler." The corner of one of these envelopes was slashed with Lorraine's angular writing and the red ink which she liked to use. "Fowler—interesting."

He glanced at that letter. Yes, it was interesting. Was Lorraine in the office? Not this early, usually. . . .

He reached for his long brass letter opener and slit the envelope from Hospital Administrators.

He turned his chair to face the window; he drew out, and read, the letter which was a reply to his own. He read it through, and he read it again. He folded it and tapped one corner of it against his knee.

The answer had come quickly; they must have answered at once, considering the dates. The letter had been on his desk since Thursday afternoon, perhaps. Certainly since Friday. Had Lorraine seen it? How much inter-office investigating did she do? She would feel privileged. Besides, she had assumed an especially proprietary manner with Sam; this was part of his discontent. If she had brought her "interesting" letter to his desk, she well might . . .

Slowly, thoughtfully, he unfolded the page again and read

the letter for the third time. In the glass of the big window, he could see himself as he sat there in the curved-arm chair, holding the white letter in both hands, reading it intently. An important letter, obviously.

He turned the chair around in time to see Lorraine's lavender-flowered hat, her pearls and dark gray dress, coming toward his office. He tipped forward and slipped the letter under his desk blotter, then he picked up the red-inked memo just in time to look up when she came into his office. He could drop it to the pile of mail, stand—and smile. He could say, "Hello, Lorraine. You're out early!"

She shrugged and sat down in the chair which faced his own. "Don't you expect me to be here in the morning? Is that why you look so guilty?"

He swallowed his irritation. She *was* out early! "Do I look guilty?" he asked.

"Very. Where do you have the body buried?"

He managed a laugh. "Even my wastebasket is empty. I have been here for less than half an hour."

"But what have you been up to?"

"You know where I went last week."

"I'm still tracing your present air of guilt and hopeful concealment."

Her tone was archly challenging. So far he had remained cool and grave. He wanted to look at his desk blotter to be sure that no corner of the letter showed. What in the devil had he done with the envelope? He picked up the letter which her red pen had called to his attention. "It's your way of popping in unexpectedly," he told her. "I don't suppose I'm the only one who dislikes it."

She leaned back in the chair and crossed her handsome legs. "I have some privileges," she told Sam.

He sat gazing at her, his head nodding up and down. She did have privileges. And their glass-walled offices made privacy impossible, though a man liked to do some things in privacy, or to think he could.

38

"I'm not ashamed of washing my teeth," he said dryly, "but I always close the bathroom door."

She laughed. "Oh, Sam . . ."

"All right, then. I've read this letter, and I suppose you want to hear about my trip."

He suspected that she did not want to hear, primarily, about the business of the office. But he held her to such talk.

And finally she left, unhappy, as he could see. Which was only fair. He supposed, sometime, she would follow up the conversation which she had started a week ago before the fire down at her mountain home. Up to now, he had evaded a direct answer to her, and he hoped things could continue that way. He wanted neither an affair nor marriage with Lorraine Harper. This was a decision in which conceit played no part. Lorraine wanted a man. Sam was available, single, presentable; he probably felt some obligation to her as his employer—she thought—he probably would be dazzled by the life she could offer to a country-boy doctor. Cars, homes, travel . . .

Sam snapped his fingers in exasperation at himself. The situation was not of his own making. He had been courteous and cooperative with Lorraine, no more. He had done his job, and pretty well. Now he still could say what would come next.

With Lorraine's lavender hat still bobbing up and down at the far end of the office space, he drew the Administrators letter out from under the blotter and read it again. To suit his convenience, he was asked to come to the offices of Hospital Administrators for a personal interview at any time in the near future.

He flipped the pages of his appointment calendar; he thought about the Hauser report which he must get in shape. If he worked hard all morning and ate a quick, late lunch . . . At two o'clock, he walked briskly down the wide, handsome street to the Doctors Building. This too was a tall, square edifice of glass and steel. Blue, whereas the one in which he now worked was silver. Between panels of blue enameled steel there were large windows. This great block of offices stood on piers or columns. At street level, one went in under the shelter of the building itself to a courtyard of trees, flowers, a tinkling fountain, and shops. There was a drugstore, an optical supply shop, a restaurant. In a central core there were elevators. All visible from the street, a miniature shopping center, arcade, bazaar—call it by any name! Sam hoped there also would be a directory near the elevators. This was a fairly new building; he had never been in it.

As he passed the windows, he looked at the people seated in the restaurant. It was a pleasant place with round tables, maple chairs, waitresses in crisp uniforms. And—his head went up—he thought he knew the man sitting at a table near the window. Sam had an absurd impulse to lean against the glass, shield out the lobby lights with his cupped hands—He did step closer, and he did look back. He couldn't recall the man's name. But he knew him! He had known him. . . .

In Ashby Woods! That was where! He had known that man back in Ashby Woods. In an instant, he was returned to the dusty fields, the "woods" of scrub pine, the gullies and the back roads. The old doctor and his hospital.

Sam Fowler had gone to medical school on a scholarship accepted with the promise that he would do rural medicine. To fulfill that obligation, he had gone to Ashby Woods for the Medical Association to further its efforts to establish clinics and hospitals in rural communities. He had stayed on there to work with old Dr. Downes, to learn from him. Working there, he had paid off his debt; there he had come to know Judy—and the man who today sat in the restaurant of the Doctors Building, eating spaghetti out of a green casserole.

That man—Sam struggled to part the thick curtains of memory. He had been—a dentist? No, that wasn't right. The

40

drugstore! Yes. He had worked in the drugstore. And what was his name?

Sam bit his lip in concentration. Harry . . . Harry something. Ginsburg! That was it. Harry Ginsburg had been the pharmacist at the drugstore. And the store . . . Sam smiled grimly to remember. It had been a good store, and modern in its way. But it still held the aroma of drugs ground by hand in a wood and porcelain mortar; those drugs were still kept in rows of porcelain jars on the shelves. One could buy remedies for animals as well as for humans. Fully as well. The owner talked of putting in a soda fountain, but he had never done it. There was a place, at the back of the store, where chairs and a bench welcomed those who must wait for a prescription, or needed human companionship and talk.

In Ashby Woods, Sam had been called "Young Doc." He remembered. How *much* he remembered!

He glanced back at the man who was eating spaghetti and reading the morning newspaper. Then he went down to the men's washroom, needing to get himself back into the mood, the feeling. . . .

Ashby Woods. Do Lawd! The people there had used that expression. They were good people, simple people; Sam had liked many of them. He had come there, glossy with all that his big medical school, his internship and residency, had taught him.

He had found Dr. Downes, and Ashby Woods. The old doctor still ready to drive out into the country to deliver a baby, ready to agree that the town needed a hospital, and to build one.

He had listened gravely to the young doctor's talk about rural clinics, and the help available from AMA. It all sounded fine, said Dr. Downes. Where would the doctors for a clinic come from?

"They'll come if you have patients and the facilities to care for them," Sam had assured him.

"We'll see," said Dr. Downes.

On his second day in Ashby Woods the old gentleman had himself been stricken ill. Judy had come for the young doctor; she said her father thought he had a ruptured appendix.

He did have one. Sam went into the small hospital, scrubbed, and operated.

Then— Someone must care for the doctor's patients. There was a delivery imminent, and another one. A man got shot in the neck, a woman became violently ill with hepatitis. . . .

Sam found himself working night and day, taking care of things. Because the calls would come to his house, Dr. Downes had Sam move to a guest bedroom there. Sam remembered. He kept the telephone, a flashlight, a pad and pencil on the floor beside his low bed. He learned to handle these night calls, to quiet alarm over the telephone, and to answer a real emergency in person. He had kept office hours, he—

He had come to know Judy, that small, dark, quiet girl. She was young, and sweet. From Judy he had learned much. From Ashby Woods he had learned a great deal. He had not established any clinics in that neighborhood. Dr. Downes already had his own hospital, built literally with his own hands and determination.

He was a great man, Dr. Downes. Sam could not have written his novel if he had never known the doctor, the town, and Judy. Should he give the town credit?

The town and the hospital would still be around, but whatever had become of Judy? He and Judy had been a little in love. She had been eighteen, he brand-new in his profession. . .

Why had he ever left Ashby Woods?

4

Sam straightened his back, squared his back, squared his shoulders, and went out again to the elevators, pushed the button for the floor which the directory indicated to be that of Hospital Administrators. It was on the third floor from the top— Did the company use all those top three floors?

It certainly used all of the fifteenth one. The elevator discharged him directly into a large, well-decorated reception lobby. Carpeting, lamps, plants about—chairs, couches—and a receptionist in a blue dress with a silver medallion on a silver chain about her neck. She was young, pretty, and pleasant. Sam walked toward her.

"I am Dr. Samuel Fowler," he said. "I was asked to come . . ."

The young woman waited. Her brown hair was well cut, burnished.

". . . for an interview," Sam added.

"Oh," said the receptionist. "Oh, yes."

She looked at a list on her desk. "Dr. Fowler," she murmured in confirmation.

"There was no fixed time," said Sam.

"I understand." She opened a drawer of the desk and took

out a paper. Actually it was several papers—pages—folded once to form a thin book.

She got up from her chair, smiled at him, said, "This way, please," and she led him to a door which opened into a short hall. There she opened another door. "In here, please," she said.

The room was a small one, a small office. There was a desk, a chair, a lamp. The receptionist put her booklet on the desk. "You're to fill this out, please," she told him, smiling reassuringly. Sam took a deep breath. "And bring it back to you?" he asked. "Yes. If you will, please." She was a nice girl. Sam smiled at the receptionist and said "Thank you." She left, closing the door behind her. Sam sat down at the desk, and hoped he had sufficiently cleared his absence at the Foundation. This questionnaire would take time.

All right. He would get through with it. Name. Age . . . He wrote busily, using the desk pen, which was a good one. At the bottom of the first page he considered the blanks which he had left.

He was not married, he had no family, he owned no property. He lived in an apartment hotel, he owned and drove a car—he belonged to a church, he attended at intervals. . . .

He had given that last term some consideration.

On the next page, and the next, were questions concerning his hobbies, interests. . . . Not to be used for reference purposes, he was asked to name and identify ten friends. The degree of friendship. There were a half-dozen questions concerning sex. These were particular enough to bring a flush to his cheek, and he went back to try to write something about his hobbies. Actually, he had none. There were things he liked to do. Try to write a book, listen to certain kinds of music, read. He read a lot, but doubted if it were a hobby. He enjoyed boats, but didn't own so much as a canoe paddle. He was good at golf, using the city links, or playing on a guest card at a private club.

44

Friends. The Chaffines, Carole—or did she belong under sex? Should he mention the Downes' of Ashby Woods? Lorraine?

Education.

Family ancestry.

Previous employment.

Present . . . Oh, dear. Best to be brief there, too. Succinct was the word.

Finally, there was a beautiful blank sheet on which he was asked to give a short account of his life and aims. Now why should they want that? From sex to bank account, he had already told the whole thing. From his grandfather to his prospective bride . . .

Did "they" want to see what he would think up to say? For ten minutes Sam considered the slant one might take. Dramatics, pathos . . .

He drew the page closer and began to write upon it. He could cover only a section of his life. And of his aims. So he chose his profession as being applicable. As a young boy he probably had been ambitious to study medicine. He had chosen high school courses with that idea in mind. During his last year in medical school he had become interested in the developing fields for doctors. They no longer needed to start with a private practice. They could add many facets to doing the work of a doctor. It amounted to a specialization. He wrote briefly of his obligation to do rural medicine, he mentioned the assignment to seek out places for rural clinics, he mentioned his year at Ashby Woods. Then he spoke, for a paragraph, of the sort of work he did at the Foundation, the detection and analysis of worthwhile research projects which in itself required an overall picture of what medicine needed and might accomplish.

He filled two-thirds of the page, trying to keep his style concise, and honest, he hoped, without any portentousness. Certain only that he had not been "cute," he folded the

6067

pages together without checking what he had written, and he took the packet out to the receptionist.

She smiled at him, took the papers, and without looking at them, she put them into a manila envelope. "Can you wait, Dr. Fowler?" she asked. "Or would you prefer to come back at another time?"

Sam looked at his watch. It was three o'clock. He could wait.

He selected a magazine, and settled into the corner of a couch. Surely it would take an hour, or more, to evaluate the questionnaire. Or would it? A rapid reader could gather the facts in ten minutes, and categorize them in a computer, mental or actual. Oh, well, he had already shot the afternoon. And he'd been wanting to read this article by Norman Mailer.

He sat there for about forty minutes—there must have been a computer! Sam read the article and looked over the other people who came into the foyer, and waited. He played a game he enjoyed of assigning these strangers with backgrounds and purposes. He—

"Dr. Fowler?" It was the receptionist.

He got to his feet, laid the magazine neatly back on the table, and approached her desk.

The girl smiled up at him. "Will you go up to the seventeenth floor and see Dr. Moir? He will be waiting."

Right again. The company did use the top three floors. The seventeenth was probably called the Penthouse. There was a foyer there, too, but no desk and receptionist. Just an expanse of brown carpet, and a pin-neat man coming toward him, hand outstretched.

For a swift moment, Sam considered his own appearance as this Dr. Moir would be seeing the applicant for a job. A slender man, he would see, almost six feet tall, wearing a suit a shade lighter than his red-brown hair. His tie was neat, his suit fitted well, his carriage was erect. Did those things matter?

Appearance mattered to Sam, when he first met a person and wanted to evaluate him. A curling shirt collar, unpolished shoes told a story, not to be labeled bad or good. Just a story.

Dr. Moir, on his part, was baby-clean, his face pink and white, his white hair shining. This doctor was not a young man. His handclasp was firm, his greeting hearty though not effusive.

"We want a little conference, several of us," he told Dr. Fowler. He led the way through a door to a huge room, made to seem even larger by great windows that extended from floor to ceiling and brought the sky itself inside the room. At the far end was a large desk and a half dozen chairs about it. It was to this end of the room that Dr. Moir led Sam; before they could select chairs, they were joined by another man—a Dr. Connors—and quickly then by three others, not doctors. Sam found himself sitting comfortably in the circle, listening and talking, in fair balance.

Dr. Moir wanted to know how he had learned of the position opening. Sam thought there was no harm in mentioning Don Chaffine. He was identified as a pediatrician. "And a good one, I understand."

Sam agreed. Don was good.

Dr. Connors then made a crisp little speech about the organization which he represented. It was one of trained men, he said, who could, and did, analyze the various problems which had to do with the administration of hospitals.

These men went out in the field, he said; they were assigned to hospitals for reorganization and help. In the case of new hospitals, or ones in the planning stage, they organized. If there were specific problems in any hospital, the matter could be referred to Hospital Administrators.

What sort of problems? Oh, say one hospital found itself changing administrators too often. H.A. set itself to find out why, and devised ways to correct the situation.

The organization devoted its resources to finding administrators and training them, as well as to setting up hospitals which could be administered.

Hospital administration, in this organization, was considered to be a science.

"At least a trade," suggested someone.

"Or a skill."

Dr. Connors accepted all the terms. "We believe we can instruct—teach—the business scientifically, and effectively."

"We analyze," said one of the non-doctors, a big man with a florid complexion. "We find out what is wrong with a hospital's setup, and then we devote ourselves to correcting those faults."

Sam was encouraged to ask questions, and he did. In fact, he became intensely interested in the discussion, and talked freely, forgetting, almost, that this was an interview.

The talk went afield. These men seemed to know all about him, his hobbies, or lack of them. They asked why he had not married.

"My fiancée thinks it is because I have a woman boss," said Sam wryly.

The men laughed. Dr. Moir asked keenly if that *was* the reason. "I know Mrs. Harper," he added.

Sam conceded that his wish to make a change could possibly be traced to that consideration. "Though Mrs. Harper has been most gracious and cooperative."

There was some talk about the Foundation. Sam told about Dr. Hauser, in general terms.

It was a pleasant hour and a half. Sam realized that these five men were coming to know just about all there was to

48

know about Sam Fowler, and especially about his Foundation work.

Then little Dr. Connors asked about bedside doctoring. Wasn't he interested in that?

"Very much so," said Sam. "I have done it, and perhaps I would do it again. But I seem to have got into organization work. . . ."

"Do you keep in touch?" asked Dr. Moir keenly.

"Yes, sir, I do," said Sam. "I have to for an understanding of the work I do for the Foundation. There, you see, my work deals with day-after-tomorrow medicine. And for that I have to be well aware of what was done yesterday, and is being done today."

Abruptly, Dr. Moir stood up. Sam looked at him in surprise. For a second his eyes had wandered to the city lights spread out in panorama below the windows.

"I am going to take you in to see Dr. Robins," the big man explained.

For as much as sixty seconds, Sam did not move. What had all this been about? Were these men pleased with him, or not? Was there, had there been, a chance that he never could be shown the great man himself? He knew of course that Dr. Patric Robins was a big shot—they didn't come any bigger. But this sort of approach?

Almost angrily he jerked to his feet. He tugged at his coat, and mentally tugged at the muscles of his face. He must, at all costs, conceal what he was feeling. That he did not like this set-up, that he wanted nothing just now except to escape from this place.

Escape? Why, no one was holding him! The choice was his. And would be, even after he saw the Great Man.

He followed Dr. Moir's well-tailored back through the door and down along a short hall.

"Have you ever met Robins?" Dr. Moir asked him.

"No," said Sam. "No, I haven't."

"He . . ." said Dr. Moir. "Well, I'll only say this by way of preparation. Robins likes his little jokes." He turned his head to look at Sam.

And he found Sam frowning. Was this Robins, he was thinking, a sadist, a—?

"Don't worry about it," Dr. Moir said quickly. "I just thought I'd warn you. It is usually better to go along with him. But of course you should take him seriously, too." He smiled at Sam, and put his hand against the wide door of Patric Robins' office.

Not knowing what to think, and certainly not what to expect, Sam followed his guide.

The *sanctum sanctorum,* he thought wryly. The holy of holies. The— He caught himself up short. This was an interview! With two sides to it. And he was accustomed to interviews. He knew how to note and evaluate every point. Well, let him get to it! And evaluate.

He stepped inside the room. The carpet under his feet was a dark beige, the draperies were a lighter shade; some of them across a window were sheer, and creamy white. There were blue chairs, and a white bowl filled with stalks of blue larkspur. There was a huge desk with a white leather top on a brown marble base. And seated behind that desk, now rising to extend his hand to Sam Fowler, was a man.

Sam went the rest of the way, hearing Dr. Moir's voice, but looking at Patric Robins. He saw a tall man, with a craggy, rugged face, heavy eyebrows, deep-set, watchful eyes. A deep indentation from nose to upper lip. He wore casual, "country" clothes. A cashmere sport jacket, small-checked, over a green shirt, with a green and blue scarf knotted into the throat of it.

He shook Sam's hand, indicated the chair in which he wanted his visitor to sit, glanced at Dr. Moir, who turned and walked back to the door. Dr. Robins fished a pipe out of his pocket, and, still standing, lit it, all the time looking at Sam.

Then he sat down, and Sam sat in the chair facing him. He knew better than to sit below the man talking to him. That position put one at a disadvantage.

He caught Robins' slight nod, and he himself relaxed. "Smoke if you like," said Dr. Robins.

"Thank you," said Sam. And he waited.

"I hope," said Dr. Robins, putting his burnt match into a tray, "that you aren't here scouting for a spot to make a Harper Award."

Sam looked up, surprised, and his eyes brightened. "I hadn't thought of that idea," he said quickly.

"We do some good things here," Robins assured him.

"I'm finding out that you may," said Sam.

"I'd hope if I ever got awarded," said Dr. Robins, "that the dinner would be better than the one I did attend."

Sam pursed his lips. "Which one was that?"

"You mean they don't have breast of chicken at all of them?"

"I haven't been to all of them. In fact—"

Dr. Robins smiled at him. "Good man!" he said. "We don't run to bashes at H.A., but you get out of all you can. If you join us, that is."

"Well, sir . . ."

"I don't mean to belittle what Harper has done for the medical profession," said this surprising man, leaning toward Sam. "It isn't the value of the award, naturally. But the prestige your organization has attached to that word has certainly speeded up research and turned it toward realistic and productive goals."

Swiftly, Sam thought of Dr. Hauser, and the stack of papers on his desk which he should be attending to, and—

He glanced again at Dr. Robins who, wreathed in pipe smoke, was watching him.

"I understand you are a moving force at Harper," he said. "That you do everything from picking the individual graduate students to work in selected fields to taking an active interest in cancer and cardiovascular research."

Sam sat back in his blue chair, and his fingers cupped the polished hardwood of the arm. Had he written any such things on his questionnaire? No, of course he had not. But since his letter of application, these people had had four or five days to look into the matter of Sam Fowler; they evidently moved with speed, concentration, and, he hoped, discretion.

Modestly he disclaimed the importance Dr. Robins had sought to attach to his service at Harper. "I investigate people," he said quietly. "I examine the work they are doing, or claim to be doing. People who may merit awards, you see."

"Are you good at judging men?"

Sam shrugged. "I do a bit of it. I hope I've gained experience."

"Fair enough," said Robins. "What noble contribution do you think you could make to our organization?"

Sam suppressed the stiffening which, without Moir's warning, would have been instinctive. Instead he managed a small, but creditable smile. "As I grow older, I might even contribute something noble to Harper," he drawled.

"Don't brag, eh?"

"Oh, yes, sir, I do. Where I think it might be effective, or tolerated."

Dr. Robins tapped his pipe into the big ash tray. "What are your positions on an early dinner?" he asked unexpectedly.

Sam looked at his watch. It was six o'clock. "I can eat at almost any hour," he said. "I learned that as a hungry intern."

"Good. So did I. Then we'll go eat now. There is a place to wash up. . . ."

52

They ate at a small round table in what must be the Executive dining room of this organization. The waiter was quiet, deft, and unobtrusive. Their meal was excellent, a small bowl of perfect soup, a small steak broiled to their taste, good wine. Robins had not offered a cocktail.

He talked, and listened to anything Sam had the opportunity, skillfully given, to say. He ranged far afield in his own talk, but about the time the steaks came in with the tiny green beans and onions, he revealed that he knew that Sam had done some general practice.

Sam looked up alertly, his face and smile showing his surprise. "How did you know that?" he asked forthrightly. The interlude had been wholly a happenstance during the Dr. Downes and Ashby Woods experience.

Dr. Robins laughed. "I'm a brain picker," he said readily. "A peeker into a man's secret past."

Sam nodded and picked up his steak knife. He felt oddly uncomfortable. He had not much of anything to hide, but—well—a man liked his personal privacy.

Robins read his thoughts as he would have read a billboard. "I never evaluate on a man's own account of himself," he said.

"Not ever?" Sam's lifted eyes were cold.

"Oh, yes. Ever. What a man says of himself is valuable. But—tell me. Did you like doing private practice?"

Sam thought about that. He thought about Ashby Woods, and the experience there. "Yes," he said slowly. "I liked it. I had better. You see, at the time, I was trying to sell rural practice to other doctors."

"But it wasn't enough to hold you?"

"It could have been," said Sam. "There's a lure, you know. Working in a small town in the mountain areas can be carried out with a lot of gracious living on the side."

"But it took a bit more to hold you than pine-scented air and a back yard full of trout?"

Sam laughed. "The place where I did G.P.," he said, "offered neither of those things. It ran more to coyotes and rattlesnakes. But in other parts of the country I saw such idyllic retreats. I will say that all those areas, needing medical care, and getting it, were ready to give a deep appreciation seldom expressed in a city practice. A man could be sure, every day, of a warm handshake and a friendly 'hello.' "

"Sounds luring to me," said Dr. Robins.

"It is luring," Sam agreed. "I could still respond to it. But, you see, I was primarily doing organization work, even then. I am doing it now." He looked across at his inquisitor. "Can you read the future, too, sir?" he asked.

"I'm better at *post facto* guesses," said Robins, easy, relaxed, and ever alert.

"I think it only fair," said Sam, "to tell you that I have done no administrative work in the medical field. Even during that year as G.P., someone else was running the show."

Dr. Robins was refilling their wine glasses. "At least you're an honest one," he said, his tone almost indifferent.

"I came here this afternoon," said Sam a little heatedly, "with the prospect of coming to work for you. If I should place in this organization, I would want to do a good job. And, yes, of course an honest one."

Robins set the wine bottle down with a small thump. "If you place with me," he said, "you will do such a job, or there would be no job at all!"

Sam heard the ring of steel, he saw its flash. And he felt better than he had since noon. He straightened his shoulders against the back of the chair. Now, he thought, that in itself was odd. But—an affable man, a steel hard one—which should be easier to approach, or to work for?

He waited while Dr. Robins took a telephone call. It was the second one which had interrupted their dinner. He spoke cryptically, saying little more than *Yes. No. I see.* Then he stood up abruptly.

54

"I'm sorry, Fowler," he said, extending his hand. "I'll be in touch with you."

And still abruptly, he was down the length of the room, and away. "Leaving me with the check," thought Sam ruefully.

He drained his wine glass, he accepted a cup of coffee, but shook his head at the offer of dessert. The coffee drunk, he too walked out. In a matter of a minute, no more, he was walking out of the blue and silver building. As he crossed the ground floor court, he looked around, absurdly, for Ginsburg.

"I'll have to tell someone," he thought, his head feeling a little giddy. Not from the wine, surely. "But who would believe me?"

He walked the several blocks to where he had left his car; he looked up curiously at his own building. He supposed it was still his own. He had not cut the cord there; and certainly Hospital Administrators had not made any commitment.

Taking out his keys, dropping them, stooping to pick them up, he went back, and back, over the strange afternoon. All the way back to the questionnaire, and the "essay" which he had written on Sam Fowler, doctor and job hunter. Should he have slanted that essay elsewhere? Or anywhere? Yes, of course it had to be slanted.

What he had said, what he had left out, both could be important. How he had said it—

A man could be entirely honest, and give a dozen pictures of his life, flash light on a dozen faces of the prism. Well . . .

He drove easily, swiftly, thinking back over what had to be called a weird afternoon. He hoped he had said enough of the right things so that he would have a chance at this job. If only to see what would come next. That Robins . . .

Imagine his knowing that Sam had done G.P. work in the

field. Sam had, in listing his experience, mentioned his work for AMA. Mentioned it, that was all. Then how did Robins know about his months with Dr. Downes?

He had checked with AMA. What else had their records told him? It could not be much. On the whole Sam's record was a good one; he had never been fired from a job.

He drove his car into the garage, and spoke to the attendant. He went up to his apartment, turned on the lights, hung his suit coat in the closet, glanced out of the window, stood looking down at his long and crowded desk.

Did Robins know that he had written a book? How far did the man's research capabilities extend?

Sam picked up the telephone and dialed Carole's number. She did not answer. What could she be doing? Where could she be?

Well, any one of a dozen places, of course. She had a lot of friends, and varied interests.

He put the phone down, got an apple out of the refrigerator, turned on the TV, and sat down in the deep armchair. He was tired. As if he had really done a lot that day.

Had he? Maybe.

He gazed at the TV screen, seeing the dancing figures, hearing the music and the talk, but at the same time looking at and considering what he had done and seen, heard and said, that day.

He had come out with one net decision. He did not know at all precisely what H. A. did, but he was convinced that he would like to do it. Grinning at himself, he let the events of the day spin through his mind again. The questionnaire, the interview, Dr. Robins' cashmere coat and his craggy face. His forehead was knobby, his cheeks furrowed—and he knew about Ashby Woods, and Dr. Downes.

Much as Sam had reviewed the afternoon, he now thought about that year in the southwest. It had been new territory for him—

Raised in the tree-shaded mid-west, accustomed to a plan of roads and streets and organized towns— He had trained medically among doctors who relied upon each other, and their assistant workers. . . .

Then he had come into Ashby Woods, and he had met Dr. Downes. That one man, taking it upon himself to provide medical care for the ranchers and the people of the communities widely scattered around the town, ready to agree with everything Sam said, friendly, interested, and most interested himself. A real character. He talked to Sam, and took him to his home for further talk.

There Sam had met Judy. Eighteen years old, lovely, shy. Caring for her widowed father and his big house. A sweet, gentle girl, excited at Sam's coming, pleased that he stayed, sorrowful when he left. A slender, dark-haired girl. Sam thought of her always as silhouetted against one of the blazing sunsets of the southwest, her chin lifted, her lips parted in a smile, her eyes bright. From the first she had had an obvious crush on Sam. She knew it, and had laughed about it ruefully. "We don't often get a young man from outside our circle," she had told him. She had had a circle—of friends, and of knowledge. She kept her father's home, she worked in the church, there were parties. She ordered clothes from Houston and from Kansas City. But she never went to those places, nor did many of those people come to Ashby Woods. Until Sam arrived, and stayed for a year.

He came to know the Downes' very well. He rode the doctor's horses, and watched him make trades. He worked in the office and in the hospital which the doctor had built, literally, with his own hands. He marveled at the land which the old man owned, which he had bought as an investment.

Sam worked in Ashby Woods, doing what Dr. Downes had been doing for years. Delivering babies, both in the small, excellent hospital, and out in a wind-swept shack an arduous forty-mile drive from the Woods, looking at inflamed throats, treating a man for snakebite, a woman for a severe hemorrhage, trepanning a skull during a norther because there was no one else to do it, and the patient would have died if the pressure had not been relieved.

Pictures formed vividly now in Sam's mind. He stood again, reflector on his forehead, a stethoscope about his neck, with proud new grandparents at the nursery window to see the baby he had delivered the night before. He sat again in someone's yard for a picnic supper. There was a table being spread with food, a circle of chairs, children, dogs, and busy women. He sat on the side of an iron-rim wheeled wagon, his medical bag beside him, and talked to a weather-bitten farmer. The horse stamped and swished his tail at the flies. Once again Sam could feel the heat, smell the dust. . . .

He finished his apple, and nibbled on its stem.

The main thing he remembered about Ashby Woods was Judy. Her crush on the young doctor who had come to their town had been a pleasant experience. Sam could have married the girl.

What if he had? They would have had, would be having, a good life together. That's what. But things had moved in another direction. Sam had got the offer from the Harper Foundation, which was a very big thing at that stage of his career.

He had come back here to the city, where he had studied medicine and had friends. Of course he could have brought Judy with him, and together they would have lived in the city. Or in a pleasant house in a pleasant suburb, as the Chaffines did.

When he returned here to work and live, there had never yet been any mention of marriage between him and Judy. But, yes, he could have married her.

By now—well, for one thing, there would have been no Lorraine problem, and there also would have been no Carole in his life.

That was not to be considered. He and Carole . . . She alone made his change, his return to the city, and his taking up the Foundation work the right thing for Sam to have done. There was no reason for him to feel guilty about giving up Ashby Woods and all it had meant to him. The work, the old doctor, the bright little hospital . . .

He should not feel guilty at all, but somehow, and to some extent, he often did feel that way.

Not about Judy. She had been a warm and friendly person. Eighteen then, anxious for life and love. By now she probably was happily married, with at least six children.

But her father—yes, there Sam had some regrets. And some reason for a feeling of guilt. He owed much to Arthur Downes, M.D. and general counselor. The old man had, for one thing, given Sam material for the book which he had written. Material, characters, setting—not the story, but the philosophy, the significant incidents—

The whole thing had grown from a single seed, and Dr. Downes had given that seed to Sam. The story of the novel had developed from a murder trial. Downes, and his character, had changed the course of the trial, the course of many lives. Downes had told Sam about it. Sam could again hear the old man.

"There was this trial for murder, you see. We don't get many of 'em. Oh, yes, we have murders. Quite a few, in fact. Man gets mad at his wife, his woman—man finds his wife, his woman, two-timing him, and he shoots the other man— things like that. But we don't often bother to bring the matter to trial. Extenuating circumstances, natural causes—all that sort of reasoning.

"But we did have that one trial, and before a jury, of course. Well, one of the jurors developed a boil on his arm. They had a doctor treat him. Man happened to be in town because he was to be a witness for the prosecution. I didn't like the fella—the prosecutor, that is. And I put a bug in the ear of the defendant's lawyer. . . ." Sam remembered how old Downes had said de-fen-*dant,* accenting the last syllable, flatting the *a.* "Case ended in a mistrial."

"Because . . . ?" Sam had asked.

"Well, there's no doubt that a doctor who is to be a witness in a homicide case should not be called to treat a juror —or jurors. Perhaps the trial was not set aside on that grounds alone. But in that case, there were a number of errors, and a new trial was called."

"What happened then?"

"I don't rightly recall. If there ever was a new trial, the accused must have been acquitted, because he's farming two hundred acres of wheat out northeast of here. Good farmer, too. Pays his bills."

It was that story, remembered, and thought about, on which Sam had built his book, enriched with all he had experienced in Ashby Woods. The old doctor's character, the people, the "one-man clinic." Sam had so titled his book, liking what it signified about a man who would try to do things his way, and alone.

Indeed Sam had written his book because he had known a man like Arthur Downes, doctor and horse trader, civic figure and land speculator.

His book was fiction, but he could not have written the novel without the things that Dr. Downes had implanted in his memory, his knowledge, his background.

Sam had taken so much from Ashby Woods, and he felt that he still had a debt unpaid. One day he should go back there and look at the books, seek to strike a balance.

Sam thought he might not sleep that night, stirred up as he had been by the H.A. experience, and all that it had revived for him of the past. But he must have slept quietly and well, for he woke the next morning, revived and ready, almost, to face a return to his desk at the Foundation.

His afternoon's absence had done nothing to clear the stack of work and mail in his office; he had the Hauser report to formulate. . . . He hung his jacket over the back of his chair, and got down to work in earnest, scribbling on his legal pad, talking into the recorder, reading his mail and other reports which came in to him. He did some telephoning, he talked to two of his co-workers, but shook his head at their suggestion of a break.

"I'm still up to here," he explained, drawing his hand across his throat.

Working as steadily as he was doing should pay for yesterday's defection. It might let him catch up by the end of the month. He had an impulse to call Don Chaffine for lunch, but again he told himself that he should not tell anyone before Carole that he had gone far toward making a change. Carole first, and only if something actually developed.

He did not let himself take time to wonder how soon he would hear from Robins. Or, if not Robins, Moir—or—he snapped the switch of the dictating machine and began to talk.

He stopped at twelve-thirty and went downstairs to the cafeteria for a roast beef sandwich, a dish of sliced peaches, and a glass of milk. Before he went back to his desk, he would walk around the block. He would—

At fifteen minutes before two, without Sam's being aware that she was in the office, Lorraine came into his square of glassed-in space. For a small woman, slender, she did give the effect of sailing, of bearing down, of—

Sam looked up at her in surprise, and scrambled awkwardly to stand, catching one foot in the pedestal-foot of his chair, and flushing at his awkwardness. He must look guilty or something or other. Just as Lorraine looked angry, cold, disapproving—of something or other.

"Well, hello!" he said, sounding phony. He scrambled to pick up his coat and to get it on.

"Are you warm, Sam?" she asked coolly, seating herself in the chair beside his desk.

"No. Just busy. Shirt sleeves are more comfortable. I've a lot to catch up on."

"Didn't you get back until last night?"

She knew when he had got back. He sat down, ready to watch her and wait her out.

He wouldn't make any excuses for his absence yesterday afternoon. Long ago he had ironed out with Lorraine his need to conduct his work in his own way. "I can hang over a bridge rail, watch the river go by, and still be working," he had told her.

This day Lorraine wore a brown dress, faintly striped in bands of darker brown, or black. Her hat was of flower petals, as usual, but they were green. Pale green. Like snowballs not yet come white. Hydrangeas, maybe. . . .

She asked Sam about his trip.

It had gone very well.

As for Hauser, she could evaluate his report better than listen to him tell about the man. Sam had been favorably impressed.

"Good." She set her purse upright, and pressed its catch. She drew out a folded sheet of paper, glanced at Sam, and unfolded it. She pretended to read it.

Then she folded the paper—a letter, obviously—and tapped it against her other hand. "We had this inquiry about you, Sam," she said in her best la-de-dah voice and manner. "Are you really thinking of ditching us?"

The expression did not fit her lofty manner, nor her broad *a*'s. Sam almost laughed. His eyes probably did.

"Not *ditching*, Lorraine," he said warmly. "Not you, nor the Foundation. . . ."

"We've been good to you." She spoke plaintively.

"You have been. I've enjoyed working here."

"But now . . . ?"

"Now it is a matter of the future. My future, There

doesn't seem to be any glittering promise in this place. I'm at an age . . ."

"Do you want more money?" Her lofty tone had dropped to a flat harshness.

"That enters into it," he agreed.

"But, Sam, you know the Foundation . . ."

"I know quite a bit about the Foundation, my dear," he said quickly. "But I cannot afford to do its sort of charity work. So . . . Money is not the whole picture, of course. I want an opportunity to do more work, and to have increased activity and responsibility."

"We have given you a great deal."

They had not. Not really.

"It's advancement, primarily," he continued, "that I have in mind. A chance to make my name mean something in the work I do."

She shook her head, then leaned toward him. "But," she said softly, "in leaving the Foundation, you would be ditching me, too, lover."

Sam held tightly to the muscles of his face. "I doubt," he said quietly, "if ever, anywhere, a man could find so beautiful a boss."

She sat back in her chair, and Sam watched her. Her feeling, her thoughts, drifted like clouds across her face. She was being torn between pleasure in his flattery and a suspicion that he had rebuffed her.

He knew what she was thinking, and he was surprised at his vision about the woman. But he was equally aware that action was called for. He really should not raise this anchor before he knew if his services would be welcome at Hospital Administrators.

As things now stood, the Foundation could make its own offer to hold him—should Lorraine want that. The whole thing rested with her, as did all the major decisions of this office.

Before Sam could begin to wonder how he would react to

such a bid, she stood up, closing her purse with a snap. Sam got to his feet.

"I'll write you a recommend," she said in her familiar half-whimsical manner. "And send it to these people."

She did write her "recommend." Within the hour Sam had on his desk a flimsy carbon of that letter, brought in along with other interoffice material. Had she circulated that matter to any extent throughout the other offices?

Feeling furtive, Sam looked around at the other desks, at the people behind them. Perhaps he flattered himself that his possible departure would create a stir. None was in evidence.

He picked up the thin page and reached for a sheet of white paper against which to read it. Her letter was both glowing and sarcastic. She spoke of his record with the Foundation, of his devotion, and of the hard work he did. His reliability, his talent. Her final paragraph voiced her regret that the Foundation could not pay him "what he would be worth probably to you." Her charity funds, she said, must go elsewhere.

Sam took a deep breath, shook his head, sighed, and even laughed a little. He dropped the carbon into his wastebasket, then leaned over to retrieve it. He folded it small, and put it into his billfold.

During the next few days Sam went to the Doctors Building for various purposes, another interview with Dr. Moir, a not-too-exhaustive physical examination, a conference on his finances. He needed to spend no more than an hour on any of these things. They were set at times suiting his own convenience—a courtesy which he appreciated.

He became familiar with the building, he came and went easily through its lower court, each time realizing, and puzzled by, the knowledge that he was dreading an encounter with Ginsburg. "I'd probably dodge behind a pillar," he told himself.

Such wariness was ridiculous. Ginsburg was only—Ginsburg. Sam probably would never see him. That first day the man probably had just come to the restaurant for lunch. It was a good restaurant. Sam ate lunch there himself one day, and told about it when he returned to the Foundation. "They make wonderful *lasagna*."

And then, on Monday, he was asked if he could have lunch with Dr. Robins and Dr. Moir. Again he was asked to set his own time, and he did.

During the past week, Sam had found out all he could about Patric Robins. He read about him in magazines and files at the Public Library; he asked about him discreetly among the doctors he knew at the big medical center here in the city. His net conclusion was that Robins was reputed to be a genius for organizing people, and getting things done. Reading about his accomplishments, and from his own personal knowledge, Sam must grant his skill.

That day at lunch, that Monday—a week after he had first met the man—he found Robins handsomely dressed in a charcoal-gray suit, a yellow-buff shirt with a bronze-gold tie and handkerchief. Very nice, Sam thought enviously.

They were to eat their lunch in the company dining room, their table was set into a corner before the big windows, a corner which Sam would come to know as Robins' own. He never ate there alone, preferring to have solitary meals sent to his office. But with two or three others, he would sit, his back to the room, his eyes on the fog of that day, or the vista across the city to be seen on a clear day. He would talk, but he listened more than he talked. The words he dropped were significant. Joking words often, outrageous often, serious rarely, but important.

That day—their lunch was of sweetbreads on toast rounds, a green salad, a light beer that was delicious.

There was ten minutes of talk between Sam and Dr. Moir about beer, and Clydesdale horses, and grass for golf greens.

Then Robins rested his fork and leaned toward Sam to ask him why he was making a change in jobs.

Sam touched his napkin to his lips and launched into a generalization. He mentioned his age, the wish to make some sort of definite contribution. . . .

"Do you want more money?" Robins broke in.

Again Sam could have been nebulous; he could have mentioned security, fitting rewards. . . . "Yes," he said flatly. "More money. Yes."

Robins grinned and glanced at Dr. Moir, who was busily eating his sweetbreads.

"That," Sam continued, "to be earned by doing more work, if I am given a chance to do more work."

"Do you want to do more?" Robins demanded.

"Yes, sir, I do."

"And express your own ideas? Good, bad, or indifferent?"

This time, for sure, Sam must be cautious in his reply. He had good ideas, he was capable of them. He could say, "They would be there to be used." Something like that. But in this group—with Robins—somehow Sam did not think the smart lip, the brash retort, was exactly—

Before he could speak at all, Robins was asking him, "Just what sort of ideas would you have, Fowler? For instance, what are your ideas as of this hour—twenty-two minutes after one, if the damned clock is right. What are your ideas on the administration of a hospital? Any hospital."

Sam poured the rest of his beer into the tall glass, he watched the bubbles rise like bright amber beads. "Careful, boy," he was saying to himself.

"I'd expose you to a lecture, Dr. Robins," he said, glancing at the man.

"That's fine. Expose me." He began to clear his plate methodically.

Sam glanced at Dr. Moir, who nodded to him. Encouragingly?

"Well," Sam began, "hospitals are run by a board of trustees. Most hospitals. I don't know too much about private, proprietary hospitals. The hospitals I know are run by a board of trustees. These people are usually businessmen who never in the world would operate their own corporations as they try to run a hospital." He paused to look across at Dr. Moir, who had coughed. Or choked? His face was red, and he waved a hand to Sam to continue. Dr. Robins was solicitously handing his assistant a glass of water.

Sam reassembled his thoughts.

"The administrator," he said slowly, "a man or a woman, though most of them are men, is appointed, hired, to do the actual work of running the hospital. This person has two choices. He can really run the organization, or he can be a figurehead, at the mercy of the board of trustees on one side, and the head nurse, the staff doctors, et cetera, on the other."

"Mhmmmn," said Dr. Robins. "What do we, as an organization, do in the way of hospital organization?"

"My information on that, sir, is that Hospital Administrators is a company to direct the hospital project to its best advantage."

"Mhmmmn," said Dr. Robins again. "You do have ideas, don't you?"

"I suppose every man has ideas, sir."

"Ah, yes. Good, bad, and indifferent."

"Well, as to that," said Sam, "a man's ideas are usually a matter of his experience, conclusions, and solutions."

He drained his beer glass. Moir and Robins were looking at each other. Patric Robins was smiling a bit wryly. But smiling. He signaled to the waiter and said they would have dessert.

Sam had an absurd impulse to refuse to eat a dessert on

this man's say-so, but when it came, it was a particular prune pastry of which he was very fond, and anyway . . .

"Sam," said Dr. Robins, "would you like to join us here at Hospital Administrators?"

Sam put his fork down. "Yes, sir," he said readily. "If we can come to a satisfactory arrangement."

"As to your salary and your duties, you mean?"

"What else is there?" Sam asked.

"Not a lot. Shall we start with salary?"

"All right." Sam picked up his fork again, and stated the salary which he had determined to ask

"I happen to know what you are getting at Harper," said Dr. Moir.

"Yes. Last week we had a discussion of my financial situation. What I earned, what I had saved, what I owe."

"It turned out in your favor," agreed Dr. Moir in the friendliest fashion. "How does this number strike you?"

It was a compromise between what Sam had asked and what he was now earning.

"With a chance for advancement?" asked Sam.

"Advancement is possible," said Dr. Robins. "Attaining it would be up to you. Do you want coffee?"

Sam shook his head and finished off the prune kolachy.

"I secure my executives," said Dr. Robins, "in much the same way, by much the same standards, as I secure and train hospital administrators. I want 'em relaxed."

"Isn't that difficult, sir?" Sam asked. He was feeling very good. Sure of himself.

"Certainly it's difficult. It will be difficult for you, I'll bet."

"Why?"

"A man gets stiff from having his back to the wall, Sam."

"Yes, sir?"

Dr. Robins stood up. "Hospital administration," he said, in the tone of a teacher laying down a principle of absolute truth, "running a hospital, and in your case, knowing how to run one, is the world's most complicated business. There's no black bound book, you know, that will answer the questions you are due to run up against."

Sam rose and set his chair under the table. "I can hardly wait," he said.

He had the job! He had the job!

He could not wait to tell Carole! She must be the first to know. And then he would tell others, the Chaffines, and other friends. Lorraine, of course. *There* would be an abrasive time!

But Carole must know first. When he was leaving the building, he went into the booth on the ground floor and dialed her office, asked to speak to her.

She answered, a little breathless. "Is something wrong?"

"No. Of course there is nothing wrong."

"You don't usually call me here."

"Well, today I did, and it isn't usual. Just tell me—can we have dinner together?"

"Sam . . ."

"I know it isn't our usual dinner night, but I have to see you. How about—let's see. Could you come to my place?"

"No." He knew she didn't like to do that.

"All right then. Your place? Or some place? How about Tony's?"

"If you have talking to do . . . Tony's can be noisy."

It was always noisy. "Look," he said, "I'll pick you up a little before seven."

"Sam . . ." She was going to tell him that she had other plans, an exhibit at the Art Museum, some personal tasks. . . .

"By, now," he said. He heard her hang up. Smiling, he hung up his own phone, went out of the booth, and on through the court, this time not thinking Ginsburg.

He spent the afternoon with interviews in his office. He must give Harper this last month, and do a good job for them. He was meticulous in his notes, and spent a final hour recording his impressions of the people to whom he had talked, the material they had provided.

If Lorraine had been in the office—She was not. She usually made a long week end, coming in about noon on Tuesday. He would talk to her the next day. Meanwhile . . .

Carole was still puzzled when he came up to her apartment, but interested enough in what he would have to say to her to have put on her pretty yellow suit. Tonight she had folded a brown chiffon scarf into its throat.

"I have a reservation at the Hunt Room," he told her, kissing her, and keeping her hand in his.

She held back. "Sam?"

"We'll talk there," he told her. "That place is like a grave."

She laughed, and he grinned at her.

The Hunt Room was quiet, and not even remotely like a grave. It was, rather, a large, handsome hotel dining room devoted to maintaining its air of Victorian elegance. From the crystal chandeliers and the wall mirrors to the silver on the tables, elegance was the theme. There were prints, hunting horns, hunt trophies. Soft music was as unobtrusive as the thick green carpet; the tables and banquettes were arranged for a sense of privacy, though the room was large. The service was the best a well-trained organization could provide.

"All this and Wednesday night, too?" Carole asked him when he seated her on the satin banquette. Its high, curving back secluded them from the rest of the room.

Sam took a chair at the side of the table where he could look at her and reach out for her hand when he wanted to. "Sherry?" he asked. "Or a cocktail?"

"Sherry, I think, and if you don't tell me—quickly—"

He nodded. "I'm going to tell you."

The waiter took their order and withdrew. Sam leaned toward Carole. "It's all decided," he said eagerly. "I am now in the employ of Hospital Administrators."

Her eyes lit up. "Oh, Sam! I am glad."

"I knew you would be."

"I suspect you did this all for me."

"Well, at an increase of ten thousand in salary I was just a little self-interested."

"But, Sam, that's wonderful! Oh, I wish we had stayed at home. I could have opened a can of soup and kissed you."

"In that order." He half rose, leaned over, and kissed her. "It would have been even better at my place," he told her, sitting down again.

"I can imagine. But—tell me!"

He told her. They drank their sherry, they ordered their dinner—and they talked. Sam told in detail about the events of the past week. The questionnaire, the interviews, the physical examination, the luncheon today, the sweetbreads. "I'm in!" he concluded happily.

"What about Mrs. Harper? Does she know?"

"Not yet. She answered a letter of inquiry about me."

"So she guessed you were thinking of moving."

"Oh, yes."

"And she wasn't happy."

"She knew I was not happy with the way things had progressed lately at the Foundation."

"Hmmmn. How did she answer their letter?"

"She spoke of my devotion, and regretted that their funds must go to other charities."

Carole laughed. "It sounds like her."

"You hardly know the woman."

"I know enough."

Sam wiped his fingers on his napkin. "We can get married, sweetheart," he said softly.

She looked up at him. "We could have been married on your old salary."

"Yes, we could have."

"Tell me about your new boss."

His Carole was a clever woman; she knew when to say a thing, and when to keep still. Appreciating this, Sam tried to tell her about Patric Robins. He had not seen a lot of him, he said. It was a matter of "by his works ye shall know him." He had built up what seemed to be a fine organization. Yes, he could tell her what he looked like. "And you'll have to help me there, Carole."

"How?"

"With my clothes. The way that man dresses . . ." He told her about the cashmere coat, the charcoal suit. "As you know, I run to the conventional three-button suit, and I let the clothing store salesman tell me what shirts and ties to buy."

"Are you going to try to be like Dr. Robins?"

"I admire him." Sam squinted his eyes at her. "No," he said. "If you mean, change myself into his pattern. No. I won't try for that. But this matter of clothes—I don't suppose I could make you understand, but I would like to feel I could talk to the man somewhat on his level."

"Will a cashmere coat do that for you?"

He laughed and shook his head. "I suppose you're right. So I'll stick to the clothing store clerk. I do think I look neat, don't you?'

Carole laughed aloud. "Always," she said. "Always. Besides, you look like you. And I'll take that."

"I'm lucky," he answered smugly.

"When do you move your desk plate to the new office?"

"I told them it would take about a month to wind things up at the Foundation. And of course I'll have a session with Lorraine."

"She'll dodge it."

He looked up, frowning. "Why should she?"

"Women . . . Well, maybe she won't. I don't know her well, do I?"

He restrained his impulse to say she was lucky. He knew there was little profit in pitting one woman against another, with a man in the middle. He had made a change in jobs for Carole's sake. She must know that he had. He would take such benefits as came his way.

They finished their dinner, and decided against dessert. But coffee, and a brandy—they lingered at the table, conscious of people moving about them, of the music, of the comfort of this handsome dining room.

"Will this be a demanding job?" Carole asked him, rather surprising him by her return to the practical.

"I don't know what I shall do, specifically," he told her. "I'd not think I would begin by administering a hospital. But—from what I've seen of the organization, I'd say, yes, the job could be demanding. I'll have to keep my wheels well-oiled, too. And be relaxed. Robins told me that his ideal was to develop relaxed administrators."

"I can tell you think that will take some concentration. Do you think you'll make it?"

"I certainly plan to try."

"Good! I'll help you."

He smiled at her. "And how will you help?" he asked.

"Oh, if I know things have been tough, and you need help —a soothing hand, a good meal, and quiet . . . Maybe we could work out a sign. If you'd come home from the office all frazzled, loose ends—and I would know that they were loose —I wouldn't pounce on you with the annoyances of my day. You know? The children misbehaved, I smashed a car fender, the hot water heater sprang a leak . . ."

Sam laughed aloud. "You make marriage sound so promising!" he told her.

She shrugged. "I thought it was what you wanted."

"It is what I want. The sooner the better. And I'll let you relax me, too."

"What sort of sign . . ." She frowned, trying to think.

"I'll come home with my tie knot down. Then you'll know."

"I thought your line was going to be neatness?"

"Oh, yes. Well, we'll find something. I'll kick the door in or—well, maybe I'll be relaxed all the time."

"Or never relaxed at all?"

"The way you tell it, the new job sounds such fun! Now, let's talk about all those kids, and water heaters, and things."

The next day, Lorraine was in the office, but she did not come near Sam. The day after, he attempted to see her in her own office. She sent word that she was busy.

That afternoon he wrote a formal letter of resignation, and sent it to her desk. He did not see her again before he left the Foundation. She had decided to go to California.

Sam was troubled by the way things had gone in that area. He wished he might have handled the situation better, though Lorraine must remember, and realize, that a woman always put a man on the spot when she propositioned him. After that scene at her mountain home, and his withdrawal, he could not have stayed on at the Foundation.

Of course she knew that as well as he did. But there must have been some better way to handle the delicate matter, even to have changed jobs, without offending Lorraine as much as he seemed to have done. He decided that he definitely was no genius with people.

5

On the first day of the month, he moved to the Doctors Building and the offices of Hospital Administrators. A little fuss, though not an embarrassing amount, was made over his advent. He was assigned an office on the intermediate floor of the organization. It was a pleasant office, its window had a view, and he was given a secretary, Mrs. Drozda, a woman of thirty-five, perhaps. Very slender, very well-dressed, she had a perfect skin, and taffy-gold hair which she wore so neatly and beautifully dressed always that Sam immediately planned to have Carole come in and tell him if she wore a wig.

Sam found that he was classed as an executive; he could eat in the dining room and take guests there by appointment. He was given keys to the executive men's room, and to the express elevator.

He attended the regular executive meetings, he had his own form-fitting chair at the long table—and sometimes he felt that he even "executed" a little.

He did not find any "black bound book" on hospital administration, but he was given a thick folder of speeches and articles which had originated in H.A. offices. There was a directive on the cover of this book. "We in no way suggest that you copy or repeat this material, but we think it fair to acquaint you with the policy of the organization, as well as its accepted stand as maintained to date."

He read the contents of the folder; he spent a day thinking about what he had read, and another day using a red and blue pencil to mark those passages which he approved and those about which he had doubts. Then he put the folder on his bookshelf.

He worked. He reviewed a correspondence file between the board of a hospital and H.A., condensing the material into a report. He was asked to look into, and report on, the matter of good Samaritan laws in their state, and the two most closely neighbor to it. Also, on the position of a list of hospitals on these laws, and their practice concerning such cases. This took him away from the city for several days. Working up his report took as long.

Meanwhile he was getting the feel of the organization for which he worked. It was made up of trained men; in all respects they were trained. The work they did was to set up administrations for whole hospitals, to reorganize those already established, to solve single problems of all sorts, big and little. Reading about those problems, hearing about them at meetings, Sam came up with a decision that was to draw notice to him, and which was due to be quoted far into the future.

To him, it seemed an obvious thing to have said. He knew that H.A. sold service, and that hospitals bought their service. He knew that individual hospitals in their administration also sold service to the patients who entered. The situation was unique in that the administration's customers did not have a normal buyer's frame of mind. They were people who were sick, or related to the sick. If the hospital team carried the ball, or fumbled it, a matter of hope, fear, and life itself was placed in jeopardy. Babies were born every day in any hospital, and people died in them almost every day. This created a dramatic environment where almost anything could happen.

It was H.A.'s assignment to anticipate these crises, and solve them before they happened, or as soon afterward as was possible. Sam sat at meetings and heard about these problems. Sometimes they did not seem too important—to him. The matter of traffic flow in and out of elevators, the matter of angering a patient by serving carrots when that patient had specifically *said*—the matter of relatives conducting their own consultations in the sunrooms— The man reporting on this last was a good mimic and one could vividly see the groups of anxious mothers, husbands, children. They came up with diagnoses of their own, they borrowed grievances, they asked for a change in doctors. . . .

Yes, this was a problem.

"It seems to me," said Dr. Fowler, "that this problem is basically no different from all your problems. And that doesn't have too much to do with the size of the sunroom, or the menus. Your one big problem, gentlemen, as seen by a green-horn at this business, the problem of any hospital, seems basically to be the patient. Take care of that, and you've got the whole ball of yarn unraveled."

There was a silence. Sam was startled by it. He looked at the men around the table. Dr. Moir was getting red in the face. Good Lord, what had he said!

Now the men were all looking at him. *What* had he said? He fumbled for words to—

The man next to him turned in his chair and held out his hand. "Shake, doctor," he said.

Sam stared at him, beginning to get angry. He'd only said . . . "I suppose I sounded naïve," he began.

"You sounded no such thing." It was Dr. Moir who spoke.

"We've hunted that button for some time, Sam. And you come in here and put your finger on it. The patient is our problem. And nothing else has precedent. Wait till I tell Robins."

Sam supposed he did tell him. Though if he did, Dr. Robins made no mention of it to his latest executive hireling.

Within days, however, small, bright cards were tucked prominently under the glass of every desk of the organization. In dark green letters on a shiny white card, Sam's words stood out for everyone to see. "The patient is our problem."

Well, if the organization was pleased, Sam would be pleased, too. Though he still didn't know why. When, on Sunday evening, he told about the incident to Carole and the Chaffines, they seemed to understand at once, and were amused at Sam's inability to see what had happened.

"Let him alone," said Don. "He's a distillation all his own. I'm just glad he's where he may be appreciated. Could you get me one of your cards, Sam?"

"I'll bring you mine. You deserve it. I think you're nuts, too. Why in hell anyone gets into the health business and has to be told—"

"Everybody but you, Sam," Don assured him. "Everybody but you."

The next day Sam was given a problem of his own to solve, and it was one which, for a while, put all other matters out of his mind.

He had no previous idea that H.A. was operational twenty-four hours a day, though he did know there was an answering service. It was his obligation to "keep in touch," and he did. But why should one ever be called out to decide what to do about sunroom gossip?

"Learn to live with it," he'd told the executive meeting. "The patient has to have visitors; they have to be put out of the room occasionally; of course they will gather somewhere and talk to other visitors."

That morning he was awakened at a quarter to six. His first reaction was anger at the hotel switchboard. The girl had got her rooms mixed up—and as long as he'd lived in the place . . .

"Hello!" he shouted into the phone, fumbling for the light switch.

He listened, settling down. Would he please plan to fly to Richmond on a plane leaving the airport at 8:20? Number of flight, everything, was spoken briskly into his ear.

He opened his mouth to ask . . . "A letter of information will be waiting at the desk when you pick up your ticket. Thank you, Dr. Fowler."

Well, he'd be damned. He looked at the clock, he rubbed his knuckles down along his jaw.

His first impulse was to tell Carole. She'd murder him. At that hour . . . Besides, he didn't have time. He'd wait until he was safely at the airport, and—

Doggone! If Carole had married him by now, she could be packing his bag while he shaved, showered and dressed. The office certainly had given him no time . . . It took forty minutes to drive out to the airport. He hoped they'd pay for valet parking. They should give a man *time!* No emergency was so urgent. . . .

He packed a bag, probably, he grumbled, leaving out various essentials. Which Richmond was he going to? He knew of at least two. Of all ways to handle things. What if he just was late, and—

He had better not be late, he admitted, as he whooshed his car out of the garage. Not for the money. They probably were doing this to test him. Well, damned if he wanted to *be* tested!

He got his tickets, he made his plane, and he opened his letter of instructions. He read it and wondered if he would get breakfast on the plane. Just let someone offer him a cup of coffee. He'd snap.

Let's see . . . A death had occurred, a lawsuit was foreseeable. His task was to get all the facts, as quickly as possible, with a report to be made in detail.

He had his coffee, he reached the proper town, he went into the proper hospital, and asked to see the administrator, giving the desk clerk one of his new business cards. By then it was a little past midmorning. The sun was shining.

The hospital administrator had a problem all right. He greeted Dr. Fowler with an amount of relief which indicated the size of that problem. "You got here quickly," he said thankfully.

Sam nodded. "I was lucky." He was going to watch himself, and not reveal, if possible, how new he was at this game. When in doubt, he would say nothing. He hoped he could work along that line.

The administrator took him to his office. "We've had a terrible thing happen here, doctor," he said.

Sam sat down. "All right. Tell me."

"I thought you knew. The baby died, and—"

"You tell me."

"Er—yes." The administrator was probably efficient under ordinary circumstances. Now he was badly shaken.

"I have to blame myself," he began.

"Just tell it from the beginning." Sam took out a small notebook and his pen.

"Well, there was this baby. Delivered her in the hospital a week ago. Normal. Mother recovered well. No complications. None at all. Then—" He stopped and stared at the wall beyond Sam's shoulder.

"What happened?" Sam urged after a minute's wait.

"What . . . ? Oh! Well, plenty happened. You see, the mother's mother died. . . ."

"Is that . . . ?"

"No, no! Her death had been expected. But this woman, our patient—"

"The baby's mother?"

"Yes, that's right. Mrs. Sparks. Fine young woman. Well, she'd recovered well—and she naturally wanted to go to her mother's funeral. In Cincinnati, it was. So she asked if she could leave the new baby in our nursery for two days . . . while she was gone."

"A well baby?"

The administrator wiped his brow with a large, clean handkerchief. "I *know* it is unusual, doctor. We just *never* do it. And I promise we won't do it again!"

"But this time . . ."

"This time we did. Yes, sir, we sure did." He slumped down in his chair, his head wagging from side to side.

"Tell me," said Sam quietly, feeling his skin prickle.

"Yes," said the hapless man. "She left the baby in our nursery, where he had been right along, you know. A healthy, normal baby."

"When?"

"She left yesterday morning. She was supposed to be back tomorrow, but of course . . ."

"When did the baby die? I suppose it was the baby who . . ."

"Dear Lord, yes!" cried the administrator.

"Now, sir . . ."

"Everybody tells me that death happens in a hospital." The man sounded angry. "And it does. Though our rate here is only twenty-seven in a hundred patients. Well, anyway—we had this healthy baby. He took his four p.m. feeding normally, and his eight. But Dr. Fowler, when the nurse picked him up for his midnight—*he was dead!* He had died without a whimper of distress—just dead."

"Then . . .?" Sam's pen moved across the page. He only glanced up at this nearly hysterical man.

"*Then?*" the administrator shouted. "Oh, I am sorry, Dr. Fowler, but it was a terrible thing!"

"I'm sure it was. However, I am remembering in what capacity I am here, and in which I was summoned. Evidently your hospital administration was set up by us."

"Yes, it was. We—Up to now, it has worked beautifully. Efficient, and all that."

"Good. So tell me what was done."

"Yes, sir. I see what you mean. Though we all rather fell to pieces there at first. The mother gone, and all."

Sam waited.

"Well, the intern called the staff pediatrician, and the O.B. head nurse called me. The situation was so unusual, you see. Of course, after the pediatrician had seen the baby, we notified the parents—a dreadful shock to them, of course."

"Have they returned?"

"They'll be here in an hour or so."

"Autopsy?"

"Dr. Fowler!"

"Doesn't your hospital require autopsies?" He knew that was a fixed policy for H.A.

"We include permission on all admissions. But a newborn baby . . ."

"Your position doesn't cover that?"

"Not clearly enough to justify our doing it until this patient's return. The mother, I mean."

Sam closed his notebook. "You should have a blanket rule, sir," he said. "Post-mortem examination for cause of death and effect of treatment is one of the best measures of any hospital staff's conscientiousness and efficiency."

"Yes, sir. I know you are right."

"I'll talk to the parents, if you like. You must have that autopsy. Meanwhile, could I see the nursery, talk to the nurses, the intern and the doctor?"

He could. He did. He ate lunch with the pathologist; the two men talked about football, and snow removal from the city streets.

The administrator interrupted them with word that the baby's parents were in his office. Sam told the pathologist he would be seeing him, and he went upstairs.

The poor devil of an administrator had already gone through the hardest part of their encounter, but Sam still had work to do. He met the father and the mother, attractive young people in their mid-twenties, and of course crushed by what had happened. Sam could tell them that he had been called in as a consultant. "Up to now, everything seems to have been done for you and your child," he said in his quiet, warm manner. "We want to be able to continue to give that sort of care and service in this hospital."

"But what happened, Dr. Fowler?" sobbed the mother. "What *happened?* Did somebody give our baby medicine, or mix up the formulas. . . . ?"

"We don't know what happened, Mrs. Sparks. I have inspected the nursery, and talked to the personnel. Everything seems to be, and to have been, in order. Now we have just one other line to pursue, for our own information, and for your comfort."

"Our *comfort?*" cried the outraged father.

"Yes, sir. You will find it a comfort to know what happened."

"What are you talking about?"

"I am talking about an autopsy, Mr. Sparks."

The mother moaned.

"A post-mortem examination," Sam continued, "will tell us what may have happened within the small body of your son. If he was fed improperly, if some medicine was given, if there was some physical defect or condition which he brought into the world when he was born."

"He was perfect," sobbed the mother.

"He looked perfect," Sam agreed.

"I hate the whole idea . . ." said the father.

"You should not." Sam talked for ten minutes, rewarded at last by a grudging permission.

"I want to watch it done," said the father, white about his lips.

"No," said Sam. "But I'll watch, and I'll make a first-hand report if you like."

"Why can't I . . . ?"

"Because you haven't studied medicine. You wouldn't know what you were seeing. And because your wife needs you with her."

It was settled. Sam found himself gowned and masked, down in the autopsy room. The only abnormality found was an abscess of the thymus.

"It might or might not have caused death," said the pathologist with characteristic, scientific objectivity.

Sam did not quote him precisely to the parents. The situation, he said, would have prevented their baby from ever becoming a normal child. They were reconciled, and, yes, comforted.

As for the hospital administrator, he was embarrassingly relieved. "You saved my life," he told Sam when he drove him to the airport. "Your organization is wonderful."

"Change your rules to include all autopsies," Sam told him.

He was back in his own town before midnight. He had not needed to pack a bag. Carole wouldn't know that he had been away.

But he had solved his first "problem." And he would tell her about it. Of course he had an office report to make, with recommendations. But that could wait until he was back at his desk.

As it happened, he made one before he quite reached that desk. Patric Robins was holding the elevator for him when he had parked his car the next morning. Brown slacks, pullover sweater, cream-colored, a scarf tucked into its neck. "You didn't call in," he told Sam.

Sam turned around to stare at him. "I didn't get home until one a.m."

"I like to know where my boys are at night."

By that time Sam was getting somewhat used to Patric Robins, the amazing amount of work he did, his ability to insert a wisecrack, a hyperbole, a bit of shock treatment into almost any occasion, and as on this morning, the human touch.

"Did they give you a hard time, boy?" he asked Sam now.

"I've had better days."

Dr. Robins followed him to his office, and said good morning to Mrs. Drozda. "We'll buzz you," he dismissed her.

"Supposed to be one of our sexier," he told Sam. "Does she quiver you?"

Sam grinned, and opened his briefcase. "My girl is a blonde, too," he said.

"I'd be afraid to muss Drozda's hair." Robins sat down with a groan. "Up all night," he explained. "Waiting for your call."

"Well, next time you'll know you don't need to."

The doctor chuckled. "Not afraid of the old man?"

"Just afraid to let him know my state of nerves. Now, this case, sir—"

"All right. Sit down and tell me."

Sam did tell him. He was feeling pretty good; he had done a good job back in Richmond. This interview, while unexpected, was giving him no "quivers."

"I'll get all this down in a report," he concluded.

Robins got to his feet. "Next time, call in and report your whereabouts," he said. And it was, absolutely, all he said. Unbelieving, Sam watched the door close upon him.

Well!

He hunted for paper. He asked Mrs. Drozda to find him a legal tablet—he indicated the size. "They are yellow," he told her, "with blue lines. . . ."

His report was made, and after a day or two of no comment, he attended an executive meeting where he was assigned a definite job. As a preliminary, his Richmond report, Xeroxed, was passed around. There was a stir of interest, with everyone looking at Sam. "I should have worn my new wide tie," he told himself absurdly.

"Dr. Fowler did a commendable job," Robins said, when everyone had read the report. "New to our organization, he did the right things at the right times."

"But I didn't report in on my return to the city," Sam told himself.

". . . especially important that autopsies should be required of all H.A.-served hospitals," Dr. Robins was saying. "This has long been our policy. The fine point of the permission's being extended to the newborn probably did need clarification. But now, after some consultation with the offices of the American Medical Association, our organization is going to conduct a campaign to make autopsies a matter of routine in all accredited hospitals. There will be some opposition to this. Shortage of pathologists will be mentioned, unnecessary trauma to the families of the deceased—you know the flap we will get. But I think the thing can be sold, and I would like to have H.A. do that selling. Do I hear any objections?"

Someone mentioned time, and money. Dr. Robins nodded. "Popularity can be lost," he agreed. "Especially in places where it's not yet been established. But if that is all we can think of to stop us, and since he already has shown interest in the matter, I am going to suggest Dr. Fowler as the one to do that selling."

Sam sat up in his chair.

"I know," Dr. Robins drawled, "that he already is doing intensive research on the handling of delinquent accounts and the difficult subject of paint matching, but I believe this can take precedence over those pursuits."

Sam slumped again into his chair. Robins had his needle

out. He would listen, pick out the significant from the nitty-gritty. . . .

But it all added up to what looked like a real assignment. He was to work up some talks, speeches in the formal sense, arguments as a means of presentation. Clearance had been given for him to use the case of the dead baby. "If he tells me not to mention names, I'll walk out," Sam promised himself.

Robins didn't tell him such a thing. "We'll talk about it," he promised Sam, as the meeting disbanded. Sam took his notes and the doodles he had made back to his office. There he put his hand on the stack of legal-sized tablets he had purchased. This part of the job, the working up of talks and speeches, could be done right here in the office.

Robins talked to him, and the talk was helpful. Again Sam was impressed with this man's knowledge and his energy. He probably had the individual situation of every hospital in the country firmly embedded in his mind. He wanted, he told Sam, material provided to cover every possible question which could be asked of hospital administrators, the doctors, the boards . . .

"You must think about the women in the auxiliary, and the funeral directors, the beauty operators . . ."

Sam's head went up.

"Have you ever arranged the coiffure of a corpse whose brain has been removed?" Robins asked.

"Thank God, no!"

"Mhmmmn. Those things can be important."

"I'm a closed coffin man myself."

"All right. That may be your next campaign."

That was Robins. Sam went to work on the autopsy campaign, in which he actually did believe, and which he wanted to conduct. He started with the writing and the research. It took about two weeks to get the mass of material compressed and converted—and thought about.

When he began the actual writing, he decided to stress the

legal protection afforded the hospital by autopsies. In these days of rising costs, and especially the huge awards for damages being given by the courts and juries, he felt that this was a most important item.

He did his writing; he then dictated to Mrs. Drozda and it was all properly typed and clipped into neat folders. Dr. Moir was the first to see any of it. He came into Sam's office, asking how he was getting along. . . . Sam could point to the blue folders. He had still, he said, a few points to catch up, but Moir could look over what he had done.

Moir brought the material back later that same afternoon and placed the folders on Sam's desk. "I can see you've put in some hard work on this," he said. "But haven't you forgotten your own first principle?"

Sam frowned. "I don't understand . . ."

Dr. Moir made a thing of searching Sam's desktop for the printed card. "If it were here," he said dryly, "it would read, 'The patient is our problem.'" And he walked out.

Sam was furious. He had given his card to Chaffine. He *was* considering the patient—at least, the patient's family—in urging autopsies. He had selected and used the arguments which he felt most surely would appeal to medical societies, to hospital boards. . . .

He fumed about the matter all that night, and the next day he asked for an opportunity to talk to Dr. Robins. This was granted him immediately. Almost too soon, he thought.

But he gathered up his blue-bound folders, smoothed the set of his coat collar and went up to the boss's office. Robins was affable; he listened to Sam's remarks about the work he had done. He had, he said, thought it best not to use scattershot, but to seek a sure means of attracting attention and action.

That morning, Dr. Robins had chosen to stand at the big window and look out over the smoke-hazed city. "Go right along," he told Sam. "I'm listening."

And making it as difficult as possible for Sam.

"Dr. Moir," he said, "feels that I have perhaps lost track of the benefit to our patients."

"You don't agree with him?"

"In performing autopsies as a routine procedure, the profession is bound to learn a great deal. Knowledge certainly redounds to the patients' good."

"I can't argue with that!" agreed Dr. Robins, turning about. He glanced at the blue folders. "Leave that stuff with me," he said. "I'll look through it. Your arguments sound pretty good."

Sam nodded and stood up. "All right. I'll go back to my paint matching."

Robins frowned. Sam had not yet learned that the boss never recognized his own wisecracks when fed back to him.

"Skip it," Sam said below his breath, and he walked across the big room to the door.

"He seemed ready to accept the work I've done," he told himself, going downstairs.

That afternoon the blue folders were returned to him—with a note in Dr. Robins' own handwriting. "I wish you would try again on this, Sam," the note said. "I'll give you one tip: If you can please Moir, you'll probably reach your audience."

Sam read the note. Twice he picked up the phone; he would talk to Patric Robins! Twice he put it down again. For thirty minutes he sat staring at the folders, spread out in a fan before him on the desk. Then, without a word to Mrs. Drozda, he took his raincoat out of the closet, shrugged into it, and went out.

He was not sure he would ever return.

But of course he did. He was at his desk ten minutes early the next morning. He had a sheaf of notes made during the night. He stacked the blue folders already written, typed, and available. He put two legal pads on his desk, and sharp-ened a dozen pencils. If Robins wanted sentiment, sentiment he would get!

He tried to stick to this high level of determination. But of course he was not a writing machine. He had to express himself. He had done the research, he had come to certain conclusions—and it was damned hard to try to set down the conclusions of two other men.

By the end of that week he was a mass of frustration; by the middle of the second he was sick of the whole idea—and convinced that he was being punished for his lippiness to Robins the morning after he came back from Richmond. But—he had not been very lippy. And surely Robins was too big a man . . .

Sam gazed hopelessly at his scribbled efforts. He should dictate, or record, something for Drozda. He was going to be asked what he had done. . . .

Well, that stack of blue folders on the shelf was what he had done! A man—maybe Sam—could take that stuff, go out on the road, and sell compulsory autopsies to any number of hospital boards!

Yes, and he could—maybe should—tell Dr. Robins, and Dr. Moir, as much!

He tidied his desk. Next morning he would begin to dictate—but for that day he had had it. He was going out for a drink, and then he would go home.

The next morning he found on his desk a memo requesting that he see Mr. Dammrich as soon as possible.

In the offices Mr. Dammrich was called the "traffic cop." This meant that he did what he was going to do to Sam that morning.

Dammrich was a rather young man—as young a man as Sam. But he seemed to be a marvel of detail. That morning he greeted Dr. Fowler with the announcement that there was this assignment for him. He handed a sheet of paper across the desk. Sam stared at Dammrich, who was a very handsome man, with a coin profile and high color under his cheekbones.

Then he stared at the paper. It did look like an assignment sheet. By golly, it *was* an assignment sheet! Sam was to go to Albuquerque, via TWA flight such and such number, departing . . .

He looked up. "What is all this?" he demanded.

"Just what it says, Fowler. A schedule of trips the office wants you to make, hospitals it wants you to visit, board meetings you are to attend, medical society meetings . . ."

"Hey, hey!" said Sam. "What am I supposed to do at these places?"

"It is all scheduled. The complete route is laid out in detail—hotels, your expenses, the clothes you will need. That is an important consideration. Two days are allowed you for any replenishment or furbishing of your wardrobe. You will need black-tie clothes as well as—"

Sam gasped. "How often do you pull this sort of thing?" he asked.

"Whenever I am told to arrange a schedule. I have the whole mass of information in this briefcase. If you prefer to use a case of your own, you may transfer, but I would suggest the advantage of keeping the papers in sequence."

"Yeah," said Sam, gazing at the black leather case. "Did you mention expenses?"

"You will be given an amount of traveler's checks, a credit card—other expenses can be passed on to the treasurer here."

"Clothes, too?"

"In reasonable supply. We realize that a month's trip . . ."

"A *month?*" Sam fairly yelped.

"It may run to a bit more than that. The climates will be

varied, though I have tried to make progress as easy for you as possible. I have included a list of what should be satisfactory clothing."

"I'll bet you have," said Sam, still looking at the briefcase. "You're telling me what to do and say, no doubt?"

"What to do, specifically. What to say, in general. I believe you have been working up some material for arguments to be presented . . ."

"On autopsies?" shouted Sam.

"Yes, doctor, I think so. There are several folders included in the material. . . ."

Sam grabbed for the briefcase. Yes, sir! There were his own folders. The same ones Moir and Robins—

"I've spent two weeks tearing that work to pieces," he told Dammrich in a weak voice.

"I believe the organization considered that process as ripening or gaining perspective, doctor."

Sam sighed. There were a dozen things he could say, and to a number of people. Slowly he closed the briefcase. "You say I have a couple of days?"

"To arrange your clothes and your own affairs, yes, sir."

To tell Carole, and to explain to her what he didn't understand himself. It was going to take every minute of his two days.

Dammrich pushed the briefcase toward him. "You may take a secretary with you, if you like," he offered.

"Mrs. Drozda?" Sam asked, not believing.

"If you'd need her. There will be reports, and correspondence."

"I'll get me a Kelly girl," said Sam loudly. "I'm going to have troubles enough. . . ."

"You're not married, are you, Dr. Fowler?"

"No, and with things like this happening to me, I doubt if I ever will be."

92

Mr. Dammrich laughed and stood up. "If I were you, I'd go straight home now and spend a couple of hours getting things lined up," he said. "This is Tuesday. Your first departure is 9.06 a.m. on Thursday."

It could not be done. But it was done. Sam went back to his apartment. He gingerly examined the briefcase and gazed in awe at his itinerary. He began to make notes of things he would have to do. His Wednesday date with Carole would take care of her—he hoped. But there was laundry, the cleaners, shopping—barber—word to the hotel. He would meet Don for lunch today at the Club, and tell him. . . .

He did all those things. Not too successfully, not anywhere near as smoothly as Dammrich's schedule worked out. Don insisted on coming by the apartment that evening to see for himself all the plane tickets and the detailed program. He decided it resembled an astronaut's flight into space. "You should have been given a chance to practice, boy."

Carole . . . She said she understood. She had expected the new job to take Sam away. Could she meet him some week end? He would phone her?

"Yes, and not on the expense account."

Then he made the mistake of telling her—trying to tell her —about the autopsy work, and his frustration. Don had grasped the story at once. Carole never did. If the corporation didn't respect and trust him, why didn't they get another boy?

By then Sam was deciding that he was happy to be "their boy." He was looking forward to the trip.

Of course it was a long one. He went to New Mexico and to California, Oregon and Colorado, to Wisconsin and Illinois. For five weeks, he lectured to hospital staffs, to boards of trustees, to city aldermen, to hospital auxiliaries. He took administrators to lunch, he attended dinners; he gave newspaper interviews, always sticking to his subject and never forgetting the "patient." Repetition became somewhat monotonous.

Sending off his daily reports, calling Carole, making sure that his clothes were in order, he often wondered if he was accomplishing anything except the expenditure of his strength and H.A.'s money. Always he left a hospital staff, an administrator, a board with the suggestion that H.A. would help them in this, or on any other project.

He had no way of knowing if any word except his own went back to the offices. Certainly he did not know if Robins was pleased. He was not recalled. That had to be good.

On week ends, he found he had hours of free time. And like many doctors, he spent this time "bus-riding." There was one certain hospital, he liked the administrator of it, and he became intrigued with its problems. It was a Jewish hospital, with many patients who were not Jewish, and the matter of diet was very big. The preparation of Orthodox food . . .

"How do we keep the sweet-sour smell out of the halls?"

For one week end, Sam, in person, explored that hospital, and then spent most of his free time on four week ends making plans, rearranging the building, changing its setup and its administration.

Not asked to do it, perhaps a good prospectus could be sold to Mt. Sinai. The administrator had sounded specifically interested about making some changes in the hospital.

Sam drew charts; he advanced ideas for change—the serving of meals, the collection and handling of laundry. At the end of four week ends he had the material to organize a new, large hospital, or to rearrange an established one. He liked the ideas which he had worked out. Maybe Robins would like them. He gathered the whole thing into a neat package, wrote a letter of explanation, and sent the stuff in, telling himself that it would be fine if H.A. liked it, but if

94

they didn't, he still had found ways to amuse himself. And not get too lonely for Carole.

On week ends, they did things together. All sorts of things. They window-shopped, they explored new neighborhoods in the city and in the suburbs. Would they like to live in this place? Or that? They found new restaurants, or experimented with cooking in Carole's apartment. They nearly always spent Sunday evenings with the Chaffines. Seldom did they do anything wildly exciting. But Sam missed the companionship, the warmth of friendship. . . .

And here he was now, on the end of a string, being whirled from town to town, away from everything that was familiar to him. He was wearing out his shoes, and getting good and sick of hotel rooms, not to mention motel quarters. He would wake up in the morning and have to assure himself of where he was. It was a very good thing that his schedule was meticulously detailed. Today he would look over a 250-bed hospital, and talk informally to whatever staff was available. Tonight he would address a dinner meeting and make a full-power speech on his subject. "See Folder #3." By then he didn't need to look at Folder #3. He knew the routine by heart.

Was this why he had exerted considerable effort to work for Hospital Administrators, Inc.? To leave home, meet strangers, talk like a parrot . . . ?

Well, he had wanted to work. And work he was doing.

6

It was on a Friday, at noontime, when Sam returned to his home city; he dropped his bags at the hotel where he lived, thinking that his clothes would need a lot of attention. He got his car and drove to the office, going upstairs and out into the lobby. Everyone was busy; girls carried papers swiftly down corridors, men walked even more swiftly. . . .

He was greeted. "Hello, Sam. Glad you're back."

Mrs. Drozda welcomed him, looking as smooth, as cool, as always. There was mail, she said, personal matters. She had cared for any business matters—as he had instructed, had he not?

"That's right," said Sam, moving to his desk. "How have you been?"

She answered; she even told him a little office gossip. And she said that Dr. Moir wanted to see him at three.

Sam nodded, sitting down. "Remind me," he said absent-mindedly.

The telephone rang, and Mrs. Drozda answered it. "Dr. Fowler's office, Mrs. Drozda speaking. Yes, sir, I think so." She held the receiver against her breast. "It's a Mr. Wynburn Clark, calling from New York. He called last week—"

Sam had his mail out on the blotter. He nodded. Wynburn Clark. *Wynburn Clark!* That was the literary agent who . . . He grabbed his phone. "Hello!" he said loudly. "Sam Fowler here." Good Lord, he hadn't thought about his book for the past six weeks. And now . . .

He listened. His hand scrambled through his mail. Yes, he said, he had had a letter. "I've been away—six weeks—just got back. Yes, your letter is here. Yes, I'm glad, too." He fumbled to open the letter with one hand. Yep! There was a folded, legal-looking paper enclosed. A contract? A contract!

The agent was talking. Talking a lot. And what he said was that he had sold Sam's book—the one he had written because of the work he had done with Downes—in Ashby Woods—Dear Lord! That seemed hundreds of years ago! Sam listened, and he looked at the contract, unfolding it. Yes, he agreed, of course whatever Clark had done would be satisfactory. He was just surprised. Yes, he would talk to the publisher. Yes, he could call him, or he would take a call right here. Before three, please, his time. His fingers fumbled to turn to the second page of the contract.

He set the phone down, and wished he could turn about to see Drozda's face. Had he given himself away? He put the contract into the long envelope, and the envelope into his coat pocket. He had sold his book. There would be money for it. He must keep track of that income. He must . . .

His fingers trembled as he made a show of looking at the rest of his personal mail. How long would it take . . . ?

The call came at two exactly. And it was the publisher—in person—a man with a nice, crisp voice, a friendly manner. Sam talked to him, keenly aware that Mrs. Drozda now was a bit more than curious. It was too much to expect that she would make herself scarce.

Sam felt of the envelope in his breast pocket, and drew his memo pad toward him; he should make notes. The publisher said they would want a picture of him, something new. He should pose for it. Not necessarily formal, but a professional picture. And they would want a brief biography. . . .

Sam listened and made notes. Should he mention Downes as a background for the book? He did not. The publisher said various pleasant things, he hoped to know Dr. Fowler personally, etc. Sam put the phone down and rubbed his hand back over his thick hair. Well!

Well, well, *well!*

He read his mail, he even dictated two letters to Mrs. Drozda, not mentioning the telephone conversation.

At three he went up for his appointment with Moir, and managed a creditable account of his trip. He concluded that the office was satisfied with his work. That long journey, this quickly, seemed a hundred years behind him.

He already knew that Carole would not be free that evening, though he talked to her on the phone. She was fine. He was fine, too, he said, and would have much to tell her.

The evening stretched out emptily; he decided he was tired, and unpacking was a dismal task. A dozen times he looked at the letter from his agent. He must sign and return the contract at once, but he wanted Carole to see it, to believe
. . .

On Saturday they met for lunch, and before they could order the Reuben sandwich that had become ritual, he told her about the book.

She was thrilled, even more than he had expected. She chided him for not telling her, even, that it was finished. And sent in!

He thought back to that time, that day. He had still been working for the Foundation. . . .

Carole could talk of little else than the book. Had she been told about the final version? What had the agent said about it? The publisher?

"From now on, nobody suggests anything but that it is a wonderful book."

"But it *is*, Sam!"

He smiled at her. "Eat your lunch. Don't we have Christmas shopping to do?"

"Oh, yes. For the Chaffine children. And something for their house. But, Sam . . ."

He let her talk. They went shopping, and brought their packages back to his rooms. He showed her the contract again, signed it with her watching and he kissed her. He had brought her a gift, and he kissed her again. "I've been away a long time," he told her.

She looked surprised. "Yes, you have been! Oh, Sam, I've missed you."

That evening they were going to the Symphony; they could have dinner sent up here to his rooms. And the next day, they would go out to the Chaffines'—early in the afternoon. Carole supposed Sam had missed them. Sam had.

"Don will talk about my trip," he teased Carole.

Don did ask, and Sam talked quite a bit about the things which he had done, and said, and seen. He talked a little about H.A., Inc.'s inscrutable methods.

"But they work," he concluded. "I went on this safari completely saturated with my subject. Robins must be the genius he is reputed to be. There are quite a lot of us working for the organization. I won't flatter myself that he gives me personal attention."

It was a snowy day; they sat inside and looked out upon the patio. In the middle of the living-room floor the children played with some gadgets which Sam had brought them.

"The important thing to me," said JoAnn, "would be, do you like this job, Sam? Carole, do you think he does? All this traveling, and without much notice. . . ."

Carole smiled at Sam. "I think his going and staying for so long was arranged in a manner beyond his control, JoAnn. I miss him dreadfully, of course, when he's gone for so long."

99

"Do you expect him to do it again?" JoAnn turned to look at Sam. "Did *you* like it?" she demanded.

Sam shrugged. "I got awfully tired of hotels."

"But you live in a hotel!"

"I do. In an apartment hotel, and I have an apartment. I don't live in one room, with one closet, one bed, one dresser, one desk, one window. Those places all look alike, and smell alike. The food— In my place I have my own kitchenette, and I can burn my toast if I want to. Hotel restaurants never burn the toast."

Don chuckled. "You really didn't expect to be sent on such a trip, did you?" he asked.

"No, I didn't. I knew other men went out on field trips, and came back with reports. I'll make such a report, incidently. When I get the material together. You see, I had written all the speeches I made, and had assembled all the notes . . ."

"Oh, speaking of writing!" cried Carole, bouncing on the cushion where she sat before the fire. "Did you know . . . ?"

And she was off and away about the book. Sam should have warned her that the matter was still under wraps. Now, all he could do was sit back, nurse his drink, and listen to these good friends be excited. Given a chance to speak, he would warn them. . . .

The Chaffines were even more excited than Carole had been. They had known only vaguely that Sam was dabbling in book writing. They asked a dozen questions, they made a dozen plans. They would give a party, they declared. A real bash! And invite just everybody.

"Let me look at you, Sam," said JoAnn, coming over to stand before him. "I guess you look the same . . . but you can't *be* the same. When will your book be published?"

"I don't know, JoAnn. It takes time, I suppose."

"When in thunder did you have time to write it?" Don asked him.

"Evenings. Some week ends when Carole's conscience made her do other things. . . ."

"Like having my hair washed, or sewing on buttons," she drawled. "Like going to church, and cultivating a few interests against Sam's safaris."

Their friends laughed. "It must have been work!" Don concluded.

"What's it about?" JoAnn bored in. "*Talk* to us, Sam!"

"Do I have a chance?"

"We'll be still."

He smiled at her. "All right. I'll tell you a little. But first I must warn you—as I should have warned my gabby friend down there—that the publishers want this kept under cover. They want to—their term is *break*—they want to break the news about the book in the most effective way possible. I'll let you know when the day is set. I suppose it is a matter of publicity and sales promotion. Lord, when I realize how little I know about publishing a book, I wonder that I had nerve enough ever to write one."

"You had the talent," said Carole solemnly, "and I certainly hope they don't make me wait long to brag about you."

It was not very long. Six weeks, about. Sam let Carole select the best picture among the proofs given him by the commercial photographer to which he had gone. This picture appeared in the morning newspaper, on the front page.

"And then," Sam told later, "all hell broke loose."

A book! Written about a doctor, by a doctor—right in this very city—

The people at the hotel made a fuss, those at the office—even Patric Robins came down to congratulate him. "We wanted a writer when we hired you, Sam, and it certainly looks as if we had one!" From messenger to top brass, there was a lot of friendliness. Mrs. Drozda said she'd known for months! Friends called in. The newspapers wanted interviews . . .

"You're not going to get much work done," Dr. Moir told him.

"Nor the office. I'm sorry, sir. It can't deserve all this fuss."

"It's good publicity, Fowler. D'you mind if our Public Relations department handles these calls? You might move over there for today. . . ."

On the face of it, this seemed ridiculous. *Big deal!* Sam kept saying under his breath. He consented to the interviews. It went on, and on—

Sam was as excited as anyone, though he tried not to show it. But he heard Carole tell JoAnn Chaffine that he was "on top of himself."

Was he? Yes, he supposed he was.

At the office—at the next executive meeting—he heard Dr. Moir praise the work he already had done for H.A. He mentioned—and this came as a surprise to Sam—the excellent chart which Sam had made for a hospital's reorganization while he was on an exhausting trip for other purposes. This had to be his idea for Mt. Sinai.

"Are you going to reorganize that hospital?" asked the man seated next to him.

"I'd like to," Sam told him,"if they use my ideas."

"Have you done any of that sort of work?"

"Just on paper."

"You seem to do all right with paper."

Sam looked as modest as he could manage.

It was that day, or the next, that Sam spied Ginsburg again, crossing the street level court. This time he made a chance to speak to the man. He said he had seen him a time or two, and recognized him. "Don't you remember me?"

"Yeah, you're Doc Fowler."

"That's right. Do you work in this building? How are you getting along?"

"I work here—in the lobby pharmacy, and I'm doing all right. I guess. I've seen you, Doc, and recognized you. You don't change." Ginsburg rubbed his hand back over his own balding head. "I hated to butt in on you, Doc," he said, with a deprecating smile. "I heard you had a big job with the top-floor swells."

"Oh, now, look!" Sam protested.

"That's top-drawer stuff, and you know it," Ginsburg insisted.

"For all you know, I'm their office boy."

"Only, you're not. And I saw your picture in the paper the other day. How about that? An author!"

"Somebody has to write the books."

"Yeah, I guess so, but it's kinda funny when somebody you know . . . And we did know each other pretty well, didn't we, Doc? Back in Ashby Woods, remember?"

In those days Sam often had spent an idle hour at the drugstore, and talked to the pharmacist. Often he had had to call this man out at night for some special medication. . . .

Now he slapped Ginsburg's shoulder. "I certainly do remember," he said heartily. "Look, why don't we have a drink together one of these days?"

Ginsburg smiled. "Sure, Doc. Sure. Just say when." He enjoyed his little joke, and they parted on that note.

Somehow it made Sam feel good to have reestablished his relationship with Ginsburg. In a way, it gave him a life line to Ashby Woods and Dr. Downes. He wondered if the people back there would hear about his book, read it, maybe even recognize a thing or two in it. A scene, an incident . . .

The excitement of the book continued for him in varying degrees. The telephone calls, and the correspondence, between him and New York. In the office—he went through the motions of work, and he did work. He was sure that he did. His task for the past weeks had been devoted to setting up the proper routines in the hospitals who were adopting his suggestions for autopsy procedure. There were many details to be ironed out and unforeseen difficulties to be resolved.

But just the same, his book kept being an item. When the girl from the accounting office brought in his pay check on the first of the month, she said archly, "I guess this won't seem so important now that you're a rich writer."

Sam snatched at the strip of blue paper. "Don't get any such foolish notions into your head!" he said sternly, and the young woman laughed merrily.

The telephone girls took an unwarranted interest in his calls. This was somewhat annoying, and maybe Sam should lay down some lines there. He had no idea of how to go about doing this, or of what to say. . . .

Those days he was playing his life, and his work, five minutes at a time. He never knew quite what to expect. From receptionist to Carole, there seemed to be any number of surprises possible.

Even Robins . . .

Even Robins? That man—he called Sam at nine o'clock one Saturday morning. Sam was barely out of bed. Week ends he considered definitely to be for rest and recreation. If this guy thought he was going out on another trip—

But Robins had other things in mind. "I believe you told me once that you played golf, Sam," he said.

Sam turned to look out of the window behind him. Yes, the sun was shining. "I'm very good in the duffer class," he admitted.

"How about going a round with me today?"

"It's pretty cold, isn't it?"

"Temperature is fifty already; the sun is shining. I'll pick you up at eleven. Okay?"

Well, what did a man say?

He said Okay, and hoped he knew where his golf shoes were. What kind of golfer was Robins? Good, of course. There'd be no reason for Sam to be careful not to beat the boss. Had there been reason, he would not have been careful. Robins would see right through such a maneuver.

He considered clothes, he even considered thermal underwear. Instead he found a heavy sweater and a warm shirt to wear under it. Where would they play? He'd get to ride in the boss's Ferrari, he supposed.

And why was he going to play golf with that man? He called Carole to tell her what was cooking. "I may not get home until dark," he told her gloomily

She laughed at him. "You'll have a fine time. You know you like Dr. Robins."

"I admire him," Sam corrected. "He doesn't stand still long enough for anyone to like him."

She laughed again. "Call me when you get home. I'll want to hear all about it."

Late that afternoon, home and ready to call Carole, he decided that he had plenty to tell her. It had been quite a day, beginning with the ride in the low-slung sports car. Robins had worn a short camel's hair coat, its collar up behind his ears. He told Sam that this was a British Warm. "You should get one sometime."

Sam was glad he had brought gloves, though once on the sunny course, things were not too bad. He was intrigued by Robins' outfit of brown corduroy trousers and loose shirt to match. The things looked comfortable. The man employed a caddy and scorned a cart. "I came out here for exercise," he explained.

Exercise they got, at top speed, and a lot of Robins' talk. He told Sam a great deal about himself. He was fond of music, it seemed. All kinds of music. "My record collection contains everything from Stravinski to Herb Alpert. No Beatles, but I may come to that. I like some of the things Simon and Garfunkel do. But I don't want my Bach being clouded with stereophonic gadgetry and trickery."

Next, he asked Sam if he'd ever tried his hand at hospital management.

He knew that Sam had not.

"But you did do general practice," he went on. "I did, too, as a beginner. And in a small town. That's why your record interested me. There is nothing like small-town medicine to get a man ready for the big time. And of course I managed some hospitals. Small ones, where I was called the superintendent. And big ones with a rubber tree in the corner of my office. Same job, both places, same problems, one after the other. The main thing, Sam, is for any administrator to get the support of the bridge-table gang and community interest. Then a man can do the things he wants with a hospital. I found that out when I was learning everything needed to be known by the administrator. Lord, I even explored the subject from a patient's bed."

Sam was interested, curious, and ten feet behind the boss.

"Sure did," said Robins, swinging his driver at a dandelion head as he strode past. Knocked it off, too. "Got myself a severe case of sunburn on a beach one time. Developed a kidney inflammation—it hospitalized me. And I learned a hell of a lot. I reckon the hospital did, too. I suppose my hospital record is confidential, but it is well known that doctors do not make the best patients. And when the doctor is the administrator as well—"

Walking back to the clubhouse, still at top speed, he told Sam emphatically that hospitals were not factories—factories for the sick. "You'll hear that charge. But there's one big difference, Sam. A factory can shut down when it runs out of materials or help. A hospital never can. And don't let anyone compare a hospital to a hotel, either. Hospitals start where hotels leave off. The charge for a hospital bed pays for services no hotel ever dreamed of providing. Day and night nursing care, with all the other services available—everything from X-ray equipment to a delivery room. Room, bed, board. Sure we give that, and so much else that, while a hotel can get by with something less than one employee to a customer, a hospital needs two and a half. Three is a better figure."

He talked a lot, and Sam wished he could be making notes. He would try to remember. He would, without notes, certainly remember the story which Robins told while they ate lunch. By then it was close to three o'clock. The men had showered; they had had several hours of fresh air and exercise. Sam was starved. Maybe Robins was, too. But his order was for grapefruit juice and sliced cold roast beef—paper-thin slices, which he spread with caviar. "Never eat onion with caviar," he told Sam sternly.

Sam ordered grilled lamb chops.

Robins was still in his expansive, talkative mood. "Maybe," Sam thought, "he planned all this, the way a hospital is planned for changes in administration. Do this. A week later, do that. Robins had probably planned this day of talk with Sam. Talk to Sam."

Sam did not mind. He settled down to an enjoyment of the crisp brown chops. "I'm hungry," was his only excuse for ordering a proper meal.

Robins paid no attention to what he said or to what he ate.

"When you first came to us," he said, "you did a job connected with a baby."

"Yes, sir."

"That sent you off on the autopsy thing. I believe you're still working on that?"

"Yes, sir,"

For an instant Patric Robins regarded him from beneath his heavy brows. "I remember a baby situation before I ever started this administration thing," he said thoughtfully. "I was a resident—chief resident, as a matter of fact—at a hospital in a state university town. One of the kitchen girls came to me for an examination. She had fainted or up-chucked, or something. Her superior said she must be sick, and if she was sick—well, anyway, I examined her and found she was pregnant. No surprise to her, of course. The only complication was that she had no husband. Well, I went a bit outside my duties and enlisted the help of the social worker. She thought I was interested in *her*— You have to play all the angles, Sam."

Sam smiled and tackled his second chop.

"We arranged for the girl to go to a small town upstate, work parttime in a dairy. The G.P. there would and did hospitalize her at term. By then I had learned that all sorts of things must be handled in a hospital. And do you know? Several years later, when I was an administrator, who should come up for a job but this same girl. She told me that she had been contemplating suicide, when I was so, quote, wonderful to her. She went on to say that she had named the baby Patric. I said she could have the job, but to keep quiet around the hospital about her gratitude."

It was a good story. Sam must remember it. A definite plot could be built . . .

Robins was sipping his grapefruit juice. "What" he asked abruptly and bluntly, "what about Lorraine Harper?"

Sam gulped, and choked a little. "Lorraine?" he stammered.

"That's the name. Is there some personal angle in your relationship?"

"I would not call it a relationship, sir," said Sam stiffly. He could feel his neck getting red.

Patric Robins saw it doing so. "Don't tell me that this is none of my business, Sam," he said quietly. "Because everything about you is my affair."

He elaborated on this a little, and Sam waited him out. Then he looked across at the strange, and fascinating, man who was his host, his boss. "I happen to be engaged to a wonderful girl," he said quietly. "I would like you to meet her. We have been engaged since before I left the Harper Foundation. She's a good-looking girl, and smart. Her name is Carole Tebeau, and she works for an investment company."

"Why don't you marry her?" asked Dr. Robins.

"I probably shall, sir," said Sam. "And soon."

That had been a day. The Mt. Sinai Hospital reorganization plan had not been mentioned.

7

Sam told many of these things to Carole that night; he repeated them to the Chaffines the next day. Don wanted to know about Robins' golf game.

Sam laughed and scrubbed his ear. "I'd have to play with him a few times more to be able to say. The locker room attendant told me he plays around in something below ninety."

"Did you beat him?"

"I don't know that, either. I tell you, Don—that man races up and down the fairways so fast, and talks so much—I was too breathless to care if I won or not, and often too far behind him to know what he shot. Or me, either. I do know this: if I am going to play much golf with the guy, or ride around in his open sports car, I am going to buy *me* a British Warm!"

Don frowned and looked across at Carole. "Do you think our friend has flipped?" he asked

She nodded, smiling. "He's flipped," she said serenely.

"We talked about you," Sam told her. "Robins and I did."

She sat erect. "You— What did you say?"

"That you and I were going to be married. And soon."

"I hope he approved."

Sam chuckled. Then he told them what Robins had said about his business being Robins' as well as his own.

"I'm sure he's proud of you," Carole told him.

They were sitting out on the patio, in the sunshine, but the children had gone indoors. "It's cold out here," they had told their elders.

"If Robins has any feeling about me," said Sam, "he keeps it to himself."

"Would he, if he disapproved?"

Sam buttoned his sweater. "Probably not. But I doubt if his enthusiasm equals yours, Carole."

"It couldn't. Nobody could be as proud as I am of your success in the job, and about the book."

"Keep talking," said Sam.

"Yes, do that," urged JoAnn. "I especially want to know about this wedding. Do you really have plans?"

"I do," said Carole calmly.

"Then you do, too," Don assured Sam, who nodded. He also wanted to hear about those plans.

"Well," Carole began, "I thought we could manage by Easter. I'd like it before, but since I want a church wedding —small, but in the church—it will have to be right after."

"You and nine hundred other brides," said JoAnn.

"I like the way they used to do it out west," said Sam, getting excited. Easter was less than a month away. "You shack up together and wait until the preacher gets around to you."

Carole ignored him, though he got a laugh from Don and JoAnn.

"He's just the boy to do it, too," said Don.

"Easter doesn't give us much time," Carole was saying. "To find a house and—"

"A house!" cried Sam. "You mean—a—a *house?*"

Her eyes were wide and dark. "Yes, darling. I want a house. We can have one now, can't we?"

Sam turned up his sweater collar. "Either I'm in shock, or I'm freezing to death."

"We'd better move inside," Don agreed. "But I'll tell you first, Carole, he can afford a house."

They moved inside, Don lit the fire. JoAnn went for coffee. "Put something in mine," Sam called after her. "For the shock, you know."

"I know just the house for you two," she announced when she brought back her tray of mugs. "It's roomy without being huge, and the grounds are planted. You know that stone house, Carole—you pass it as you come here. It's right after you turn into this road. Stone, with a slate roof, just down the hill—"

"Oh," moaned Carole, "that would be perfect! Bay window— Come on, Sam, I'll show it to you."

He did not move. "I still am freezing," he complained.

"You'll come anyway. We'll be right back, folks."

She led him outside, to the far end of the patio. "Before I look at any houses," he told her, putting his arms around her . . . His kiss was long, and warm.

"They'll see us," Carole murmured.

"They're watching," Sam agreed. "If I didn't do this, Don would call the funny wagon. Here. Just relax, and—"

But they looked at the house, too. "In the summer, with the leaves out," said Carole, "we couldn't see it from here. But isn't it just perfect, Sam?"

"From the outside," he agreed. "It's very nice. But there's just one thing—"

"What's that?"

"People are living in it. Can't you tell? Smoke from the chimney, kiddy swing in the yard . . ."

"You're probably right. But there are other houses. JoAnn was citing an example. I'll find ours. You'll see."

"Kiss me again, and then take me back where I can defrost."

They went back into the house, and the women continued, gaily, to make plans. How big the house should be—

"I'll want a room for my desk," Sam specified.

They all laughed, knowing the state of Sam's desk in his living room at the hotel. "You're going to keep on writing, then," JoAnn concluded.

"I'll have to, the way you girls are spending my money. Don't forget, unless Carole is a good grass cutter, we'll need a brick or gravel yard."

The chatter was fun. Sam was happy about the way things were going, but still Carole told him he seemed bothered. They were in the kitchen, warming the *lasagna* and hard rolls which they had brought for supper. "Is something wrong, dear?" she asked him. "Is there something about the job . . . ?" She was thinking that Robins had probably done more talking about Sam's work than he had told.

One of the Chaffine children, Augusta came into the kitchen then for napkins, and he didn't have to answer Carole more than to say that the job was all right. Yes, he was sure. Didn't they bring some wine? What about the kids?

"JoAnn would scalp me if I brought milk."

"Isn't there something more exciting we could provide for them when it's our turn to tote food?"

"They drink milk, Sam."

"I'm going to look into that situation."

They ate their supper before the fire, and the clearing away was quickly accomplished. JoAnn took the little boy, Peter, off to bed. "He just needs to get started," she explained, coming back and sitting down again on the couch. "A half hour, Augusta," she reminded her daughter.

"I *know*," said the girl. She was drawing something, her hair falling across her face. Sam had teased her about eating some of it along with her *lasagna*. She had been patient with his older-person idea of what was funny.

113

Companionable, replete, they gazed at the fire and talked of various things in a drowsy, pleasant way. Sam sprawled on the floor, his head on a square leather cushion, one ankle propped on his updrawn knee. He was, he said, still resting up from that golf game. "I wonder if Robins ever heard that a man who can't break eighty-five should never go on a golf course."

"How's he going to learn enough to break eighty-five?" Don asked. "When I was young and unencumbered and played golf on my free afternoons—now I have to cut grass, and stuff—I used to start the season flirting with a hundred. By September, I'd be into the eighties."

"That must have been a long time ago," drawled Sam.

"I'm an o-o-old man."

"So am I," groaned Sam, rolling over on his stomach, resting his chin on his folded arms.

"But he says his work is going fine," chirped Carole, and Sam looked up at her.

"Must you quote everything I say?" he asked. "And if you do, will you please quote it correctly? I said everything was all right."

"Isn't it *fine?*" asked Don.

"Well, I quibble about words, Donald. You know I do."

"Yes. What isn't fine about the new job?"

"Not much. Maybe nothing at all. It's just—well, I don't feel that I am fully busy."

"Good Lord, man . . ."

"I know. I've not been there long enough. I took that one long trip. Now and then I sally forth to talk things over with this hospital and that. My desk keeps well supplied."

"What would you consider . . . ?"

Don and Sam had been close friends for so long that Sam often said the other man was like his conscience. They did not always agree with each other, but they usually did understand what the other man was thinking and feeling.

JoAnn had soon come to recognize this quality in their friendship and kept her hands off. Carole was not yet so wise. She would like to be Sam's conscience.

"I realize," Sam said now, "that I can't be sent out to administer a hospital. I've not had the experience, of course." Though he would like to do just that for a place like Mt. Sinai. Or Sinai itself. To go there, solve its problems, set the gears meshing . . . *There* would be a job!

"I'm the dumb one of this quartet," said JoAnn, "and I probably have been told the answer to this. But tell me again. Sam, what is it you do?"

Sam turned his head to look at the pretty blonde woman. He liked JoAnn. "Me?" he asked.

"No. The corporation, or whatever it is called."

"Oh. The Ink."

"That's a funny, sweetheart," Don explained to his wife. "You see . . ."

She punched him, not lightly. "Let Sam talk."

"You be careful what you say, boy," Don warned.

Sam grinned. He gazed into the fire. "Well," he said slowly, "the organization is Robins. The rest of us are just the extra hands and feet he needs to carry out the things he thinks up. I am sure it's been that way from the first. It began, you know, through Robins' curiosity as to why hospitals change their administrators so often."

Don's head was nodding up and down. "They do," he agreed.

"Some of them," Sam agreed. "Yes, they do. And our organization sets itself to find out why. Is the man the wrong man? Are the board members fully informed as to their duties, privileges, and so on? Is the hospital plant well designed and functioning? What's wrong with the personnel? What's wrong with the key personalities?"

"My goodness," breathed JoAnn.

"There are scores of things that can interfere with a hospi-

tal's smooth operation," Sam agreed. "When there are difficulties, our organization is asked to come in and find out
why, and what. Sometimes we reorganize the whole setup.
Most of our field men are sent to these hospitals to administer them, find out what difficulties exist, or that may develop,
get things running smoothly, then train someone to take
over the operation. Sometimes the hospital administrator is
okay. He may himself know what the problem is, and can
ask for specific help. I ran into this on my trip. There was
this big hospital, built, organized, run, by Jews. It is a good
hospital, and has several outstanding services."

"They usually are good," Don agreed.

"Yes, they are. They keep the welfare of the sick in mind,
they exert compassion. Now this hospital had a couple of
problems. One, it had grown, physically. Wings had been
added, three floors built on, things like that. Another situation has arisen; non-Jewish patients are now admitted. This
develops a problem of its own. Jewish dietary laws require
certain menus. Non-Jewish patients like bacon for breakfast."

Don began to laugh.

"It can be serious," Sam assured him. "That hospital not
only has the problem of serving the meals hot, but handling
them in a way not to offend any patient. You have to have
separate diet kitchens, but do you have to have them on
every floor? With the nurse and doctor shortage, you can't always staff pure-Orthodox."

"I'd go back to all Jewish," said Carole.

"You can't do that, sweetheart," Sam told her. "For one
thing, this hospital boasts a very fine—superfine—orthopedic
surgeon. He is especially wonderful with broken hips. Cheatham, Don. Elmer Cheatham."

"Oh, yes!" cried Don. "He's a wizard. I've recommended
him for congenitals."

"And were your patients all Jewish?"

Don chuckled.

"Cheatham isn't a Jewish name," Carole pointed out.

"No. And Cheatham isn't a Jew. He is just a big, red-headed guy who knows what to do for people—most of them old people—who break their hips, but want to get back on their feet again, able to walk. Some of them are Jewish. A lot of them are. And many of them Orthodox Jews at that. They want the holidays observed, and no smell of bacon in the halls."

Don laughed and shook his head. "If your Ink can solve those things . . ."

"Maybe it can't. I spent my week ends on the trip working out some solutions. I practically rebuilt the place, had schedules of meals, service traffic patterns—I did the whole thing. Some of it unworkable, I suppose, but I'd love to see it tried."

"Why don't they send you out?"

"Lack of experience, son. Lack of experience."

"I know. You need experience to get a job, but without a job, how do you get experience? What was the Ink's reaction to your reorganization plan?"

"Dead silence. They didn't even erect a decent tombstone."

"Oh, Sam . . ." Carole protested.

"That's their right, darling. Now, let's see. What else do we do? We bird-dog. That is, we send someone out to trouble-shoot in the case of a particular and immediate problem."

"What sort of problem? Or trouble?"

"Well, we sometimes supply an administrator when a hospital is left without one."

"How . . . ?" Don began.

"Oh, one of the staff men goes, or the Ink knows where to find a trained man. We keep files, you know. A large room full of files."

"Very efficient. I wanted to know how a hospital becomes minus an administrator, on an emergency basis."

"Well, a man can die."

"That's an emergency, all right."

"It sure is. Or maybe the fellow has to be fired. There's been a big row, or he quits."

"Do you train administrators, Sam?" JoAnn asked.

"We don't have a school. But we work with medical schools and universities toward the training of such men. They need not be doctors. An administrator must be hep on all sorts of activities, purchasing, fund raising, things like that. The graduate schools of business and administration are a good source, but the candidates need special training."

"Will you be working along that line?"

"After I get a bit more hep myself. Of course I think I could handle some of the emergencies."

"What sort . . . ?"

"I told you about the baby who died."

JoAnn and Carole made sounds of pity.

"And then there was this situation which I know about only through hearsay. However, it is dramatic enough to interest the ladies. And you're young, Don, but you must remember iron lungs. And polio?"

"You bet. We still have iron lungs around, and we use them."

"I know you do. For certain cases of paralysis, injuries, and so on. But what would you do if you were working in a hospital in a small western city, had a single iron lung complete with patient, and word came to you that back in a National Park infirmary there were two cases of what looked like polio. Tourists—very sick—the Rangers were calling on all their resources to bring the sick patients over the mountain to your hospital, and would you please have the lungs ready?"

"I'd run like a deer," said Don.

"No. Not if you were well acquainted with Hospital Administrators."

"All right, tell me."

"Oh, I'm going to! You'd call our office, and we would lo-cate two lungs within three hundred miles of you—we have files on such things. And— Did I say it was storming? Rain, lightning . . ."

"I took that for granted."

"Well, it was storming. And Sunday . . ."

"But good old Hospital Administrators knew what to do."

"They really did, Don. Robins did. He realized that the lung was a heavy piece of equipment, and that most small city police forces are limited as to resources. So what does he do? He calls the Air National Guard of two adjacent states, and—"

"Now wait up, Sam. Those units, especially in the north-west, are trained on fighter planes, and—"

"And they all have a bomber of some sort. Usually called the Goony Bird. They also have plenty of beef and brawn—"

"Can they fly in a storm?" Carole asked.

"They can. They did. They solved the emergency."

"And hurrah for Ink," drawled Don. "Now if they will only solve the question of what to do with you. . . ."

"Oh, I am sure it has been solved. They just haven't put that work sheet on my desk. I suppose they will someday. Meanwhile I'm waiting, taking each day, one at a time."

"That alone can be a full-time job."

"It is," Sam agreed. "And when I am assigned . . ."

Carole sighed. "Maybe Easter will be too soon for our wedding," she said. "How about—well—June?"

"Maybe," said Sam.

He took Carole home and asked to come in. She let him, with a warning that tomorrow was a working day.

He took off his coat, and hers. Then he drew her into his arms, warmly demanding. "We can still be married at Easter, sweetheart," he told her.

"It doesn't give me much time to find a house."

"Who needs a house?"

"I do," said Carole. "I would. You have your job, but I'd need a house."

"But couldn't we still be married at Easter? Or even this week?" His embrace tightened.

"Sam . . ."

"Yes, we could. We could get our license and tests tomorrow, and be married Thursday or Friday."

She laughed a little and tucked her head down into his shoulder.

"We could," Sam assured her. "Tomorrow, you could give notice at the office . . ."

"But, Sam . . ."

"You're not going to work. I'll need you at home, cutting all that grass and tending to all those kids." He kissed her, and kissed her again. He—

She pushed him away.

"Let me stay," he whispered in her ear.

"No!"

"If you did, we'd have to get married Friday."

"You—can't stay. Sam! What has got into you?"

"I just want to marry my girl."

"You'll wait."

He dropped his arms. "You'd like it," he told her, picking up his coat.

She was too confused, and startled, to argue with him. She probably would like it, but—

She stood at the window and watched him come out of the apartment house, get into his car. A wind whipped his hair and the edge of his coat. He looked lonesome down there on that empty sidewalk. He—

She turned from the window and found a calendar. She drew a circle around Friday, and a darker one around Easter Sunday.

Sam didn't think a house was important.

8

Sam's book, *One-Man Clinic,* came out in April. Sam received ten copies, gave one to Carole, one to the Chaffines, and wondered what he would do with the others until people at the office began to hint that they would sure like to have one. He put a copy on the shelf in the reference library.

He considered sending a book to Dr. Downes and Judy in Ashby Woods, but they probably would have forgotten him.

The book immediately got good reviews. It was called a fine, well-developed story about a horse-trading doctor working in a small town. The two sides of the man—passages were quoted. "The sweetest sound in the world was the plop-plop-plop of hoofs in the dust as a fast trotter rounded the three-quarter pole, knees high, and head cocked." Horse trading, training, gaiting, racing his horses, built this doctor's hospital and clinic. The story was that of a determined doctor and his quarrels with the townspeople necessary to build his hospital and care for those same people.

The book was going to be popular.

The publishers gave a cocktail party to introduce this new writer to the literary world. Sam was interviewed and photographed. He didn't mind one party of that sort, but wished he had taken Carole to New York with him. She would have liked that, too.

The Chaffines gave their party, and Sam did really enjoy that one. "Nothing like your friends to get your head down to size," he told Don and JoAnn.

A department store in the city arranged an autographing party. Sam was ready to refuse this honor, but the publishers thought he should do it. He did, and vowed never to do it again.

To sit there behind a table stacked with his books, to smile inanely at the kind people who came to see him, to say the same things to them, inanely, over and over . . .

JoAnn and Carole were there, in Carole's lunch hour. "The women love you!" JoAnn told him.

He wished they had not come. "They make me feel like a fool," he grumbled. "Go home, will you?"

He didn't like the autograph party, he said. But it was good to be noticed, to be a success at something which he had done on his own, through his own efforts and abilities.

Then, at the beginning of the second week, he got an urgent telephone call from his literary agent. Could he come back to New York?

"Of course not. I have a job to hold down."

"The publishers want to talk to you."

"They have talked to me."

"This is very important, Dr. Fowler."

"Couldn't I call them, and talk to them?"

"You could try that, but if they insist, I'd like you to agree to come in. . . ."

Sam made the call, sending Mrs. Drozda off on some errand. That smooth blonde listened too well, and drew some fantastic conclusions. That morning she could have drawn some really gaudy ones.

He reached the switchboard, then his personal editor. "Will you wait a minute, Dr. Fowler? Mr. Boyer may want to talk to you himself."

The Big Man. The top. Sam waited. Having been there,

he could picture the offices—big, busy, pleasant. The windows of the president's office overlooked a small park and the busy streets of New York.

The president came on. How was Sam?

"I'm fine, sir. I had this call from Wynburn Clark; he asked me to come to New York, but I'd find that rather inconvenient just now, sir. Could you tell me . . . ?"

"A personal confrontation would have been better, Sam. But I realize your position. So—let's see. There are some questions . . ."

"About the book?"

"Yes. It seems to be going quite well, incidentally. I believe Clark has sold some rights."

Sam waited.

"Er—yes," said the voice at the other end of the wire. "Now, let me see, Sam. Could you tell me something about the research behind your book?"

Sam frowned. He had done some research. The story was placed in the twenties and thirties. He was himself too young. . . . "I used newspaper and magazine files, sir, for the time material. Clothes, home decoration, things like that. I checked on automobiles, medical equipment available during the period."

"Mhmmmn," said Mr. Boyer. He was a very nice chap. "You understand we would want to give proper credits, if credit should be given."

Sam frowned, and turned a pencil end for end, point, eraser, point again. "I don't understand," he said.

"Well, tell me this, can you?" asked Mr. Boyer, his tone brisk. "When did you write the book?"

"When?" asked Sam stupidly.

"Yes. When did you begin to write it? How long did it take?"

"Oh," said Sam. "The idea—the beginning—as much as five years ago. I don't remember exactly. Intensively, the research you mentioned, and the getting things in line—I'd say the writing took three years—first draft, rewriting and all." Easily it had taken that long. He had begun before he knew Carole.

"Yes," said Mr. Boyer crisply. "Now tell me this. Is there an identifiable character? Something that could be identified?"

Sam stared hard at the memo pad beneath his pencil point. All at once, he felt nervous and depressed. He wanted to hang up the phone, get away. . . .

"Are you talking about libel?" he asked his publisher, hearing hoarseness croak in his voice.

"Well, libel, doctor. You understand that you would have to use a person's name, and draw a picture no one could mistake, with unpleasantness broadly implied. But sometimes . . ."

"The characters in my book," said Sam stiffly, "are based on real people, but not too exactly. Some of the incidents are true. In my experience. But the story is my own!"

It was. He had placed the story back thirty-five or forty years, and it told of an appealing young doctor, and the girl who loved and believed in him. That girl had been drawn from what Sam remembered of Judy Downes. But the doctor —perhaps it had been a dream picture of himself, doing some of the things which Dr. Downes had done. Building a hospital out of his dreams, against the town's belief in its possibility. . . .

"The book was entirely my own work," he said stiffly. "I even did the typing."

As he talked, he found himself, swiftly, back in Ashby Woods. Had his book reached there? Was its bright jacket displayed in some store window, and at the library? Had Dr. Downes read it, recognized things he had told Sam—Would he make trouble? Was he doing it? Oh, he wouldn't!

But—would he? In the short time—How had he found out that there was a book?

124

Ginsburg? Ginsburg would have read about Sam and his book in the city newspapers, and seen his picture. Curiosity might have led him to buy a book and read it. . . .

Did he have contacts in Ashby Woods? Ginsburg was the type to decide Sam was a "big shot" and brag about knowing him. He probably had told someone in Ashby Woods about the book, and stirred things up there.

Sam told Mr. Boyer that he was sure there was no basis for a libel charge. But he continued to worry because the subject had ever come up. He didn't have to go to New York, even over a week end. He tried to put the matter out of his mind. He did not talk about it to anyone.

But on a beautiful week end, the first one in May, he told Carole that he didn't think he wanted to go out to the Chaffines' that Sunday evening.

"Is something wrong, Sam?"

"What could be wrong?"

"I don't know."

"We don't have to go out there every week."

"No, we don't. And we don't go. When you are out of town, or when I have the flu, as I did in March, or—"

Once the Chaffines had gone on a trip with the kids.

Sam said nothing.

"There is something wrong with you," Carole told him. "It's been wrong for about a month—give or take a day or two."

"Oh, now . . ."

She put her hand on his arm. They had gone to the park, had spent an hour in the art museum, and were now strolling back to where they had parked the car.

Sam covered her hand, and smiled down at her. She was wearing a straight dress of checkered wool, red, white, and blue—hound's tooth—and a little round red hat that clung to the back of her head. "You look cute," he told her.

She snorted delicately. "I am not the cute type, and you know it. So tell me what you are worrying about."

Sam sighed.

"Is it your work, Sam? I often think . . ."

"The work is fine, Carole. It really is."

"All right, then. Are you worrying about me?"

He was startled, and turned to look at her. "You?" he demanded. "Should I worry about you?"

"Maybe you shouldn't be worried at all. That's why I am quizzing you."

"But you asked me . . . ?"

"I am a large part of your life. I think I am?" She looked up.

"You are," he told her, smiling. "And I'd like to make that part larger."

"I know," she agreed. "You wish I would have married you—or a reasonable facsimile—that chilly evening when we'd been out at the Chaffines'."

"I love you, Carole. A man wants certain things from the woman he loves."

"I know." She reached up and kissed his cheek, and he caught her arm strongly in his hand, drew her against him, not gently.

She pushed away. "Sam . . ."

"There's plenty of smooching going on in this park."

"I know you are right," she agreed, laughing, recovering her hat from where it had fallen.

"If I'd take you home, would you smooch?"

"Oh, *Sam* . . ."

"I want to, Carole. Don't you want to? A little?"

"If I didn't want to, taking me home would present no problem."

He gazed at her, and nodded. "Let's go home and see what happens."

"You sound seventeen."

"I sound thirty-seven, and like the frustrated man I am."

"Sam, darling . . ."

"All right, all right. We can be married this summer, and I need not be frustrated any more. And to answer your recent question: I am frustrated, I get angry at you, but I do not worry about you, Carole."

"Good." She let him put her into the car. When he joined her, she asked, "But you still don't want to go to the Chaffines' tomorrow?"

"Oh, we can go. But if they start asking questions . . ."

"They may. You have something gnawing at you, and the teeth marks show."

"Let's take some Chinese food out to the Chaffines'," he said. "Peter really goes for those little spare ribs."

"I'll call JoAnn. Tell me, is Lorraine, by any chance, giving you trouble?"

Sam jerked with surprise, and the car bucked. "Lorraine?" he shouted. "I haven't seen Lorraine but once since I left the Foundation. You were with me. At that symphony thing where we drank beer and danced Viennese waltzes. Only you wore a tight skirt. . . ."

"Never mind my mistakes. And I asked you. . . ."

"I don't hear one damn thing from Lorraine." He was shouting again.

She smiled. "All right, Sam," she said softly. "Let's go home. I have some frozen lobster. I'll make Newburg."

"And smooch?"

She smiled. "A little," she agreed.

"I can make a lot out of a little," he assured her.

"We'll see."

Sam was sorry that he'd let Carole detect his worries. They didn't amount to that much. He'd heard nothing further from the publishers, or his agent.

And he had spoken truthfully. He had no worries about his job. He was working, wasn't he? Perhaps still in training, but it was work, and well paid.

The training idea came from the request that he go to Detroit and sit in with the administrator of a hospital there, not offer any advice or comment—just observe. When he came back . . .

When he came back he would make an evaluation report. Yes, he knew the routine. He went to Detroit, wondering why, of the seven thousand plus hospitals in the country, Robins had picked this one.

He went to the hotel, called the hospital and asked how early their administrator started his day. "I am Dr. Fowler, from Hospital Administrators."

"Oh, yes, doctor. Dr. Goris, our executive director, left a message for you. He asks that you come to his office here at eight o'clock. Is that convenient?"

Executive director, eh? "I'll be there," said Sam, and prepared to go to bed. Early hours was one big trouble with these hospital types.

He found Dr. Goris to be a pleasant man, about his own age, though inclined to be chubby. Rotund. His office was decorated with examples of his Sunday painting; he talked to Sam a little about his hobby. He seemed to know better than Sam did why his visitor was there.

"We are going to start today with a conference of physicians," he announced.

"I hope you didn't arrange things. . . ."

"I didn't. If enough things don't happen to interest you, call it a most unusual day. This conference has been scheduled for three days."

The conference of physicians had Dr. Goris firmly in charge. One of the several men who came in was a courtesy staff doctor who was informed, though gracefully, that his mortality record was too high. "You've been warned about that," said Dr. Goris, looking down at a sheet of figures. "We are going to ask you, Dr. Crawford, not to do major surgery here except under the supervision of a senior attending surgeon. That can be arranged. . . ."

There was a little blustering protest, and self-justification.

"The situation well can be self-terminating," Dr. Goris said pleasantly. "Now, Dr. Dillard, we have here a record of several charges that—while you are conceded to be a skilled surgeon—you are also temperamental, to the impairment of the nerves of the o.r. personnel."

Dr. Dillard was a man in his late fifties. "I yell at a nurse who drops sponges on the floor, yes," he agreed. "And the quickest way to train interns is to scare hell out of 'em."

Dr. Goris nodded. "Nevertheless, Dr. Dillard, I am going to ask you to stop relieving your tensions by screaming at the interns and nurses."

The silver-haired doctor stood up. "No doubt you'll be checking."

"I shall be," said Dr. Goris pleasantly.

Why am I here? Sam asked himself. This executive director seemed well in charge.

After the conference he tried to keep up with the director's rapid progress over and through the acres of hospital which he supervised. He met with nurses, dieticians, engineers. He stopped on this floor and that for a bedside chat with a patient. "I'm the head operator around here," Dr. Goris would identify himself to a patient. "How are you getting along in our hospital?"

He told Sam that, from the mood of the patients, whether they complained or did not, he could tell a lot of what was going on in the hospital. "We have three hundred beds," he said, "and they are so continuously filled, emptied, and filled again, that we get in from eight hundred to a thousand patients a month."

At noon he took Sam with him for lunch with a man who, he hoped, might be persuaded to give the hospital $20,000; he could take most of it out of his income tax.

In the afternoon there was a conference with the comptroller on delinquent patients' accounts. He even did, what Robins referred to so often, paint matching, down on his knees with a paint-crew foreman and an array of color samples.

He gave a two-hour lecture at the university medical school.

In between he attended to mail and answered three telephone calls from program chairmen of women's clubs. Yes, he would like very much to talk to their group about the hospital.

When Sam was ready to leave, realizing that he had seen a good cross section of the big hospital, from o.r. to the sump pump in the basement, and of the work done by the easygoing director, Sam asked Dr. Goris why, he supposed, Sam had been sent to spend the day with him.

"Robins organized this hospital, trained and organized me," said Goris readily. "He checks on his work regularly."

"Do you mind being checked?" Sam asked curiously.

"Not at all. I want the job done right as much as he does."

Sam went back to the office and made his report, again with no resultant comment or reaction. He wondered—he often wondered—if he was doing his job right.

Once Don suggested that Robins might be testing Sam's patience. The very thought infuriated him. Was Robins so poor a judge of men that he had to *test* them? If the end justified the means, said Don, it might pay.

Sam refused to explore the possibility. He often wondered what, if anything, had been done with the reorganization plan which he had drawn up in such detail for Mt. Sinai Hospital? That had been a good piece of work. Some mention of it should have been made to him. Some action taken. Once he was tempted to write to that hospital administrator, or even to use his own time and money to go out there.

His plan might need adjustment. He was ready to admit that. But basically it was a good plan, and he would like nothing better than to work on it further. Or, even, to be given the job of stepping in and administering that hospital for a year, or whatever it would take. He was half inclined to speak of this idea to Robins. But before he could summon the rest of that inclination, his attention was diverted by a piece of legal paper brought to his office one morning and handed to him after he had properly identified himself.

"Yes, I am Dr. Sam Fowler. What . . . ?"

The man gave him the folded paper, said "Good morning," and walked out.

"It's a subpoena," said Mrs. Drozda from her desk.

Sam glanced at her.

"You'll have to appear in court about something," she told him.

Sam tapped the still-folded paper against his left fist. "If you can tell me what about," he said, "I won't need to open this."

She smiled at him, brightly, and resumed typing whatever it was she had been—

Sam unfolded the paper. It was a legal document, all right. He read it, and read it again. "My mother should have raised me to be a lawyer," he muttered.

"Does your mother live here in town, doctor?" Mrs. Drozda asked pleasantly.

Sam did not answer her. He was reading the paper again. As near as he could make out, this was an order to stop the publication and sale of "one novel" . . Why, Lorraine Harper was trying to make trouble about his book! Of all the . . .

He went over to the window and stood looking out, tapping the paper, folded again, against the glass. What concern was it of hers? She wasn't in the thing. If she was the one who had caused all that talk last month about characters identifying themselves . . . She was *not* in it! Not remotely!

He remembered that he had used to think she would hope —that she *did* hope—he was writing his novel about her. He couldn't remember just how she had found out that he was writing a book; he didn't talk about it to many people. And he really had not talked much about it to Lorraine. But, in her oblique, arch way, she had used to say . . .

Oh, if he should pay her a compliment on a costume, she would say, "The color is dusty pink, Sam. Men aren't very exact in describing women's clothes." Things like that.

He went to his desk and called the office of his publisher in New York, telling the switchboard, as he always did, that this was a personal call. His mood was such that he wondered if she would listen in. Well, let her. The conversation was bound to be interesting.

The call went through, he talked to his own editor, and was put on to the president. Yes, Mr. Boyer had expected him to get in touch. He wished Sam could have come into the office a month ago—

He took a deep breath and told about the legal paper which had been served on him that morning.

The publisher knew all about it. They too had been served.

"Just what sort of trouble is Mrs. Harper trying to make for us, sir?" Sam asked, and humbly.

"I'll try to interpret the legal terminology," promised Boyer. "But first I'll say, if you like, we'll handle the legal end of this suit."

Sam liked. Of course he was ready . . .

"Yes, there are a couple of questions."

"I did not write the book about her!"

"No, that seems evident."

"When I talked to you before, you said . . ."

"Then we knew only that she was about to make trouble for you over the book. Libel was our guess. She's a well-known person, she has resources . . ."

"I think she rather hoped I was writing the book about her, sir."

132

"I see. She knew then that you were writing it?"

"But not the subject matter."

"Now, that is very interesting. Because, you see, she is claiming that you did the work on this book while you were employed by the Harper Foundation, while your time was hers."

Sam gasped, he sputtered. He was so immediately angry that he could not speak. He had not been employed for twenty-four hours of his time each day. He had written the book, done his research—everything—after hours and on week ends. Even on vacations. He could produce witnesses. Yes, and right in the Foundation offices. Glass-walled, everyone knew what everyone else was doing in those offices! Lorraine had known what he was doing. Writing a book caused considerable litter. He would go to that woman and tell her. . . .

Mr. Boyer managed to get his attention, and sternly forbade Sam's talking to Mrs. Harper at all. Sam was not to see her, not to write a letter—nothing. The wrong word, and just one wrong word, could be disastrous.

Still angry—his ears burned with his anger—Sam agreed to let the publishing house deal with the matter. Yes, he would be available. Yes, if it really were necessary, he could come east. But Mr. Boyer must consider his employment. . . .

Drozda came back, and Sam was still fuming. He needed to think, to settle down. . . .

"I'm going downstairs for some coffee," he said, walking out.

He did not stop for coffee. He strode down the street, toward the Harper offices. Realizing this, he turned the corner, and then another.

Now his excited anger was simmering down into a deep concern and worry. He was still angry, of course, that Lorraine should reach her fingers into his affairs, that she would, after all these months, act upon her chagrin at Sam's deserting her. Well, she had had no business declaring herself to him. He had never given her grounds. . . .

If this thing ever came into open court, he would tell the world. . . .

He groaned. It must not ever come into open court. Even the suspicion that something was wrong—Drozda knew about the legal service—Sam's job at the Ink could be in peril. At best, his work there would not, ever, advance.

He need not say one thing. Robins would know. Robins knew everything.

9

Because, in the beginning, Boyer had asked Sam so particularly if he had written his book about identifiable characters, that point still was a part of his continuing concern and worry. He wished he had not promised the publishers to keep silence on the subject. He would have liked to talk to Don, and to some lawyer right there in the city. He wished, grimly, that he could go to Lorraine Harper and tell her, roughly, just what was wrong with a woman like her.

But having promised to keep still, and not trusting himself very far, he had little to say to anyone. Carole and the Chaffines decided that he had something big on his mind.

"I wouldn't push him to tell you," JoAnn advised Carole. "But—"

"He'll tell you when the right time comes. Men have their reserves, darling, and they cherish them."

"I thought, just now, he might be cherishing me."

"He will. He does. If you'll just sit patiently, and lovingly, through this hard time."

"What hard time, Jo? *What* hard time?"

Unaware of this womanly concern for his well-being, Sam did appreciate being allowed to stretch out on a long chair in the sun and not have to talk. Everyone else seemed busy.

Carole and JoAnn were in the house, busily making, of all things, sourdough bread. Don had grass to cut, then a professional call took him away for almost two hours. Peter and Augusta were down the hill splashing in a neighbor's pool.

Sam could just lie in the sun and feel some of the kinks straighten out of his nerves. He did some thinking about Lorraine and her demand to stop the sale of his book until certain rights had been defined. He even began to imagine the scene should he have to go into court and answer her charges. He could picture her, in her flowered hat and her straight, deceptively simple frock.

On Monday he felt better, though he was still bothered and inclined to break off whatever he was doing for a minute or two of contemplation of what was threatening him.

When he went downstairs at noon, thinking that he would walk several blocks to a restaurant, for the exercise—sun and air seemed to do well by him—coming out of the elevator, he literally ran into Ginsburg.

The man was hurrying in one direction, Sam . . .

Sam caught at his arm. "I'm sorry," he said automatically. Then, recognizing the fellow whom he had almost floored. "Hello, Ginsburg!" he said heartily. "I'm glad to see you."

Ginsburg gave himself a shake. "Almost too glad . . ." he said with a nervous laugh.

Sam laughed too, and continued to hold his arm.

"Look, Ginsburg," he said on impulse. "How about your eating lunch with me?"

"Well, I don't know, Dr. Fowler . . ."

"It's your lunch hour, right? I belong to the Professional Club—that's only two blocks away. They serve a very good pot roast on Monday. Or you could order whatever you want."

Ginsburg didn't need a lot of coaxing. He was happy to walk down the street with Dr. Fowler, happier still to go into the Professional Club—among all those doctors—to sit at a small table, to be introduced to some of Doc's friends . . .

And to talk to Sam—to let him talk—about Ashby Woods, and the people there.

"Well, Doc," said Ginsburg, diligently attacking his plate of pot roast. "The town doesn't change. Still the jumping-off place, far as I'm concerned."

"Has it grown?"

"What's to grow? Farms all around—big ones, little ones. The town doesn't have any industries to speak of. There's a small factory, makes gloves. Canvas gloves. And the quarry, of course. The railroad station is being used by some church, no passenger service any more. One store will put up a new front, another one will close down. They built a new high school about two years ago. And I guess as many as a dozen houses have been built since you left. Not what you'd call a development."

"But the hospital . . ."

"Yeah, it still works around the clock. All the country people, small towns within fifty miles—it's good to have the hospital."

"And Dr. Downes? He must be getting really old. What about his daughter? Judy?"

Ginsburg glanced up. "I remember you used to be sweet on her."

"I suppose the town thought so. If any young doctor had gone in there for a year . . ."

"We thought you liked each other."

"I did like Judy. She was a fine girl, and of course, taking the doctor's place as I did, living in their home, we saw a lot of each other. There was never anything . . ."

"Naw, Doc. I'm sure there wasn't. But you know how a town that size talks. There were people who felt sorry for Judy when you left."

"I felt a little sorry for myself. And if there had been anything between Judy and me, she could have left with me."

"That's right, she could. Only she had Doc Downes to look after. She wouldn't ever have left him."

"The subject never came up," Sam said stiffly. Too stiffly. Again Ginsburg looked up at him.

"My mother still lives in Ashby Woods," he said. "I go back there occasionally. And her letters keep me up on town affairs. Boy, do they ever! She tells me every little thing, who painted his house, who had a baby—what girl gets into trouble— For the last year she's been telling me that the old Doc has been sick. You knew he had diabetes?"

"Yes," said Sam, eating his own pot roast.

"Well, he had to have a leg taken off about a year ago. A horse stepped on his foot, and . . ."

Sam made a deep sound of regret.

"Yeah, it was bad. I don't guess he easily gave in to a thing like that. If he can't get around the countryside—you know how he drove!—or try out a horse on his dirt track . . ."

"Does he still train horses?"

"Trains 'em, swaps 'em, breeds 'em. Or he did until this happened. Judy takes care of him, I understand, though I think she has some sort of job. Downtown. I saw her the last time I was home. She's secretary or something in Judge Rogenhofer's office."

"I remember him."

"Sure you do. I don't suppose Judy earns much. In that size town."

"I wonder why she works. Do they need the money?"

"A woman likes to get out of the house. I don't think they would need the money, Doc. I could find out for you. Just asked cold, I'd say the Doc was well fixed."

"Still," said Sam thoughtfully, "a young woman would almost have to have a rough time, nursing a sick old man. Downes was quite a character."

"He was that, and I guess he still is."

"Yes, and characters aren't easy to live with. Not usually. I'm surprised Judy hasn't married."

138

"No, she never did."

"That's too bad, because she was a very sweet girl."

He glanced up and found Ginsburg leering. "I guess you'd know about that, Doc," he said meaningly.

Sam nodded. "And that's all you're doing. Guessing."

Ginsburg scrambled to recover status. "I was only kidding, Doc. You know how it is."

"I do know," said Sam. "Are you married?"

He was, and for ten minutes Sam listened to Ginsburg's account of his wife, his two children. He looked at pictures of them and of Ginsburg's home on the north side.

As he listened, Sam wondered if he should get in touch with the Downes'.

He watched Ginsburg eat a slab of apple pie, and then heard him say, "Gosh, I'm late before I ever start back. Care if I take off, Doc? It was real nice! Real nice!"

Sam sat on, finished his coffee, and thought. . . .

He had some work to do at the medical school library; he called Mrs. Drozda and told her where he would be "most of the afternoon." He did the work, too, but by three-thirty he found himself walking briskly downhill to the park which overlooked the river and where, before now, he had done some heavy thinking. Parks were supposed to be dangerous places those days, and perhaps even this one was. But that afternoon, children played on the grass and rode tricycles along the gravel paths, watched by their mothers, who clustered together on benches and visited.

Sam sat on a bench, under a tree, and looked down the steep hill to the river which gleamed like dull brass. And he thought about Ashby Woods, about Dr. Downes and the work which Sam had done with the old man ten years ago.

It had been good work. Several times in the intervening years Sam had known a desire to go back into the active practice of medicine. He had wanted very much to sit again beside a patient's bed, to scrub and go into the operating room. In recent years, he had known that any such move would require a brush-up residency to bring back skill to his eye and hand. But he had liked the practice of medicine; there was a certain warmth which only the particular relationship between doctor and patient could give a man. Sam had known that warmth in Ashby Woods. He could know it again. Somewhere.

When Sam arrived in Ashby Woods, Downes was working alone in his office and in his hospital, a widower for fifteen years. There had been a son, but that young doctor was killed "in the war," leaving only Judy in the home.

The "old man" had diabetes, he was a horse trader, he worked with the bank. He had built his hospital—

No person with writing ambitions and a knack could fail to pick Arthur Downes as a character. When Sam knew him, he was an old man, but listening to the stories about Dr. Downes, it was not difficult to imagine, and write about, the young man he once must have been.

Coming to the dusty southwest town with a brand-new wife, a brand-new medical degree, ready to treat any ailment brought to his attention, and charging the going rate—fifty cents for a cold, eight dollars for a delivery. Traveling, sleepless, by foot and horseback to halt a milk-borne epidemic that killed a fifth of his patients in and round town. . . .

As the years passed, he was the school doctor, trustee of the library, member of the board of health, using his spare time to edit the district medical journal and write articles on diabetes, a disease which he had acquired when serving in the army during World War I.

Sam had marveled at the old doctor, a man of two faces. With his long white hair and ascetic features, he looked like a member of a string quartet. But in reality, the doctor was a horse trader of the first water. He knew medicine and practiced it, but his inner heart was in harness, and his happiness was in the seat of a low-slung road sulky as he tried out a good horse on a fast track.

He made some money at his horse swapping; he had bragged to Sam that the money he made by buying a horse and selling it for a two or three per cent profit, or by training a promising horse himself, gaiting it, and driving it in a winner-take-all race on one of the nearby small tracks, had put his son through medical school.

He was a man to spot an opportunity and make something of it. Or himself to make that opportunity. The young Dr. Downes had not been in Ashby Woods a week before he had arranged with the management of the quarries to take care of their employees at a dollar per man per month, the money to be taken out of the pay envelopes. This had brought the doctor twelve hundred a year right off, a living in those days, and a shoal of quick experience.

As fees increased, he bought pieces of real estate and sold them at a profit, or kept them as rental properties. Along this line, he had acquired the twenty-room mansion, a monstrosity of a house, where Sam had lived while helping the old doctor that year. The house had been built by a New Yorker sixty years before. Living in it . . .

Sam shook his head. To practice medicine, to train horses, and concern himself with town affairs, took time. The doctor —Downes, and for that year, his locum—was up at dawn, starting his country calls by seven to give himself time for his hospital work.

The hospital. Old Dr. Downes, when still middle-aged, had recognized that the only way to check the migration of doctors from the rural areas would be to establish hospitals for them to use. A hospital in his district would do much to guarantee health care for his widely scattered "neighbors."

From his first days in Ashby Woods, Dr. Downes had known that he could serve his community better if he had a hospital. During his first term as mayor he had suggested that WPA labor be used to build a community hospital. His friends told him that such a project would be impractical in a town the size of Ashby Woods.

A swimming pool was built with WPA labor, street lights were installed. A hospital would be a waste of public money.

But not his own. Dr. Downes borrowed on his life insurance, he borrowed $25,000 from the bank, and he began. Several former patients agreed to pay off unpaid bills by hauling sandstone from the quarry. The first unit of the hospital opened, containing eighteen rooms and an operating room. The first patient, a child with a fractured skull, was saved because the hospital was there, not a death-dealing fifty miles away.

It took doing to persuade the rugged people of that district that a hospital was anything but a place in which to die. The women had to be convinced to have their babies there. But once a mother had come in, been given the comfort of a light anesthesia, known the luxury of bed rest and being waited on, the thing was sold to the women of the whole neighborhood. News traveled fast in those parts.

Young Dr. Sam Fowler had not had to sell Downes the need for hospitals in rural areas. The doctors of the neighborhood, from fifty miles around, sent their patients in, or brought them. Dr. Downes engaged these doctors in talk, in the discussion of their patients; he put them to work. He was a one-man clinic if such a thing ever was possible.

When events felled him while Sam Fowler was in town, this man had already so inspired the young doctor that he took a leave of absence from AMA, rolled up his sleeves and worked with Dr. Downes for a year. Learning much, gaining much—he'd done big jobs, and little jobs . . .

Sam looked at his watch, got to his feet, and started back to the office.

He remembered especially one patient, a man who had

been cut up in a Saturday night tavern brawl; the doctor had been called out of bed early on Sunday morning by the jailer, who said he had a man . . .

And indeed he did have a man. There was a long, jagged cut, from his ear down to below his armpit, through the area of the parotid gland, and the carotid artery. . . . Sam's fingers still could feel the small scalpel . . . interchangeable blades of razor steel . . . especially sharp. . . . He had injected antibiotics, trimmed away the dead tissue, sewed the healthy tissues together, dusted the whole thing with sulfa drugs, and helped his operating room nurse wheel the man to a bed; he watched him—

Angry at the jailer for having confined a man so wounded, he told Downes about the work he had done, adding, "If such a thing happens again . . ."

Downes had stopped him. "A surgeon, Sam, says, 'When a thing happens . . .' It always does."

Yes, it had been good work. Sam had done that work for a year with Downes; he had lived in the rococo Downes home, and he had had dates with Judy. . . .

Now, walking past the bright glass of a shop window, seeing himself reflected there, Sam could also see himself as he had been ten years before. A young doctor, more than a little green around the edges. An eager, idealistic young man . . .

And Judy. A sweet girl, a dear girl, with smooth brown hair, an upward, trusting way of gazing at a man . . . They had liked to do things together. To join the square dance club on Tuesday nights, to pack sandwiches and hike out to a certain creekbank on a Sunday afternoon. They waded, caught sunfish and crawdads, talked, laughed—and returned home, sun-warmed, tired, and happy.

Only once had there ever been anything like a love scene between them. At night, they were walking home from something—perhaps a square dance session. Judy had made a misstep and would have fallen, but Sam caught her strongly in his arms. Caught her, and held her, and then he had kissed her.

Later, coming into the big, shadowy house, he could have followed Judy up to her room. . . . She had been soft and warm in his embrace, loving.

Yes, he could have made a life with Judy Downes. But he had not. His year was up and he had a job to do, one not in Ashby Woods. They didn't need a clinic there. The whole town was Dr. Downes' and he cared for it.

Sam reached the Doctors Building; he went up in the swift, silent elevator. There was a conference; he had all but forgotten it. He nodded to Drozda, gathered up some papers, and went out into the hall again, to the elevator.

He was the last to arrive, but the meeting had not yet started. With one ear on the reports being made, his pencil making some meaningful notes, he still thought of Ashby Woods, and the Downes'. The doctor now really old, and really sick. And Judy?

She would be twenty-eight. An even lovelier age for a woman than eighteen. He owed much to Judy and her father. He could not have written his book, or perhaps any book, without the two of them. The girl in his story got her glow from that swift, sweet companionship—that love, really —which he had known with her. The tone of her voice, the light in her eye, the feel of her hair against his cheek—her laughter—the sight of her slender bare foot through the brown waters of the creek. . . .

Sam gave himself a shake, poured a glass of water from the carafe, and drank it.

Downes had given him the rib-work of his main character. Sam had had to imagine him, create him, as a young man, a lover, a husband, and tell about that young man.

Sam put aside his preoccupation to join in a discussion of

144

a problem; after the meeting adjourned, he lingered for ten minutes talking to his colleagues, accepting an invitation to dinner with one of them.

"I'll get you a girl," said this man.

"Don't bother."

"No bother. They are standing in line."

Sam shrugged, and went on to his own office, to sign some letters, to say "Good night" absent-mindedly to Mrs. Drozda —No, she didn't need to stay; he was leaving in a minute or two.

Before he did leave, he found himself thinking again of Ashby Woods, of Judy. . . .

What had happened to her? Ginsburg said she had not married. Why not? Sam could not have been the reason. He was not vain enough to think that he was. With her father's money, and her own desirable person, there should have been many men, both presentable and willing.

And what had happened to Dr. Downes' work? He would have had to have help. During the past ten years, the old man had got no younger. He had needed help when Sam was there; he would need it increasingly with each year. Surely he must have brought in someone, formed some sort of partnership.

Downes' practice needed to be cared for. Now if he were completely disabled . . . Oh, surely he had trained a new man. If not, could he find and train one now?

Sam was trained. After ten years, he could go into that hospital, into Downes' office, and—

Oh, nonsense!

He went to the washroom, took off his coat, his tie and shirt, and freshened himself. The long, disturbing day seemed to stretch endlessly behind him. How much about it could he tell Carole when they met for dinner? Could he tell her anything? Could he conceal any of it from her? The things that had happened, the things he had thought about, and remembered. . . .

Could he tell Carole, this woman whom he loved, about Judy, the girl he might have loved?

Judy. What was her life now? Twenty-eight was darn close to thirty. What future lay ahead for that young woman who already should have grasped a life of her own? But now, to take Ginsburg's word, she might be tied to an aging invalid. Could Sam rescue Judy? Could he, or someone acting for him, offer to pay a nurse, and let her escape?

Perhaps the Downes' were paying for their own nurse. Perhaps . . . The way the old man had juggled his money, no one, even ten years ago, could tell what, to use the local phrase, Doc Downes would "cut up to." By now, through bad horse trades, bad bank loans, he could have lost even the appearance of wealth.

Sam went down for his car and started to drive to Carole's apartment. He hoped she would have some ideas about where they would eat. He had been spending his thinking on the Downes'. But what *had* happened to them? They could be comfortable, and content. Perhaps Judy had a full and satisfying life.

But he still was curious about them. Should he go to see them? He parked the car and glanced up along the tall building to Carole's windows. He must begin to think about her. His thoughts that day, she might feel, had been disloyal to her. Should he tell her about the Downes'? All about them? Could he take her with him on a swift week-end visit to Ashby Woods?

He laughed grimly, nodded to the doorman, and went into the apartment vestibule. Neither Judy nor Carole would welcome such a suggestion.

10

He found Carole ready to welcome him—a weary man at the end of a warm day—comfort him, restore him. Her apartment was shaded against the still-bright sky of the hot day which, to be truthful, Sam had scarcely noticed. He had eaten pot roast, he had walked blocks and blocks. . . .

Carole's bare arms were silky under his hand, cool and round. She wore something thin, a little floaty—a rosy brown dress, dotted all over with big white "coins," the neckline simply, and artfully, draped. Her hair was drawn up and back on her head.

She kissed Sam, complimented him on his dark blue summer suit. "You should wear a straw hat," she told him. "A boater, is it called?"

"I'd call it a strawcaty," he laughed. "I don't own a straw hat."

"Do you own any hats?"

"Oh, yes. For cold days. My hair gets so blown about, you know? And I have a knitted cap. That's for cold weather, too, when the Chaffine kids want to go coasting."

"Sit down, I'll bring you a cold drink."

"I can wait till we get wherever we are going."

"Would you mind dreadfully if we ate here?"

"I'd mind washing dishes."

"You won't even need to help put the food on the table. I'll get the drink."

He would be happy to stay here and eat crackers and cheese if Carole would let him make love to her. She would not. A kiss, a sometimes-warm embrace, constant friendliness and interest—that seemed to be enough for her. Often it was not enough for Sam.

She brought a small tray with tall, frosted glasses.

"Lemonade?" Sam asked suspiciously.

"Not lemonade. I had them sent up from the bar downstairs."

"And the dinner?"

"And the dinner."

Sam tasted his drink and lifted an eyebrow. He reached for her glass and tasted her drink. "Mine's better," he said. "What'd you do? Get a love potion to put in it?"

She smiled at him.

"I'd switch glasses," he told her.

Sometimes, alone in his hotel suite, Sam imagined himself forcing Carole to submit to his desire for her. He could take her into his arms, use his strength, his urgency . . .

And, gaining her for one night, he would lose her forever. But how long could a man love a beautiful woman, and continue to be held at arm's length? Or, at least, the fourteen inches which now separated him from her. Sometimes, he thought, too, of finding another girl, someone who would be warmly responsive, ready to love him and marry him.

The trouble was, he did not want that other girl. What he wanted was Carole, warm and responsive. If ever he should achieve that miracle . . .

Tonight she was letting him sit in silence, to enjoy his drink, and unwind whatever knots his day had tied into his nerves. His warmly responsive girl would have been snuggling against him, wanting him to think about her; she would have asked him what was the matter, what was he thinking about . . . ?

Carole just sat there, drinking her lemonade—it really was lemonade—and waiting for him to be ready to talk. Well, he should be ready, and right now.

He should already be talking to her about the things which he had had so constantly on his mind that day—Ginsburg and Ashby Woods, the old doctor, and Judy. Would she understand his feeling about those things? Could she understand?

Probably not. To her, he would be talking about a dusty small town, an eccentric doctor, his teenage daughter who had had a crush on Sam, which was pleasant to remember, but which had not been actually pleasant enough to hold him to Ashby Woods, or make him do more than dream about returning to the place.

How would his thin worsted suit, his polished black shoes, his regimental tie go in Ashby Woods? No one wore a suit coat there in hot weather. A necktie would be ridiculous. Judy had used to wear summery dresses, and they were fresh, pretty—

Carole's dress—even the color would not be the choice of any young woman in Ashby Woods. She would know it; he would.

No. He had better keep that year, and his memories of it, close in his thoughts. With his book he had done his best, his very best, to project the experience which was a thing unique to him. If now he would try to talk further to Carole about that experience, she—or any woman—would listen and gauge his concern. She would, when he finished, decide that his obligation to the Downes'—to Judy—must go deeper, much deeper, than he was telling.

Sam loved Carole. . . .

Murmuring something about putting their dinner on the table, she had slipped out of the room. He could hear her moving about, the ring of silver, the soft clash of china—he called to her, and offered to help.

"Sit still," she said.

He sat still, and this time he thought about her. About the first knowledge he had had that he loved the slender, golden-haired girl.

Carole had to call him twice to get him to come to the table for dinner. "You were really deep into something," she told him.

He smiled at her and seated her. "I was thinking about you," he said.

"Now, really—"

"I was thinking about when I first met you."

"Three years ago," she agreed.

"I picked you up off the ice at the rink."

"I never fell at the rink. But you did pick me up. We were riding the escalator at the airport."

He'd seen her there, and he had picked her off the ice, too. Then he had seen her again at a Friends of the Art Museum show.

"I called you, and you agreed to have dinner with me," he told her now.

She nodded. "It must have been the end of the month."

"If so," he laughed, "it would have been with me, too."

"That's when we began to do interesting things together," she remembered, in her turn.

"I even took you to the dentist's office, and waited . . ."

"Oh, you really did!" she agreed. "Sam, that was a terrible thing for me to ask you to do."

"I liked it. You had to go."

"We've had fun together. The little restaurants we have explored."

"And the big, expensive ones."

She nodded. The sun was going down, and seated there before the window, they could see the shadows taking over the park and the streets; car lights began to weave ribbons between the buildings.

"We spent one evening a month working at the blood center."

"We still do."

"Yes." It was about the only doctoring Sam did these days.

"I remember," he said, "the very night I fell in love with you."

Carole remembered, too. The swift color in her cheeks said that she did. "We were at a party of some kind."

"The Historical Society dinner. There were big round tables . . . twelve at a table. And beautiful flowers, tulips, freesia, jonquils. Everybody dressed up. You wore a white dress."

"Probably not really white. I don't look well in dead white."

"It looked white to me, and you looked fine. You sat across from me. The dumb hostess liked to mix her guests."

"Ye-es. You said, that night, it was a dumb thing to do."

"My social graces . . ."

"You do all right."

"I decided before the dinner was over that she had not been entirely dumb, because, sitting across from you, I could look at you. Your hair curled a little against your neck, you were being very gay, and very lovely. There was some glitter on your dress . . ."

"I remember! I still have that dress. It is a very pale yellow, with a sequined jacket. It . . ."

"Shut up. I'm telling this. You were talking, and you said something . . . I looked at you, the way your eyes were set in your face, your cheekbones, the way you gestured and talked. You showed control, but you were very witty, too. And all at once . . ."

Her eyes were soft. "In front of all those people, you

leaned across the table and you said, 'You're cute. I think I'll chase you.' "

"I did not say 'cute.' "

"You did, Sam. A girl remembers such things."

"All right. And I remember what you said. You said, 'I think I'll let you.' "

"And you did chase me," Carole said softly now. "You did."

"Yes. I was in love with you. Of course you . . ."

"I enjoyed being with you, Sam. From the first. The things we did. Everything we have done together. You taught me how to play a pinball machine, you shared the Chaffines with me; we had fun together, we got to know each other, our tastes . . ."

"I had fun, too," Sam assured her. "Even when you made me go to the meetings of that dinner bridge club, or whatever it was."

Whatever it was had been a loosely organized group of eight couples, most of them married, who met irregularly, usually once a month, for dinner, to play bridge, sometimes to go dancing. They took their turn being hosts.

This past year Sam had lost track of the club. He didn't know if Carole kept in touch or not.

"We went to church together," he mentioned. "And took drives to interesting places. I even got you to go on a week end trip downriver."

"But the ski trip was my idea."

"Yes, it was. And my back has not been the same since."

She ignored this. Sam had, at the time, complained bitterly about the dormitory where he had had to sleep.

"You took me to the Professional Club . . ."

"That's when we began to eat Reubens on Saturdays."

"And going out to the Chaffines' on Sunday."

"That's when I first asked you to marry me," he reminded her.

"Over a Reuben sandwich."

"Is that why you said no?"

"I said yes, later."

"You didn't mean it."

"I did, Sam. I did."

"I only know that you let me give you a ring, we became engaged. And three months later, you gave the ring back to me."

She sat turning that same ring on her finger. "I told you—"

"That you liked your work, and your independence. That you were not ready to marry."

Carole lifted her eyes to his face. "I had my doubts, Sam. About myself. Not you."

"It might have been better if I had come on a little more strongly."

"But we still . . ."

"Oh, sure. We still went to the symphony, and ate Reuben sandwiches, and you got jealous of Lorraine Harper. Then —"

"I put your ring on again. And last spring we almost did get married. Only—you got masterful."

"Well, damn it, girl . . ."

"That's the way you talked."

He had made her go with him to apply for a license, and to get tests. . . . "And you backed out again," he said.

"I still wasn't ready. You were busy. . . ."

He got up from the table and went to stand at the window before the couch. She followed him and put her hand on his shoulder. "I was being silly," she admitted. "That time I didn't stop wearing your ring."

"For all it means," he grumbled, putting his arm about her waist.

"It means that I am going to marry you, Sam."

"When?"

"As soon as possible."

"You'll need to define possible."

"I can. It means as soon as things can be right for us and our marriage. It means a house of our own in the suburbs, a wedding. Not large, but dignified and solemn."

Sam sighed. He wanted those things, too, certainly if they meant he could have Carole by having them. So—tonight, again, he would tread easy. Not to deceive her, but to avoid bringing up things about which she could deceive herself.

He would not talk to her about Downes and Ashby Woods.

He would not mention Lorraine Harper.

"Let's wash the dishes," he said aloud.

"I promised you . . ."

"Your promises aren't worth a penny, sweetheart. That's what I've been telling you."

Lorraine Harper was not going to be able to make much trouble for Sam. The publishers and their lawyers almost at once were able to sidetrack the threatened lawsuit. Various ones in the open offices of the Foundation had shown themselves willing to testify that Dr. Fowler had done no book writing during his hours on the job he had held with Mrs. Harper. They would testify that he had done a full job for her.

"Does she know who these people are who would so testify?" Sam asked. Heads would fall. . . .

"We have been able to keep the names a matter of privileged communication. They could be produced. . . ."

"I must have friends."

The publishers also had the letter of recommendation which Lorraine had written when Sam applied for his job with Hospital Administrators. Now, where had they got that? he asked.

"Dr. Patric Robins sent it to us, free will."

But how had Robins known about the threatened lawsuit? Sam had said nothing. . . .

He had not needed to. Robins' spies were everywhere, his antenna reached into every possible corner. The man was a real wonder. Relaxed, almost indifferent, he was in the office, he was not there; he gave no evidence of what must be a seething brain and octopus fingers. But the brain and the fingers were there. The man was there.

"I wrote the book while I was employed at the Foundation," Sam said thoughtfully. "In my spare time."

"That's understood, Sam. And your employer had no claim upon such time."

Though when he worked for her, Lorraine often had claimed a good bit of his spare time. The week end trips to her mountain home. A dinner with her to talk over some award applicant. . . .

"We are going to make up a new dust jacket for future editions of your book," said the attorney who had come to talk to Sam in person. A pleasant gentleman, bald, solid, assured. He took a sheet of paper from his briefcase. "This is to be the new blurb," he said, giving it to Sam.

Sam read it. There had been added a statement that he had formerly been employed by the Harper Foundation.

"Does that do anything for them?" he asked, giving the paper back to the lawyer.

"It does for their vanity."

Sam nodded. "I suppose." He had a rising, strong impulse to tell this big, clean, well-tailored man about Dr. Downes. Sam, from day to day, ever since his book had appeared, had felt, was feeling, that the doctor had a claim. . . .

Perhaps not legally, and that was the basis on which his caller would consider the matter. But ethically, morally—

"Is something still bothering you, Dr. Fowler?" asked the attorney. He had put his papers back into his briefcase.

"No," said Sam. "Not really. I was just thinking. This

matter of bringing forth a book is a complicated business, isn't it? So many things go into its writing, alone. Each person you meet, each thing you read or experience—Whether you are conscious of it or not, you use all of those things, and those people."

"Do you plan to write another book, doctor?" asked the visitor, standing up.

"Oh, yes. I expect to."

"Then don't let yourself be troubled about your source material. As a fiction writer, I mean. Just avoid drawing a recognizable picture of a person doing things that same person has been doing, in settings where he lives, and behaves not creditably."

Sam walked with him to the door and out to the elevator. "I've been told that one person in ten wants to write, and thinks he can. Why should they, sir?"

"To give guys like me a job." The big man smiled. "Good-by, doctor. I'll see you again."

"I sincerely hope not."

It was, of course, a relief to know that the threat of legal action had been removed. For one small thing, Sam would not need to tell Carole about Lorraine's behavior, and stir up anew all of her dislike of the older woman. Sam no longer worked for Lorraine; she need not be any part of his life with Carole. He would forget about the whole situation.

Which he really did, for a time. Later the same day, he attended a staff conference where he heard the job of reorganizing Mt. Sinai Hospital—*his* Mt. Sinai Hospital— assigned to one of the other men. Young Dr. Curry. Younger than Sam . . .

"Go out there and survey the whole setup from possible termites to starlings and pigeons on the roof," Robins told this fellow. He was really a nice chap, but Sam hated him!

"Dr. Fowler—Sam, here—has worked up a schedule which you may find it possible to use. I'd like you to get at this no later than the first of the week."

They were using Sam's plan—as of course they had a right to do. It belonged to the Ink. And it must be a good plan, or they wouldn't use it. They might have said it was good. They might have assigned Sam to this project. . . .

He was bitterly disappointed. And again he wondered about the job he held, the work he was doing on that job.

He maintained this mood of uncertainty, of vague plans to make some move to straighten things out. He would go to Robins—or, more likely, to Dr. Moir—and ask just where he stood, what his job was, where his future lay. A man had to make plans!

For days he did nothing but worry, and that not too acutely. At the end of the month he put Carole on a plane to go visit her mother, who lived in California, in what she called a leisure village, but which Sam, and Carole sometimes irreverently called an "old folks' corral."

"She has a wonderful time," Carole assured Sam when she returned. "She has friends, she keeps busy, they take trips . . ."

"I'll make reservations for us twenty-five years from now," he told her, nuzzling her hair, her ear, her throat.

"Sam?"

"Hmmmn."

"Is something—has something happened?"

"You bet. My girl went away, and now she is at home again. I'm in the mood to enjoy that fact."

"How are the Chaffines?"

"Don't change the subject."

"I think it is time. Did you go out there Sunday?"

"I did. I did everything you told me to do before you left."

"Good boy."

"I don't want to be a good boy."

But he was, of course, and at the end of the week he had a reward—of sorts. Because, all at once, things at the office took a turn for the better.

They were better in his private life, too. On Friday evening Carole told him that she had a house she wanted him to look at with her on Saturday.

"Where is it?"

"In Skyview."

He whistled. Skyview was a new luxury development in a wooded area out in the county.

"You should be able to afford this house, Sam. And I'd rather go into a new suburb than one of those which are running down at the edges."

"Skyview's fine, but a long walk from here."

"Now what does that mean?"

"That my car is in the shop. It will be over the week end. In fact, it's been there since last night."

"What happened?"

"Ever hear of the one-horse shay?"

"Are you saying . . . ?"

"I'm saying that I am without a car now, and I may be with a new car next week."

"Oh."

"I have the money, Carole. . . ." He thought she was having thrifty second thoughts about the house. Didn't she know he would buy almost any house if she were ready to marry him and move into it? "I just don't want to walk clear out to Skyview— Where'd they get that name, anyway?"

"Why can't we use my car?"

"I thought you'd never ask."

She laughed and promised to pick Sam up at nine on Saturday morning.

"Not *nine!*" he protested.

"I want to make a day of it. If we like the house, there will be nine million things to do. If we don't like it, we can look for one we do like."

He groaned, and agreed, and told her to hang up. He would start getting his sleep for that night.

But before he did go to sleep, he thought quite a bit about a house where he and Carole would live together. He thought about homes he knew, and liked, about those he didn't. The Chaffines' bright, ultramodern, steel and glass house was right for them, but Sam wanted something—well —warmer. A stone house maybe, set back among trees, with a deep hearth, rich wood. . . . He was not intrigued by flat walls and square corners. A curving staircase was better, a bedroom under the eaves. . . .

These things stayed in his mind, and he was still thinking about them when Carole showed up the next morning. He was eating breakfast, and offered her some coffee.

"Oh, no," she said. "It's too hot."

"Hot?"

"As blazes. Outside, of course."

Her little car was not air-conditioned. "Let's go buy my new car right away," he suggested. "We could take one for a trial run. . . . I'll finish my oatmeal and we'll get busy."

He bent his attention again to his breakfast, which did not feature oatmeal.

Carole moved restlessly about the room, straightening the papers on his big desk, looking out of the window. She wore a straight dark blue linen shift, piped with white at the arm-holes and the neck. She had drawn her pale golden hair into a thick club at the back of her neck, and tied it there with a red and white checkered scarf.

Sam liked to look at her, and did not hurry with his last piece of toast and his coffee.

He was wiping his fingers on the napkin, ready to get up

and go with her, when the door buzzer rasped rudely. "Now what?" he muttered. The maid would have opened the door a crack and closed it again immediately.

"Probably your laundry," said Carole.

"Prob . . ." Sam threw the door open and stepped back. "Dr. Robins!" he cried, not believing his eyes.

"Dr. Robins," agreed Sam's boss. "May I come in?" By then he was already *in,* and looking at Carole.

"I'm sorry," he told Sam. "I should have phoned . . ."

Sam pressed his lips together. "Miss Tebeau," he said tightly, "my fiancée. Dr. Robins, Carole."

Dr. Robins went swiftly to her and took her hand. "I am delighted," he said. "Surprised, but delighted."

Sam waited. What was Robins stirring up now? Besides the things he was thinking, and the gossip he might engender. Sam would not explain. . . .

But Carole was explaining. "Sam's car is in the shop," she said in her cool, clear voice. "I came to pick him up; we are planning a day in the country."

"How nice for Sam," said Robins. "Too bad I have to spoil things. Except that's the best thing I do."

He glanced around at Sam, who was still waiting to find out . . . Carole, too, was becoming curious. Her first reaction had been to set things straight.

"How do you plan to spoil things?" Sam asked, never doubting for a minute that Robins would do it.

"Well, I've a little trip in mind, and unless Miss Tebeau— What's your first name, my dear? I am sure I won't want to address you formally."

She blushed; Sam would mention that to her later.

"Her name is Carole," he said truculently. "And what sort of trip?"

Robins did not even look at him. Now he was over at Sam's desk, straightening the same piles of paper which Carole had tidied. "Trouble-shooting," he said over his shoulder. "When did I ever do anything else?"

Sam had small idea of the things this man did.

"And you need Sam to go with you?" Carole was asking.

Patric Robins turned and smiled at her. "I *want* Sam to go with me," he said softly.

She turned to look at Sam.

"Go pack your toothbrush, boy!" Robins barked at him. "The plane leaves in an hour and ten minutes."

"Where are we going, and how long will we stay?" Sam asked, not moving an inch. "What sort of trouble-shooting?" It need not be any big crisis. Robins often liked to do jobs himself. To keep in touch, to check . . .

"I'll brief you on our way to the airport. Miss Tebeau, can you drive us?"

"I'm afraid my car holds only two." Her voice was like clear water. She probably was greatly upset.

"Then we'll have to invest in a taxi," said Robins. "Which is one of my pettest peeves. Sam, aren't you going to pack?"

"I suppose I am, but . . ."

"You don't like this sudden sort of thing. And I don't blame you. Not one bit. Come along, Carole, if you know where he keeps his undies. . . ."

"I don't," she said crisply.

"Well, we certainly can find the things. You'll want to change, Fowler?"

"Where are we going?"

"Texas, first."

Sam groaned, and went into the bedroom. "For how long?" he called back.

"Just a small bag—be quick. You can get anything you may need."

"On the expense account?" asked Sam, coming back to the doorway.

Robins turned to look at him.

"I'll be quick," Sam agreed. He didn't want to close the door. But if he were going to change from his rust-colored slacks and yellow knit shirt into anything matching Robins' mouse-gray suit and pink shirt—with a brown tie, yet!

He closed the door, hearing the guy say, "I love to use my muddling stick."

Well, Carole could scream or walk out. She was a girl who knew how to take care of herself. But that guy—flippant, wisecracking, and most maddening of all, so damn cool and nonchalant—

Sam took clothes from the hangers, he brought down a medium-sized bag from the shelf. Texas, eh?

He changed quickly into a lightweight suit, hung the tie on the lamp, and he began to empty drawers. Undies, indeed!

He went to the living-room door. Carole could tell the hotel, the garage . . .

She was sitting on the couch; Robins was talking on the telephone. Sam beckoned to Carole, who came quickly to him. "I'm sorry, darling," he told her.

She was frowning. "I can't figure him out, Sam."

He laughed and turned back to his packing, counting over the items. Toilet gear, razor—another suit, a sweater, the slacks and shirt he had just taken off. "Nobody figures Robins out," he said, not speaking softly.

"He must really be a big shot," said Carole, handing him the stack of shirts. "Do you have ties?"

Sam selected three. "Will you go look at the house?" he asked.

"I'll go home and wash my hair."

"It doesn't need it."

"You probably don't need to go to Texas, either."

Probably he did not. Nor Robins. But they went, and Sam hoped Carole was as understanding as she could be under the circumstances. As the men got into the taxi, she waved from the steps of the hotel.

"A really nice girl," Robins told Sam.

"I know she is. I wouldn't, myself, put her through a morning like this."

"Does she know anything about the work you do?"

"As much as I know."

Robins chuckled. He seemed to be enjoying the whole episode. A puppet master, loving his strings.

They went to Texas; they went to two hospitals in Oklahoma, and, finally, on a rain-swept night, they ended up at Sam's Mt. Sinai Hospital.

Now, really—

"I thought Curry was reorganizing this place," Sam said accusingly to Robins. The last few days had told him much about the man—he could hardly wait to talk to Carole!—but he still had questions, and questions.

"I sent Curry," Robins agreed. "You were upset that I did."

"Well, I'd worked out that plan. . . ."

"Mhmmmn. We'll look around here a little tonight, and come back tomorrow."

"I've looked this place over pretty carefully within the past six months."

"I know you must have."

"Could you tell me why you didn't send me out instead of Curry?"

"That's what the board here at Sinai asked me."

"And what did you tell them?"

"That you were a bright young man, but I didn't believe you had figured out a way to be in two places at once."

Sam looked at him. But he did have the sense to keep still. "Curry hasn't worked out," Robins rewarded him. "I told him he might use your plan. . . ."

"I remember." Without any recommendation, or—

"He junked it. And the board . . . Well, they don't think they will like his solutions."

"What were they?"

"They may tell us."

The board did tell them. Curry thought they were too folksy at Mt. Sinai. For efficiency, economy— "But we are dealing with people!" said the chairman of the board.

"The factory syndrome?" Sam murmured to Robins.

"I see you are immunized."

"Yes . . ." Robins had told him about illegitimate babies, and things that perhaps he had not told Curry.

"We must have slipped up on Curry."

"Perhaps he should listen to, or even deliver, some of the lectures I've written for the office."

"You did one on hotels, too, didn't you?"

"Yes. Wrote 'em, didn't give 'em."

"Sometimes I think you are not happy with us, Sam."

Fortunately, again, Sam turned to look at the man. "I'm not apt to settle down and be *happy* anywhere," he said gruffly.

His answer must have pleased Robins, because they had hardly started their tour of Mt. Sinai the next day—a telephone call came for Robins and he finished it, looking at Sam speculatively. "Will you determine if Curry left your plan for this hospital anywhere around here?" he asked.

"I'm sure he wouldn't have done that, but I have a duplicate in my office."

"All right. I suppose you remember enough . . ."

"I like things down on paper."

"So do I."

It was the first time Robins had said as much. Then—"I'm sending you to Philadelphia," he told Sam abruptly.

Sam stared.

"They have a problem. See what you can do with it."

"In *Philadelphia?*"

164

"Not in the city. Out along the Main Line."

"What sort of problem?"

"You'll find out."

Sam did find out. By that night he was in Philadelphia, talking to Carole for a quick five minutes. Had she bought a house? What about his car? Did she love him?

"I can answer one of those questions."

"Take the last one."

"Yes, I love you."

"That's enough for me. How about you?"

"What are you doing in Pennsylvania?"

"They have a laundry strike in this big hospital. . . ."

"And you're going to run the washing machine?"

"Listen, girl, do you know what happens when a hospital doesn't have clean linen?"

"No—not really."

"They've been bombed, sweetheart. Everybody, everything, is crippled."

"But what will *you* do?"

"That's my job. To do something."

He did. Beginning the next morning. Tenser than Robins would recommend, he called the commercial laundries. They could not help. The strike was not mentioned. But they said they were working to full capacity. Four thousand pounds of sheets, gowns, drapes, diapers, uniforms . . . Oh, no! They could not handle a load of that sort.

Sam went down into the bowels of the big hospital. A few workmen were around. There were some who knew about the laundry and, having gained that experience, had moved to other jobs. They would come back and man the machines. They would need help, of course. If that could be provided, they might keep things going.

Sam went up to the office of the manager, a slender, alert-eyed young man in rust-colored slacks and a yellow knit shirt. He asked how many members were on the board of trustees. Thirty. He asked for a list, with telephone numbers. No, he would speak personally to each one.

He determined the members of the various hospital committees. The members of the women's auxiliary. Within twenty-four hours, the hospital laundry was operating under a full head of steam, with crews of Main Line women working the day shift, and their husbands, home from their offices, coming on in the evenings. Dr. Fowler took his turn manning the clothes driers.

On the second evening, he called Carole. Would she care to come and help?

Why, Sam, she had a job to do.

"You won't need a job, as my wife."

"I am not your wife."

"I'd like very much to change that. And any day would do."

But she again said, no, she would not come.

"There are all sorts of women here, ready to help me. Maybe I could pick one of them."

"Would you?"

"Certainly I would."

It took ten weeks. "Ten!" Carole reminded him, when she met his plane.

Without a topcoat, Sam shivered in the cold September wind. "I know it," he said ruefully.

"Did you pick a girl back there?"

He smiled at her. "I met a dozen girls. Those women . . . They were the grandest people, Carole. All sorts. The thin, ride-to-hounds, short-haired sort in tweeds and tailored linens. The perfectly groomed symphony-on-Saturday night, run-up-to-Bergdorf's-for-clothes type, with their diamonds and manicures. The young wives in striped chambray, who had to hire a sitter for the children while they did

166

the grubbiest sort of work. The grandest people in the world. You know? I could go back there to live. The scenery is marvelous, their cricket clubs, their . . ."

"Did you see much of that scenery and their cricket clubs?"

"No," said Sam. "No, I didn't."

"But you did see the ladies?"

"Darn good thing I did. The way they came in, exchanged their pearls and their faultless suits and sweaters for the baggy laundry-room smocks, tucked their expensive hair styles under the caps—they called them mop-covers—and went to work! For ten weeks, Carole. *For ten long weeks!*"

"Yes, I know," said Carole, driving carefully.

"I stayed. The office knew where I was, and what I was doing. A goddam washerwoman!" He laughed happily and stretched his legs as far as he could in the small car.

"Was that all you did? The laundry?"

"No, it wasn't. I worked out some plans for other emergencies which might arise. Everything I could think of, from a massive power failure to riot in the streets."

"Why did it take so long?" she asked, turning into the hotel's driveway.

"We had to get an equitable settlement. On both sides."

They went upstairs, and Sam took Carole into his arms. She loved him, she still loved him, but—

"I'm sorry, darling," he told her.

He said he probably would burn the clothes he had taken with him to Texas; he'd worn them so hard. Had she bought him a new car? What about the house?

She said he could take up those things, now that he was home. "I don't think you want to talk about a house. It sounds as if you had a lark," she added.

"Not a lark. Though, yes, we did have some fun. People of that sort, working together . . ."

"The Brooks-Brothers, Chanel-suit bunch."

He put his hands on her shoulders and turned her so that he could study her face. "You're bitter?"

"I've been lonely for ten weeks," she pointed out.

"So was I."

"Oh, Sam . . ."

He kissed her. "We have a lot of things to work out, don't we?"

He insisted on taking her back to her apartment, and then getting a taxi to the garage where he picked up his old car. She still loved him, with reservations. But how could he complain about reservations, and still feel it right to go off the way he did?

Maybe something could be worked out.

Twenty-four hours after he returned home, Dr. Robins ordered him out on another assignment. He was to make a tour instructing hospital administrators, already installed and working efficiently, on what to say to the public. He was to conduct indoctrination courses for bettering relations between hospitals and the public. Rising costs, crowding—this had become a necessary thing.

Sam demurred. He had not had time to see his girl. . . .

"You had last night."

"After my being away for nearly three months, she was not ready to make it all up in one night."

"Mad at you or at me?"

"She was not mad. Just cool. Besides, my clothes are a mess."

That Robins would listen to. He would give Sam forty-eight hours. Dammrich would arrange his schedule.

Dammrich's schedule already provided for the forty-eight hours. Carole laughed at this revelation. Sam did not. He wanted . . . "I'll take two days off and shop with you," she offered.

She did just that, and they had fun. They had one dinner

alone together, they spent the second evening with the Chaffines. Sam bought a new car, and told Carole to use it, to keep it in use.

"How long will you be gone?"

"The schedule is for three weeks."

"What will you do, Sam?" Don asked him.

"Not laundry, please God."

"Doesn't solving these crises, as you solved them, help tie a hospital organization together?"

Sam glanced at Carole. "Tell her."

"I did tell her. I told her she was missing some fun, too."

"And I spent the ten weeks," Carole admitted, "growing back the nose I had cut off when you asked me . . ."

This time he went off on a better note of feeling. This time his bags held well-cut suits, good shoes, shirts and ties. He wore a perfectly fitting topcoat and scarf. Carole wanted him to buy a hat. "Don't reform me all at once," he told her. "There's a tomorrow."

He traveled; he saw administrators, he advised them. Yes there were things to say to the hospital boards, to the patients he would meet when he addressed the public. "You'll be making speeches," he assured them. "Rotary, noonday meetings, PTA. If you're not asked, make ways to be asked. We are going to have to sell our side of this hospital and being sick business."

He provided copies of the speeches he had already written, he "talked" the subject matter of those speeches to the hospital administrators, sometimes to the staff doctors, and to the boards. He wore his good clothes, and gratefully packed his bags for the last time, to return home. If he could just putter around now in his own office until—well—Christmas. He would be so glad to see home again, he might even kiss Mrs. Drozda.

He went home, found Carole cheerful and full of plans.

"Which your boss will probably tear up and throw away."

"I've already done the over-the-ropes bit," Sam reminded her.

"I'm not counting on a thing. But if you do stay around . . ."

They had a week. Sam attended an executive meeting where he heard Robins himself say that Dr. Fowler had conducted several successful operations. He was asked to tell about the laundry project, and about some of the questions encountered on his public relations tour.

"Did you meet with problems you could not handle?"

"Yes. How to get a suit or my shirts back from valet service."

"That sort of higher research takes time and maturity," Robins assured him gravely.

He had a week. He took Carole to dinner on Wednesday, they ate Reuben sandwiches on Saturday, spent Sunday afternoon and evening with the Chaffines; Sam raked leaves and ate marshmallows the kids toasted over the fire.

Monday night was their Red Cross date, and he and Carole both were glad that he was there to keep it. She let him explain where he had been for the two months' absence. She liked seeing him as a doctor in white clothes. He thought she was beautiful in her blue pinafore. He told her so when he took her home and ate the bacon and tomato sandwiches she made.

What, he asked, would they plan for the week? October's weather invited many things.

"Things your boss can throw out the window."

"It's my job, Carole."

"I know. I made you give up your job at Harper's."

"There were other considerations."

She patted his arm. "It's big of you to say so. But I know how I acted. And I should remember that you are a doctor. You could be practicing and called out at all hours for stomach aches and things."

"Robins seems pleased with what I have done these past weeks."

"And that's important, I know. But I still hesitate to plan."

"Then let's play it by ear. Find a house on our next week end, get married on the next one . . ."

"You know?" she said. "You have a one-track mind."

"Hop aboard."

"I just may do it."

But she didn't. Not just then. Sam thought they might follow his "track" because Robins was in Chicago, or somewhere, working out plans for a large, new—not-yet-built—hospital. The office buzzed along, Sam with it—until Tuesday afternoon when a call came through for him.

"Dr. Robins on two, doctor," said Mrs. Drozda brightly.

Sam stifled a moan of protest, turned his chair so Drozda could not watch his face, and said, "Fowler here."

Mrs. Drozda heard him say, after five minutes of listening, "All right. I'll bring a length of string and a safety pin."

He put the phone down, his face thoughtful, and he began making his usual notes on the big legal pad. "Call Carole." "Warm clothes." "Fishing pole." He crossed that out blackly. He *never* went fishing.

He stood up. "I'm joining Dr. Robins in Minneapolis tomorrow morning, Mrs. Drozda. He thinks I should be back by the end of the week. He is going up to talk about that Canadian hospital job."

"And he thinks you may get in some fishing," she concluded brightly.

"Yes, but he doesn't know me."

"You'll fish," she assured him.

Sam groaned. "Get me Dammrich, will you please? And don't be so cheerful."

Carole thought the trip did not sound too bad. They would miss a dinner date, but just going to Canada sounded simple enough. . . .

"Things are never simple with Robins," Sam assured her.
"I'm looking at the good side."
"You keep doing that."
She laughed. "Can I come over and help you pack?"
"You may come over. I may pack. . . ."

He went to Minneapolis, which was a beautiful, shining city of parks and lakes. Dr. Robins was all fired up about the trip into Canada. "They" were planning a hospital to serve some of the oil boom communities. Sam would not need any fancy clothes.

They flew on a jet to their first meeting with the men who felt a hospital was needed, and possible. Then they transferred to a small plane; Robins was careful to take his long slender case which was sure to contain fishing rods. It seemed one did not call them poles.

They had two conferences. Sam made notes and suggestions. This was going to be a rugged-type installation; weather would be an item, and the transportation of patients . . .

"And personnel," he suggested.

The second conference was a long one. The two doctors came out of it with tired eyes and stubbled cheeks, as well as a map of the lake country. Robins—

"We want to get in some fishing before we go home," he said.

"The fishing is good just now," someone told him. No friend of Sam's.

"Can I get a guide?"

"Yes, and rent a seaplane if you like." It seemed that Robins could fly.

Robins liked; Sam did not, but he went along. Robins hired a guide, secured supplies and gear. A canoe was lashed to the top of the little plane; it was never used. Robins and the guide fished from the plane. Sam did not fish, nor try to.

He endured the whole thing, aware that Robins was watching him. Sam didn't say a word in his own defense.

He cleaned fish, and ate them. He slept for two nights rolled into a sleeping bag. "My arthritis starts here," he told himself.

Three days of lake hopping, three days of trying to be a good sport . . .

"What do we do with all the fish?" was the only question he asked.

"Give 'em away."

"I don't have that many friends."

"To tell the truth, I don't either."

What a way to earn a living!

He and Robins returned to civilization, signed the agreement to plan and arrange for the administration of the Wilderness Hospital. Robins said it always took three days for a group of men to make up their minds.

Then they went back to Minneapolis, to the luxurious suite which Robins seemed to have reserved in his name wherever he went. Gratefully Sam took a hot bath and dressed in his customary clothing. They were taking a night plane home.

Dinner was served in their rooms. "Not fish," was Sam's only specification.

Robins leaned back, smiling.

"You make a good trail partner, Sam," he said.

Sam looked at him, startled. "Great guns, man, I didn't like any part of your damn trail!"

"I know you didn't. I never judge a man for the way he does things he likes to do. It's how he endures, how he suffers. . . ."

Sam unfolded the first newspaper he had read in days.

He put it down. "Judging me?" he asked.

Robins nodded.

"I must have flunked when I was trying to get into that

damn sleeping bag. And getting out of it was no feat of skill either."

His boss chuckled.

Their dinner came. Thick steaks. A big green salad. Sam moaned with pleasure. "I'll leave the fish and the woods to you hardy types," he said.

"I liked your type all right," Robins told him unexpectedly.

Sam ate three bites of steak before he looked across at the other man. "What was to like?"

"I also liked the way you took the Texas trip. The laundry bit—the three weeks that followed. How about your girl, Sam? Tell me about her. You are engaged?"

Sam continued to eat. "You met Carole. I think she is beautiful. . . ."

"She is. Are you planning to be married soon?"

"Lately our plans don't seem to get much play." He opened the bottle of beer, carefully filled his glass.

"Because of me."

"She knows I have to have a job."

"That's good. Many women don't know that about a man."

"Carole . . ." Sam began, then he shook his head, and resumed eating.

"I have had my eye on you ever since you first came to us," Robins told him. "I like most of the things I have observed. You are a man to know what you like to do, and to do it. You have formed your own tastes and stick to them. You have imagination—you have humor—and patience. . . ."

"Not too much of that," Sam said wryly.

"Enough to keep you out of messes such as our profession provides in amplitude."

Sam finished his steak and looked at his watch.

"I'm about through with my speech," Robins told him.

"Sir—"

"We still have an hour for me to say what I have in mind."

They did have an hour. Sam looked across the handsome room; he could see himself, distorted, reflected from the side of a silver bowl filled with red roses. There was a lamp of dark green glass, a gold-framed round mirror . . .

He sat erect. "What did you say, sir?" he asked sharply.

"I asked what you thought about becoming my number-one assistant."

Sam sighed. "That's what I thought I heard you say." He picked up his napkin and touched it to his cheek. "You didn't mean it."

"I did mean it. When you first came to us, when we hired you, I hoped you would become my assistant." He held his gaze closely on Sam's face. "I had my eye on you when you were still at Harper's. I keep a file of possible young men. . . ."

Sam threw his napkin down, got to his feet, and walked the length of the room, looked out of the window, down at the busy street, across the roofs of the city. That confounded questionnaire, the interviews . . . "Why didn't you tell me?" he asked, turning back. "Did others know of this plan? Moir? Connors? Mrs. Drozda?"

Robins smiled grimly. "Not Mrs. Drozda."

"No. She would have told me. But why in the devil . . ."

"Would you have told such a thing to an unknown, coming into the organization, if you had been me?"

But he did not tell Sam to be honest. Which chalked up one score. Sam again looked out of the window. He had, so often, been tempted to demand to know his status. . . .

Carole would not believe this. And, convinced, would she like it? Of course, Sam must give his answer, make his own decision.

"Just what would I do?" he asked, turning around, tightening the knot of his tie.

"You'd live in my pocket," Robins told him bluntly. "You would think for me, and around me. . . . Do you remember the scheme you worked up for Mt. Sinai Hospital?"

"I remember," Sam said. "It was cut away from me like a —like a wart."

Robins chuckled. "It's being put to use. But that's the sort of thing you will be doing. We offered you the opportunity to make up some plan of your own—and you did it."

Sam nodded and went into his bedroom to gather up his last items of personal property, to close his suitcase.

"This is not the kind of job," he said, rejoining Robins, "that a man refuses. Not without a lot of thought."

Robins made no comment.

11

Carole said that he celebrated his new job by buying a green suit. He did buy one, though it was more tan than green, really. "Wait until I buy a raspberry pink shirt," he warned.

She laughed. "If I see you soon enough, I won't wait a minute. Seriously, darling, I am proud of you."

"Why now? I've not changed."

She gazed at him thoughtfully. "No, you haven't. That could be why I am proud."

At the office there was no formal announcement of the change in his status. Everyone knew about it, of course. The figures on his pay check told the story. He moved up to quarters on the seventeenth floor.

"I want you to see it," he told Carole. "I have a thick rug, my own view, my own lavatory."

"Oh, I must drop in!"

He chuckled.

"Mrs. Drozda is located in an anteroom. That alone makes the whole thing worthwhile."

Carole placed a card on the low table before them. "Is it?" she asked.

"Gin!" said Sam. "Is it what?"

"Is it worthwhile?"

Sam gathered the cards, stacked them, and shuffled them with a crisp rustle. "I can be my own man," he offered.

She turned on the couch cushion. "Oh, but, Sam, can you be?"

"Why not? He said I knew what I wanted to do, and did it. . . ."

"So he grabbed you. To do what *he* wants."

Sam nodded. *To live in his pocket.* "We'll see," he said mildly.

Dr. Moir still was Robins' "assistant in residence." He kept his fingers on the pulse, the reins of the business in his hand. He conferred with Robins, and with Dr. Fowler, often. He brought problems to Sam, big ones and small. Now Sam sent men out into the field; it often was he who decided what should be done, where and how.

He found himself acting like Robins in that he made the quick decisions, seemingly on snap judgment. Now he knew the judgment was, and had to be, carefully considered.

At dinner one Wednesday evening, he asked Carole if she would like to take a long drive with him over the week end.

"How long?"

"Oh, five hundred miles—a little more perhaps. We could go down on Saturday, back Monday."

"I work on Monday."

"We might make it home on Sunday night. With a new car—hospitals operate on Sundays."

"I could take Monday off."

"And you were planning to show me a house."

She shrugged. "That never works out for us."

"It can. It will."

"But not this week end. We'll go look at a hospital."

He reached for her hand. "And be together. . . ."

"That's a long drive," she agreed.

"We'll have fun. Things always pop up."

"Not a fishing trip, Sam!"

He laughed. "I am Robins' man. I try to think like him. But you'll never catch me going willingly into the wilderness."

"The scenery must have been beautiful."

He leaned back, thinking, "Yes," he agreed. "It was. The trees—pines, I suppose. The sky and the lake water. The crisp, cold air. There were animals—deer all over, and one moose. I don't want his head over my fireplace, and I got less than enthusiastic about snow on my bed every morning."

They made their plans for the long week end—her plans, and his. He talked a little about the community hospital that wanted to find a place and way to set up a pediatrics ward. Building a wing was so damn expensive. . . .

"I'm going to look for waste space and poor arrangement. They now treat the kids in the surgical and medical wards with the grownups."

"That's not good, Sam."

"You're going to make a fine doctor's wife."

"I hope," she said sadly.

Their plans were set. Sam was to pick Carole up at eight on Saturday morning. At midnight on Friday, his telephone rang.

He cursed mildly, turned on the light, reached for the phone. "Dr. Fowler!" he growled.

"Sam . . ." The voice was strange, muffled.

He sat straight up. "Carole?" he asked. "What's wrong?" All sorts of melodramatic things could have happened, could be happening.

"I—" She stopped to cough. "I've caught cold."

"You—"

"I woke up this morning with it. I did things, took aspirin —but it just gets worse and worse."

"I can come over."

"You cannot!" she protested. "Oh, Sam. I—I can't go with you tomorrow."

"I'll stay here and take care of you."

"For a head cold?" she asked.

"You're sick."

"I'm sick. I'll stay in bed. I'll drink orange juice. And when you come back, you can tell me about it." She sneezed.

Sam laughed, not unkindly. "I'll call you before I leave."

He made the trip; there didn't seem to be anything else to do. He could have flown south, and returned within thirty-six hours, but he kept to their plan of driving. He drove a bit faster than he would have done with Carole watchful at his side.

He reached his destination in time to go to the hospital late Saturday afternoon, returning to his hotel room late that night; on Sunday noon, he met with the administrator and some of the trustees. Then he could start home, reaching there . . .

He found his road map. Yes. If he should drive fifty miles southwest, before turning toward home, he could go to Ashby Woods and see Dr. Downes.

He checked the room, the bath, and came back, ready to close his bag. He frowned, looked up, and around. Someone was rattling the doorknob, someone—he strode across the carpet, threw the door open. "Oh," he said, "it's you."

Patric Robins grinned and walked around him into the room. "I figured you'd be just about finished here," he said.

"I'm finished. I haven't written the report."

"You can do that later. I understand you're driving." I want to go to Bartmer with you, before we return to the city."

Sam could feel his jaw muscles tighten. "What's at Bartmer?"

"There's a college there, a university."

"I know about the college."

"All right. If you are through here, let's get started. I'll talk on the way."

Sam made no comment, no protest. He checked out, picked up Robins' bag in the lobby, put it and his own into the car. He consulted his road map, still folded for Ashby Woods.

Robins was acting the way he had months ago, when Sam first joined the Ink. "Do what you are told, don't ask questions."

Had something happened? Sam had thought he was doing all right, but was he? Had his smug self-satisfaction showed?

Things had seemed to be all right! The book was selling well, they were about to make a movie sale. Lorraine Harper had been quieted. And the job had seemed to be going well.

His relationship with Carole, too. That blasted cold had spoiled this week end, this chance for them to talk long and earnestly about their future. He would have been able to sell her on the fact that his home, his personal life, must be under her surveillance and her planning. He would persuade her that marrying any doctor required more of a wife than marrying another man would do. She just couldn't count on her husband—It would be the same if Sam were, say, a heart surgeon or a general practitioner.

He would have talked to her, and made her understand.

Of course she was disappointed about the house. He had so often failed to go with her to look at one which she had selected. A house seemed very important to her. And he *would* put it on his calendar to spend a week end looking at houses and buying one.

He negotiated the cloverleaf, and was on the road straight away to Bartmer.

He wished he were headed for Ashby Woods and Dr. Downes. He could have cleared up the small cloud there. That cloud, that wonder in his mind, his sense of having failed that relationship, could all have been resolved. Maybe he still could make it to Ashby Woods—tomorrow.

"What are we doing in Bartmer, sir?" he asked.

Dr. Robins sat relaxed in the car seat, his head back, his legs extended. "What were you thinking about so hard, Sam?" he countered.

"My problems. Let's hear about yours. I don't think this state college has a medical school."

"You know Bartmer?"

"I spent a year in general practice fifty miles from there."

"Ah—yes. I remember."

"Did you perhaps attend college here?"

"No. I was raised in a small college town, however. My father taught mathematics."

Sam ventured a quick glance at Dr. Robins. "Mathematics?"

"He coached basketball on the side."

"I see."

Robins chuckled. "You don't, but you can guess what living in the academic atmosphere of such a place might be. My own formal education, however, was acquired in the state of Washington. College, med school. I was a champion sprint-runner, college level, but that career came to a halt one hot day when I stopped my car at the side of the road, shucked my clothes, and dived into a roadside river. I hit the hardest rock in all of Idaho. Knocked me cold, and ended all track competition for me. Taught me a lesson I needed to know."

"I'd think."

"Yes."

What other problems did Robins have? Most men had some, Sam believed.

He checked his gas gauge. "Do you have a family, doctor?" he asked. The office never spoke of one, but a man his age . . .

"Yes," said Robins. "And no."

Sam waited.

"I married when still in med school," Dr. Robins told him. "The daughter of a doctor. He got himself elected to a state office and, green out of med school, I took over his general practice in a small mountain town."

"Like it?"

"Not at the time. Now I find myself highly approving of it. I think every young doctor needs a year or so of G.P. to learn to appreciate people."

"You learn a lot," Sam agreed. "What happened then?"

"My father-in-law came back to his practice, and I took a job as admissions examiner in a seven-hundred-fifty-bed hospital in Wisconsin. I thought then that I would become an orthopedic surgeon. As it turned out, I went into administration. My first job was to help an expert redesign a five-hundred-bed hospital. Doing that, I was offered a position as administrator of a Chicago suburban place. I did that, found myself making speeches on administration, and offering advice, free. Decided I could charge for it. The rest is history."

Sam turned off the Freeway to get gas.

"You should have filled up back at the motel," Robins told him.

"I should have. What about the family?"

Slowly, deliberately, Robins took his pipe from the side pocket of his plaid jacket. He got the pipe going, and the car immediately was filled with the haze and perfume of rich tobacco.

"My wife divorced me," he told Sam, putting the match end into the receptacle. "She is raising our children. . . ."

"Too bad," said Sam.

"Yes. Too bad. I know people, Fowler; I can organize for them. But my life—I make a holy mess of that."

Sam said nothing. What was there to say? Robins' knobby face was thoughtful, concerned.

"You watch your step, Sam," he told the younger man.

"I'll try."

"My problem of this minute," said Dr. Robins, shifting in the car seat, raising himself erect, "has to do with a friend. Or—a man I thought was a friend. I'm about to find out . . ."

Sam watched the car ahead of him; it had an overly cautious driver. And he thought Robins had made this chance to talk to him. To someone. A man needed that.

It had occurred to Sam before this that Robins might be a lonely man. For all his success, his financial security, his interest in many things—yes, he probably was lonely.

"Don't mess up your life, Sam," Robins was telling him again. "Stop every now and then and think about what you want. . . ."

Should I tell him about Carole's head cold? Sam wondered. He pulled into the filling station, got out of the car and walked around. Robins stayed where he was.

"This chap I mentioned," he said to Sam when they were on their way again. "He is a young man—younger than you are. About thirty-two, or three. I helped him go to theological seminary. I let myself think I was doing a good deed. The boy had graduated from the university, and went into the insurance business. He was doing well—then he felt this call for the church. I knew him, knew about his decision—I happen to feel strongly that it is the duty of all men to further this sort of work. We may not be noble and unselfish ourselves, but—well, anyway, he went through seminary. He was ordained. And this past year he has been serving a small church in a town thirty-five miles from Bartmer, and as chaplain-adviser for the college. He is well liked, the young people talk to him. He's been holding 'talk-ins' at his home, on all sorts of subjects. The race problem, drugs, sex . . .

"He lives in a small house at the edge of the campus; the young people come there. And the good people of the town

—peeping Toms to you—push through the hedge, look in through the windows, to see what is going on. One of the things they have seen, besides untidy young people sprawling about on the floor and the furniture, was a sign taped to a refrigerator door. It read, "Cokes, 15¢; beer, 30¢."

"Thirty cents?" asked Sam mildly.

"Well, whatever it was. I don't do much traffic in single bottles of beer. George, my friend, could not afford to provide it free.

"Now, the real crime, of course, in this part of the country was that the people lolling about his living room were a mixed crowd, black and white. The *charge* that has been brought against him is that he sold liquor without a license."

"I'd say he was a mistaken man, but hardly a criminal."

"So would any thinking person. But of course with a legal charge made, the court has to take some action. The university does. And the church."

"Bartmer coming up, sir."

"Find us a place to stay for the night. We'll go back to the city early tomorrow. I'll see George this evening."

"What will you be able to do?"

"Nothing maybe. Perhaps this will be something he will have to work out, as an adult, as a man who has made his decision. . . ."

Sam nodded. A motel sign loomed ahead. The little university town was a pretty place, the streets hilly and winding, but he thought this highway would lead to the motel.

"What George probably was trying to do," he said, "was to seek to put himself on a level with the students. But your big question there is: Did the students want that of him? Wouldn't they have come to his house, and no beer served? There must be plenty of people—other students—on their own level. There must be plenty of places where they could drink beer and talk. When they sought out a priest of the church, Robins, they wanted something beyond what they themselves possessed." He pulled the car into the drive of the motel.

"You check us in," said Robins. He slid over into Sam's seat. And Sam watched his new car disappear down the road.

Well . . .

He spent the evening alone. He did not call Carole. If he told her where he was, with whom, she would have the screaming meemies.

He ate dinner, and watched TV. When Robins returned with the bags, he went to bed.

Sam did not meet the clergyman friend. On the return trip to the city, Robins was practically silent—certainly on that subject. When Sam let him out at his home, he did have the grace to turn back, lean into the car, and say gruffly, "I plagiarized your stuff, Sam, Thanks."

Sam nodded, and drove away. He would go to his hotel, check on Carole, and maybe even go to the office. Robins, probably, would get there before him.

12

Sam was busy. Time flew past. Here was Christmas, coming up again over the horizon. Last year he and Carole had said, "We will be married at Christmas." This year, nothing had been said, though they could be, of course. Six weeks from now, or six days.

Sam bought Carole a string of cultured pearls in a handsome case of blue leather and white satin. She would like them, but he was not sure they were what she most wanted.

They had their dates together, did the things they liked to do. Sometimes they did. Because Sam was busy. Carole understood, she said, about new jobs. She respected his profession, but sometimes . . .

When, a few days before Thanksgiving, he told her that he was going west again . . .

"Will you be long, Sam?"

"I should be home Sunday."

"But no turkey?"

He smiled at her. "You may come with me."

She seemed to consider this. "What will you be doing?"

"I'm to inspect a reorganization job we've been doing at Mt. Sinai Hospital."

"Sam Fowler?"

He looked at her in surprise. "Now what?"

"Is that the same Mt. Sinai Hospital—when you first began to work for the Ink, you drew up a plan, and that man gave it to someone else. . . . Is *that* the place?"

"I—yes, it is, Carole."

"Well, you can go see it. I wouldn't take the first step. After the way they treated you . . ."

He shook his head. "I was booted upstairs," he reminded her. "And even if I had not been, it would be my job to go out and see what Curry's been doing."

"Who's Curry?" She was very cross.

Sam laughed. "He's the chap assigned to the reorganizing of Mt. Sinai Hospital. He got into some trouble first. . . ."

"And you straightened him out?"

"Robins did. Will you go with me, Carole? You'll love the mountains. Maybe we could do some skiing."

"A platonic trip, of course."

"I've never felt one bit platonic toward you."

"What would Dr. Robins feel about a non-platonic trip?"

"He'd like it better than a platonic one."

"You're joking."

"You don't know the man."

No, she did not. But she still refused to go west with Sam. "We could even be married out there," he told her.

"And come back here to your hotel rooms? Or my one-room efficiency apartment?"

"Oh, Carole . . ."

She began to weep, and turned her back to him. "Go away," she said. "I don't make a good job of being noble and all-suffering."

He could not comfort her since, of course, he had to leave for the west on Tuesday night. Young Dr. Curry met his plane. A crisp, icy wind swept across the airport.

"I have a car, Dr. Fowler," he said. "I'll take you to the hotel. I thought, tomorrow, we could make a tour of the hospital. . . ." The young man was anxious. Since his early mistakes, he had been working from Sam's plans; this was his first job on his own.

Having so recently been in those same shoes, Sam could be kind to the boy. Well, really, Curry was only a couple of years younger, but— "What time do we start?" he asked, approving of his hotel quarters. He got mighty tired of motel units, all alike, all with hermetically sealed windows and no views.

"I'll pick you up at a quarter to six."

Sam whirled. "Six!" he shouted. "To look at the operating rooms on the second floor and the maternity ward on the fourth? To—"

"That wasn't the sort of tour I had in mind, sir," said the hapless Curry, his tone subdued but stubborn.

Sam nodded. "All right," he said. "I came out here to see what you had done. I'll take your tour. Five-forty-five. But don't expect me to be cheerful."

"No, sir."

"And don't call me *sir!* The name is Sam."

"Er—yes, S . . . Sam. The board will meet with you on Thursday."

"But that's Thanksgiving."

"I believe dinner will be served—and there's a staff party for that evening. Friday, you can check details. I have a small office at the hospital . . ." The man was half sick with apprehension.

"All right, Curry," Sam said. "Pick me up at five-forty-five."

Dr. Curry held up his briefcase. "I have my report written out, if you'd care to go over it."

"After I've seen the hospital. Good night, Curry. Happy dreams."

"Er—yes, sir," said Dr. Curry.

Carole would have said he had been hard on the little

man. He had not been. Women scarcely ever understood how the male person operated in his business, his profession, and how he could, personally, like the same man he fought or judged across a desk or on the job.

Robins had seen to it that Sam was trained in the hazards of the work they did. Curry, too, must be trained. Someday, he would be rewarded, as Sam was being by his present situation. He was the one to survey the way Curry had used his plan; he had the power to approve or disapprove. . . .

He was glad that Carole had not come with him. Platonic or no, her presence would have completely thrown Dr. Curry.

As it was—

Sam was awakened at five-fifteen the next morning by a tray containing coffee and orange juice. "A chunk of meat to quiet the lion," he told himself. But as he shaved, he could hear Carole's cool voice, "Give the boy a chance, Sam."

And the coffee and juice were a great help.

At six he was ready to listen to Curry when he made a nice little speech about a modern hospital's being the proper showplace to impress a visitor from Mars.

"I guess you're right," Sam said. "A great deal of purposeful and skilled activity goes on within all that architecture." He gestured toward the mass of red brick and white stone that was coming toward them.

An hour had not passed before Sam had to clutch at his judicial role. He was, again, enthralled with the hospital itself, and what went on within the great building. The 455 patients, and the many, many more people who attended them. Sam was indeed taken to the "second-floor operating rooms, and to the fourth-floor maternity department." He saw the switchboard, the kitchens, the supply center, and the cleaning and maintenance departments in the basement.

The activities did somewhat resemble those of a large hotel, but there was an overtone of drama and seriousness which few hotels ever achieved, and almost all of the guests would, by choice, have liked to be elsewhere.

The cold statistics of the day he spent in the hospital would have appeared on paper as:

Five babies were born.

Thirty-two surgical procedures were scheduled.

Forty-eight patients were admitted to the hospital, as many were discharged.

About 2,000 meals were prepared and served to the patients and employees.

One patient died.

When the two inspecting doctors first arrived, the tempo of the hospital was stepping up from its post-midnight quiet. The night admissions officer had made his count, an assistant cook arrived to start the coffee. At eight o'clock the big front door on the avenue would be unlocked.

Mimeographed and already posted was the operations schedule. Sam read it carefully. Time, surgeon's name, the kind of surgical procedure, the type of anesthesia, and—yes, the name of the patient. He nodded. In Ink hospitals no one was a gall bladder or a gastric resection.

The surgery schedule began at seven-forty-five and extended into the afternoon. Some sections were planned days, even weeks, in advance; some were performed on an emergency basis. This morning, the o.r. nurse, a Miss Meriweather, had entered the hospital just ahead of Dr. Curry and Dr. Fowler. She got the keys to the operating suite from the switchboard operator.

Sam learned that that operator had been with Sinai for twenty-three years. During the past night she had handled four emergencies, including a heart case. She had responded to about fifty telephone calls, most of them inquiries about patients' comfort and welfare. At hand she kept a file of pertinent information.

This woman, Dr. Curry told Sam, could recognize each

voice of the 450-member staff, as well as those of the fifty residents and interns. She could also recognize the sound of certain footsteps passing in the hall. "She says she knows if some pretender calls, claiming to be a doctor. She says there is an assurance to a doctor's voice and manner that distinguishes him from other men."

"Did you find a way to bottle her knowledge?" Sam asked.

"I've suggested that she personally train the other operators."

Another early bird was the food service director. Sam talked to this man with great interest. Dr. Curry should have made great changes in the cooking and serving of food here at Sinai. He had. "But the quality of food has always been good here," said the director. "Of course the patients have always complained. They claim any gravy is gray. They complain of the tastelessness of a salt-free diet. I do my best for them. I consider the food we serve as important as the medication. Under the new setup, when wine is called for, we cook with wine. We use spices; there are two hundred pounds of lobster in the freezer right this minute."

"Have you always worked . . . ?"

"In hospitals? No, doctor. Hotels, a country club—a French restaurant in New York. I had worked in one hospital before coming here. We have about seventy thousand meals to serve a month, and we cater as well for all sorts of meetings, parties and benefits held here at the hospital."

"All kosher?"

"No, doctor. You know better than that. Dr. Curry has given us three divisions—regular diet, special diet, and kosher. The kosher kitchens are now entirely separate units from the other kitchens. From them we serve about a hundred persons at a given time, with menus presented and choice observed so far as we can and stay within the physician's limitations.

"Meals, you know, are often all a hospital patient has to look forward to. I'm glad the reorganization around here so occupied itself with that fact."

Sam and Dr. Curry, unescorted by any member of hospital administrative personnel, descended to the basement, to the quarters of the housekeeper. To keep the hospital clean was her job, and a big one. "Staph infection has doubled my job in the years I've been the exec," she told Sam. "They resist everything!" she declared. "And I have to stop them in every possible spot."

This project, too, had been an item in Sam's plans, and Curry's application of it must be studied. "There are one hundred twelve employees on the housekeeping staff," Curry told Sam. "They operate twenty-four hours a day. The entire hospital gets a wet mopping each twenty-four hours. The plans are detailed. Six hundred rooms a day are cleaned, walls washed, by machine. O.r. walls cleaned every other week. Hospital windows washed three times a year."

"Dry dusting?"

"Not tolerated."

The housekeeper had charge of the laundry and the sewing room. A complete change of bed linen throughout the hospital each day demanded a busy, and efficient, laundry. The sewing room occupied itself with mending about 7,500 articles a month. Three seamstresses were employed. Sam studied the drape sheets they were making according to the surgeons' specifications for particular operations. He had advised, Curry had carried out his advice, that the maternity ward linens be a different color from surgery.

While still in the basement, Sam took a look at the quarters presided over by the "plant" engineer, the carpentry and paint shops, the massive boilers and refrigeration machinery, the furnaces and storerooms, the steam piping for the surgical sterilizers and the kitchen steam kettles. For the laundry, too, of course.

Walking beneath the maze of overhead pipes, between the batteries of gauges and boilers, Sam felt as if he was inspecting a battleship.

"It's different, though," he reminded Curry. "One of these electricians, I hope, makes a check regularly of the operating room floor, and the lights."

"Once a month, sir," said Curry.

Sam was particularly interested in the reorganized central supply office in this hospital. Emergency, and long-range service, required that oxygen, vital medicines, surgical supplies, be kept in good supply and readily available.

"Our main point of stress," said the central supply supervisor, "at least, our greatest *activity*—" she looked anxiously at Dr. Curry, and then at Dr. Fowler—"is the oxygen therapy service. We are keeping an oxygen unit and a technician in readiness around the clock. Of course each nursing division always has a half-hour's supply on hand, but we know we can have two heart attacks at the same time and in the same place."

"How quickly . . . ?" asked Sam.

"We deliver within three minutes on coronaries," said the supervisor.

Would Carole consider that as important as his presence at the Chaffines' Thanksgiving dinner table? Sam shook his head. She would, if she understood. He must find time, and a way, to make her understand.

He spent some time watching the personnel—some of them were volunteers—at a long table, disassembling syringes for cleaning, folding green cloths of various sizes and shapes, and assembling packages that could be parachutes but which were not. They contained clothing for surgical teams, sponges, towels, masks. Everything that would be needed in o.r. except instruments and gloves. Behind him were the autoclaves where these packs were sterilized for use.

He watched two women inspecting rubber gloves for the nicks that would make them useless; he inspected the bank-vaultlike autoclaves.

"How's the tape working?" he asked Curry. His plan had called for the use of special binding tape around the surgical packets; this would turn black after the half-hour exposure to 250°F. heat.

On a rack near the dumbwaiter to the operating rooms, the black stripes showed up dramatically. No danger of an unsterilized package. . . .

Those things were important. So was the location and comfort of the cots where interns and residents rested and waited in the maternity area.

Sam spent the whole day busily, talking to individual patients which he selected, to the doctors, nurses, interns, looking at the books in the finance office.

By night he was tired, and said so. "If you don't want to eat dinner with me, Curry," he said, "you need not."

"My wife came out for the holiday. I'd like you to meet her."

"I'd like that, too," said Sam. "I left my girl back home feeling sorry for herself."

"She has a right . . ."

Sam went back to the hotel, took a hot bath, changed clothes. He would graciously spend two hours with the Currys. Tomorrow—

He reached home too late to go out to the Chaffines' for Sunday supper, but he did talk to Carole, and told her that the trip had been tiring, but had gone well.

"Your plan works then?"

"Curry made it work."

For a second she was silent. Then she said softly, "I love you, Sam. But sometimes I hate me."

"May I come over?"

"Not tonight, dear. Tomorrow?"

He saw her "tomorrow," and she was loving, and contrite. His work was important; she knew that.

For the rest of the week, he did not see her at all, but he was back in the city for Sunday, and they went out to the Chaffines'.

"What do you plan for Christmas?" JoAnn asked them.

"With Sam, we don't plan," Carole told her.

JoAnn looked at him. "Sam?"

He shrugged. "I've been busy . . ." he said mildly, "and probably will be. I work all hours, I travel constantly. I can make no plans of my own, and the best thing I do is to break up those Carole makes."

"Is what you do so important, so necessary?"

Sam glanced at Carole and smiled.

"He should know the answer," she said. "I've asked that question of him often."

"Would it be easier if you were married?"

"She could go with me," said Sam, "on most of my trips."

"Wouldn't that be expensive?"

"On planes, and in motels, she'd travel half-fare. It might be cheaper than keeping up a house."

JoAnn did not laugh with the others. "I suppose if I knew what you did—more about it—" she conceded.

"Tell her, Sam," Don urged. "Tell all of us."

"Won't the prime ribs burn?" he asked.

"Yes. They will turn into soup beans boiled with a ham-bone."

"All right, then."

He got up from the couch, went to the kitchen, filled a glass with ice cubes, then water, and brought it back to the living room. "I'll get hoarse and thirsty," he explained. "All this talking."

"You could confine yourself to this past year," Don suggested.

"I could," Sam conceded. He sat down again, sipped of the water. "Well, let's see. I work all hours . . ."

"You said that."

"It's part of it. This past week—I should have kept notes. On Monday I went to Washington and sat in on a 'Bank-in' seminar."

"Do you know what that is?" JoAnn asked Carole.

"Yes. He called me from Washington. We'd save money on phone calls if I'd travel with him at half-fare."

"Aw, he puts his telephone calls on his expense account," said Don.

"With Robins and Moir watching me?" Sam asked. "You've got rocks in your head."

"How are you doing in the office anyway?" Don asked him. "Didn't you bump this Moir?"

"Not me. He's Robin's office assistant. I do the field work."

"You're away a lot. Do you see much of Robins?"

"He bobs up."

"He must like what you are doing."

"I don't know, Don. I find myself glancing quickly at him, hoping to catch an expression that will tell me how I'm doing. He knows I'm doing that. He is a remarkably patient man."

Beside him Carole sat straight up. "Robins?" she asked, her voice sharp.

"Robins. Yes."

"Well, *you* certainly are patient."

Sam shrugged. "I'm not Robins," he said quietly. "And he doesn't want me to be."

Carole relaxed against his arm. "Tell us about the seminar," she said.

"Didn't you read about it in the paper?" Don asked. "There was quite an article."

"*I* don't read about things like seminars," JoAnn assured her husband.

"It was a congressional seminar," Sam said, "in connection with an investigation on the high cost of being sick. It covered hospital financing, hospital reimbursement, financial formulae, bank leasing programs for hospital equipment, and general hospital economics."

"Do you like doing things like that?" JoAnn asked him.

"I like my work. Some parts of it are more interesting than others. Your being a wife and homemaker would show up the same lack of enjoyment. You like being married to Don, and having him love you—but feeding the family within your budget has to be done, too."

"Yes," said JoAnn. "It does. Go on."

Sam looked at her, frowning. "Oh, yes. The things I did this week. Well, let's see. From Washington I went to Delaware to handle the situation caused by a batch of prima donna doctors. . . ."

"I never heard of the like," drawled Don, getting up to put a new log on the fire. JoAnn told him to stir the beans, which he did. He returned to hear Sam explaining what was meant by "prima donna doctors."

"At one time or another, the doctors all develop minds of their own," he said. "Which causes the administrator to rejoice in a very low key. They decide that the hospital is a workshop run pretty much for their sake."

"As it is," agreed Don, a spark in his eye, "the patients are ours, the responsibility . . ."

"Ah-hum," said Sam heavily. "And I'll bet you are upset whenever some administrator considers his hospital morally obligated to see that the patient is properly treated."

"Oh, I never let myself get upset, doctor," Don assured his friend.

Carole took Sam's hand and stroked it. "Pay no attention to him," she said. "Just tell us what went on."

"I do like being coaxed," Sam admitted. "Let's see . . . I found that the administrator was having his troubles. One of the courtesy visitings had left orders that the resident physician should not examine his patient. He reported this to the administrator. . . ."

"Who said, 'Examine him!' " said Don.

"He did say that. Tests showed diabetes; the patient was being treated for something else. I told the administrator he was right to move in. He had called in a specialist, and told him to take over."

"Simultaneously, I presume, the visiting was moved out?"

"Yes. And do you know? In talking to that administrator —oh, he had other problems of staff doctors not letting the interns examine private patients—that happens too often to be funny, and there is always an intern who gets sassy. This administrator backed one of these."

"Oh, oh," said Don.

"Yes, he was on marshy ground there, and I told him so. But in sorting out these trouble spots, and advising the administrator, do you know? I had the weirdest feeling that I was talking in Robins' voice, that his voice was within my own—or something. I couldn't really tell if it was Dr. Robins talking, or Fowler."

"If he had on a lavender shirt, it was Robins," said Carole. "Then what did you do?"

"Those shirts cost forty-five dollars apiece," Sam told her. "Did you ask?"

"I did."

"I'm glad you can't afford them. What did you do next?"

"That's it, except for a speech I made to a board of trustees."

"And that's all you did!" drawled Don. JoAnn got up to set the table.

"In my spare time I worked out my idea for training experienced auxiliary volunteers as aides on the surgical floor."

"Doing what?" Don asked, interested.

"Relieving pressure. On the patient, and on the staff. You see, patients get scared of surgery. A pleasant woman, showing up of her own accord, as the patient will know, could come to the patient's bedside, promise to go with her to o.r. And then, if this same woman could be around when the patient comes out of anaesthesia, it should be reassuring. Where reassurance is needed."

"Would she be in o.r.?"

"Oh, no, but up there on that floor there are all sorts of things she can do, answer the telephone, take messages, run specimens down to the lab, fetch items from central supply. . . . The floor secretary can use help."

"You'd need experienced women."

"I'm specifiying that. And attractive women."

"You'll just have to look at them," Don decided. "When do we eat, Mamma?"

JoAnn came back to the fire. "Ten minutes, maybe a little longer. I'm making cornbread."

Don nodded. "Kids watching TV?"

"There's a Wild Kingdom program, and Disneyland."

"Okay, okay," said Don. "TV at their end of the house was a fine idea."

"I'm getting to be an expert on the late shows," Sam told his friends. "Nothing like a lonely hotel room. . . ."

"If you'd stay out of those hotel rooms," JoAnn said, her voice clear, "you might be an expert on some other things."

Sam glanced at her, and so did Don. "Now what does that mean?" her husband asked.

JoAnn shrugged. "It means that I think, and so does Carole, I'm sure, that Sam could do better to stay out of so many lonely hotel rooms. What I'm saying is that I think it's terrible the way he treats Carole, and expects her . . ."

Sam sat up straight. "What you are saying," he told JoAnn, "is complete nonsense."

"It's not any such thing. Look. You love the word *evaluate*. All right, Dr. Sam Fowler, why not do a little evaluating of yourself and what you have been doing lately?"

Sam gazed at the small, blond woman. She stood in the firelight, the lamplight, every muscle tense, her eyes blazing. "Somebody has to say this to you!" she cried. "You—and others—think you are a great success in your career. I don't. I think you are a complete failure. You gave up what was a good job with the Harper Foundation, and—"

"That was Carole's idea," said Don, his voice rough.

Sam turned to glare at him. "I make my own decisions," he said flatly. "And if Carole has any complaints . . ."

"Oh, she has them!" cried JoAnn. "She may even make them to you. But you don't listen. You go off on your precious job assignments and leave her stranded. Alone . . . Well, I had hoped you and Carole would make a thing of it, Sam, but now— Did it ever occur to you that there are other men around? Men who might, and do, appreciate Carole, who—"

"You're not making sense," Sam told her, leaning back on the couch again. Carole stood behind him; her hand now touched his shoulder.

"You're not bringing up that widower again, are you?" Don asked his wife.

Sam's head went up. "What widower?" he demanded. He looked up and around at Carole. "Do you have a widower?" he asked her.

She touched his hair. "On the stage," she said, laughing a little, "this performance would be called a farce."

Sam sprang to his feet and faced her. Her cheeks were pink. "What *widower?*" he shouted.

"I'll tell you what widower," said JoAnn, "He is a *very* attractive man, a little younger than you are, Sam Fowler. He lives down the hill below us in that stone house with the blue slate roof. He—'

"The house we looked at at Easter?" Sam asked Carole.

"Last Easter!" JoAnn agreed. "A year ago, Sam."

Sam rubbed his hand back over his hair, and took a deep breath. "I guess it was," he admitted. "But that house—there were children—swings and stuff."

"Rollin McCann has children," said JoAnn airily. "Two. Which is more than Carole will ever have from you."

Sam gritted his teeth. He hated to smack a woman.

"His mother takes care of the children," JoAnn was saying. "He is a commercial airline pilot, a charming man, and —"

"I suppose he stays at home all the time?" Sam asked her.

Don stepped between them. "This is all nonsense," he cried. "Shut up, JoAnn. Go look at your cornbread."

"And especially shut up!" added Sam. "This is none of her damn business."

"Watch your tone, Fowler," Don said loudly.

"What I'll watch," Sam assured him, "is my own life. My own affairs. You might tell your wife to do the same with hers." He snatched his glass of ice and water, stalked out of the room, going to the kitchen. He threw the ice cubes—diamond-hard and prism-hued—into the sink with a clatter, and set the glass on the counter with a thump.

Then he stood looking down at it for a minute. He picked it up and held it against his cheek. Were they quarreling? The Chaffines and he?

But they couldn't be! They *couldn't* . . .

He went back to the living room, to JoAnn. He bent over and kissed her cheek.

"Hey!" cried Don. "You're smooching my wife!"

"I have to," said Sam, his voice sounding odd. "I don't have one of my own." He turned to look at Carole. "Let's go home," he said gruffly.

She shook her golden head. "No." She spoke coolly. "No, Sam."

He sighed. She was right. If they went home now, they could never return. And the Chaffines . . .

"Let's eat the beans," he said. "I only wanted to smooch you, and see what I could do about getting me a wife."

They ate the beans, and the cornbread. The children helped bridge the difficult time. Encouraged, small Peter graphically told about the capture of a leopard. *"El tigre!"* he said fiercely.

The evening was saved. But the scar and the sutures would show for a long time.

Sam and Carole departed a bit earlier than they would have, perhaps. But on a friendly note. Sam promised to call Don about lunch one day the next week. JoAnn told Carole she could bring a cheesecake the next Sunday.

In the car, halfway back to the city, Sam asked Carole, "Have you been seeing that pilot?"

"JoAnn asked the whole family for Thanksgiving."

"D'you like him?"

She put her hand on Sam's sleeve. "Sam," she said, "I like lots of men."

"I thought I was the one."

"You are the one, darling. You have been for three—no, four—years."

"Is JoAnn right? Are you tired of waiting?"

"You were right, too. It was none of her business."

He took her home, parking the car in the street, going up with her to her apartment, and inside. He took off her coat, and his. Then he turned to her, held her face between the palms of his hands, and he kissed her. Then he kissed her again, and hard, his lips bruising. She would have pulled free, but his arm tightened; he kissed her eyes, her throat, and the soft white swell of her breast.

"Sam . . ." she gasped.

She wanted a wedding, a house. She wanted Sam. She leaned into his embrace, and she sighed, ever so faintly, as with regret.

He kissed her mouth again, gently, and put her into a deep chair. He picked up his coat and let himself out into the hall. Carole sat there.

She would find a house. Or choose an apartment down by the river. She wanted a place in Sam's life, a place he would recognize. Of course she knew that he was busy. . . .

Sam was busy—and not doing any writing at all; he had not done any for months. Carole was being neglected, and he determined to change both things. She had found another house; he had promised her, and himself, to look at it on Saturday. He would like it. He was determined that he would, no matter what sort of house it was. Then he would tell the office that he was going to take two weeks, absolutely free. He and Carole would furnish the house and be married. This he could do.

And he would have done it, too—except for the blizzard. He was not to blame. Carole must know he was not. Several thousand people were stranded along with him in New York that week end. Fourteen inches of snow, roads closed, no planes leaving Kennedy . . .

He had one terrible time getting to a phone to call Carole. He told her, "They are showing movies, and serving meals in some of the stranded planes. Six thousand people are sleeping wherever they can find a place to stretch out. I'm wrinkled, I need a shave. I'm hungry, but I love you. And look, my darling, if that house pleases you, take an option on it. I'll be home with a check as soon as I can get out of this concentration camp.'

"Oh, no, Sam . . ." she protested.

"But why not? I'd like the house."

"I want us to do these things together."

Sam sighed. She could hear him do it. She could look out of the window and see sunshine. It seemed incredible that he should be held up by heaps and mounds of snow.

"Lately," he was saying, "it seems to be more a matter of Robins and me together."

"Is that as good?" she asked him.

"No!" he shouted into the phone. "It definitely is not!"

"Have you tried asserting your rights?"

Sam laughed at the idea. Then he considered her question as important. "I might do that," he said, "if I knew what those rights were. In this work I do . . ."

"Why don't you find out where you stand, what your rights are?"

"I'll answer that when I get home," he told her.

"Do you really think you'll get home?"

"If I have to walk."

He surrendered the telephone booth, shaking his head at the line of weary travelers waiting to use it. He walked to one of the great expanses of glass which looked out over the runways of this magnificent airport. All of man's inventiveness, all his skill and ingenuity, had designed the place, had built the planes which now squatted like fat-logged ducks into the piled snow. A plow, tiny against the vastness of its task, was blowing snow from one place to another. Occasionally, a human being, muffled, wrapped, would appear. . . . Nature had taken over again to prove the futility of man. One wondered . . .

But of course man kept trying—to conquer nature, to control it. To conquer and control his own environment, to solve the insoluble, to stretch a line to hold to, and follow. . . .

As Sam had read of pioneers on the prairies who had used to stretch a clothesline during a blizzard to get a man safely from house to barn, and back again to warmth and security.

His now life . . .

He had no line stretched, no sure way. . . .

Someone got up from a couch near him; with long strides he went to the empty space and sat down, sighing gratefully, struck with the fact that a rump-sprung plastic cushion could feel so good, could mean comfort and rest.

He leaned back and closed his eyes, his briefcase clutched across his knees.

He had promised Carole to set things straight at the office as to his rights.

Could he also assert his rights with her? Could he tell her so? Could he . . . ? Did he have rights . . . ?

He fell asleep.

13

At noon, two days later, he reached his home city, sentimentally happy to possess his bag again, to be able to get his car, drive it to the hotel, go up and shower, to resist an impulse to put all his soiled garments into the wastebasket. He checked on his mail, then he went to the office, and, at five o'clock, without calling her first, he went to Carole's apartment.

She was so surprised to see him. . . .

"Shut your mouth," he told her, backing her away from the door. "You look like a fish in a dime store tank."

"Oh, Sam. . . ."

He kissed her. "I bathed," he told her. "But you should have smelled that place full of refugees!"

"Couldn't you have gone back into New York, and then—"

"Those were the roads that were closed. Besides, we didn't want to go into New York. We were supposed to be boarding departing planes, and we did board them as soon as we could."

"You do look tired."

"I slept all the way home. Two hours. I cleaned up, reported, and came here. . . ."

"I'll fix us something to eat."

"Can't we have something sent up?"

"Yes."

"I don't want you going 'way off to the kitchen."

She laughed. It would mean "going off" for a matter of ten feet.

He called the restaurant downstairs. He wanted a steak, he said, "a large salad . . ." His eyebrow lifted to Carole. "Make it two of everything," he said into the phone.

"I'll eat what you can't," he told her, putting the phone down.

"Did you starve?"

"Not really. But by the time you stand in line for an hour to get a ham sandwich . . ."

He sat down, and smiled at her. "Come here," he said. "Do you know? I believe, if you had been with me, you would have come out of that mess looking just as cool and smooth as you do this minute."

He was tired; she could see that. But he made a gay thing of eating dinner. And he was pleasant, not demanding anything of her, when he told about finding a job waiting on his desk when finally he did get back to the office. "I wanted to tell you about it," he said. "I want you to understand about these assignments. First, will you go with me?"

"They shouldn't send you out so soon again."

"Why not?"

"You're tired."

"They are giving me twenty-four hours to rest. You should have seen my beard, Carole. Scraggly, reddish— I'll never make it with the hippies."

"I'm glad. Wasn't there a barbershop?"

"Yes, and I had a razor in my checked bag. I couldn't get near either one."

"Oh, dear. Did you really order pie for us, Sam?"

"Sure I ordered it. I'll eat yours if you don't want it."

She laughed, and pushed her plate toward him. "Tell me

about the assignment. Though you don't have to tell me about your work just because of the foolish things JoAnn said a week ago."

"What did she have to say about the blizzard?"

"I think Don has placed restrictions on what she says."

"That won't work. For them, and especially not for us. Our friendship has always been on a frank and open basis. Did you go there Sunday without me?"

"I did, and took cheesecake. And no, Mr. McCann was not there. Now, tell me . . ."

"Mrs. Drozda also thinks it is terrible that I should be leaving again."

Carole laughed. "What did you tell her?"

"To get my itinerary from Dammrich, and to be sure she had a copy for her desk."

"Sam, aren't you hard on that woman?"

He moved over to the couch. "Come over here," he said. "I never was so full and contented."

"You should be." She pushed the table out of the way, and covered it with a cloth. Then she sat next to Sam, and cuddled into the circle of his arm. "I know you always solve special problems."

He considered what she had said. "Problems, yes. Always. Solve . . . not always. I find out what we have, and often bring the whole mess back to the office whiz boys. Special? Well, in that we are concerned with the smooth, efficient care of the sick—yes, always special."

"I'm glad you do the work you do, Sam."

That evening was all a tired man could ask. Contentment. No pressure. He left on his trip feeling that things were well with him and his girl.

The first night he was home, he called Carole. "Only forty-eight hours?" she asked. "You're improving."

He laughed. "I hope the boss agrees."

"But you must be, Sam. Aren't you?"

She didn't start it. He had been thinking along these lines for some time now. About the situation wherein he found himself.

For the next two days he was occupied in setting up an interview with a new man it was hoped could become a member of the organization. There was a tremendous amount of data involved, research into background, the man's history as he had lived it, which would be compared with what was told in his application answers. He must be observed, interviewed, talk about. . . .

Sam found himself considering the fellow—he called him "the poor guy"—as a replica of himself, two years ago, venturing to apply for a position with Hospital Administrators, Inc. Now here he was, getting a glimpse of the hapless candidate down on the ground-level concourse, listening in as he talked to Dr. Moir, being selected to have a twosome lunch with the man in the company dining room.

Sam was sorry for the man—his name was Kottler. Yet, the fellow wanted this position. So Sam should stick by the rules and conduct his personal interview. As often happened, he could hear Robins' voice and manner within his own.

Kottler would probably please Robins, Sam thought. The way Kottler dressed, alone. He was a large man, over six feet, and he must weigh over two hundred pounds. He wore, on this day, a dark blue, double-breasted blazer with brass buttons. His ballooning tie was of navy blue and white checkerboard silk, as was his pocket handkerchief. In contrast, Sam felt mouselike in his own three-button worsted, and blue on blue striped tie.

Well—he'd made the grade with Robins, whom he admired and often liked. There had even been times during the past months when—yes—he had had an impulse to worship Patric Robins. And about as many times when he hated him.

If, as Robins once had said, and as it seemed, Sam was being trained, honed, whittled, burnished and planed, to do the work which Robins did, must he become the man Robins was? Did he want to become such a man? In detail, or largely. He had not Robins' swift, probing wit, nor his complete and ruthless dedication to the work he did. To be another Robins, Sam would need to study the man much more exactly. Try to pin down, exactly, the sort of man he was.

Not the way he looked! Of course. Two men could not be more different. Robins' knobby face, his expensive, sometimes flamboyant clothes, his deep-set, probing eyes . . .

While Sam—slender, with a youthful, wide-eyed look about him. Neat, usually. Conservative, always. Custom-tailored suits, smooth leather shoes, polished to a dull luster . . .

But looks, similar or different, did not feature. Might this Kottler be deciding that he was overdressed? If so, Sam could reassure him. Though now was not the time to commit himself, or the Ink.

In this, he had learned to be like Robins. To talk, listen, observe—and never give the other fellow a thing on which to hang his own opinions and decisions.

That, and other characteristics of Robins', he had learned, absorbed, and made his own. Consciously, Sam was not an actor. But he often heard Robins' voice in his own, his words in what Sam was saying. He had liked, and learned to practice, Robins' ability to be off-hand, and relaxed. To *appear* to be. That was a pose, merely. For Robins, and for Sam. Especially for Robins.

Sam could have times when he was himself, able to show himself. With Carole, with the Chaffines—and in his writing.

Robins, so far as he knew, never relaxed. He was never simple, or straightforward. The relaxation was a pose, Sam had decided. But such a pose, in itself, must make tremendous demands. And the fiddler would come around, regularly, to be paid.

Could Sam live his life that way? Gaining much, losing everything. Depending on the way a man counted the coins of his life.

Robins was a tremendously successful man in his profession, and certainly he must be rich. He lived in a fine town house; its wrought iron, stone, and shining windows promised luxury and beauty within. But he lived there alone. He had no wife. His children were not with him. Did he have friends?

Sam had heard none spoken of; he had never seen Robins with people he could think were intimate friends. No one here in the office could boast such friendship for all of Robins' joking, casual way with his employees.

The work the man did— Sam was learning to do that work. Was he, to any degree, becoming the man Robins was? That was harder to determine. There were those occasional echoes, which could become his own voice, loud and clear. And if he could become another Robins, would it mean that he, too— Must he lose Carole, and give up his dreams of a family? Must he sacrifice his friends?

As, once before, he had sacrificed friends for his work, leaving Ashby Woods, abandoning the Downes', in order to work for the Foundation? He had come to regret doing that. . . .

And he would regret losing his comradeship with the Chaffines. He could talk over *anything* with Don. The Sunday night suppers in that home . . .

Did Robins have any life of his own? The only chink Sam had ever been allowed to see was the story, half told, of the clergyman, the priest, in that college town. That young man had reached Patric Robins; he had a hold on him. Robins had felt an obligation to help him, to seek him out. . . .

It made Robins become much more of a human being to know that he could be reached, that he would respond. . . . It gave him a kinship with Sam, who was tugged by a similar sense of obligation to Dr. Downes. He had not been able to go to see the old man. Ironically, Robins had been the one to spoil that projected trip.

But the obligation remained. Could Sam, one day, when some sort of goal was attained in his career, some mark reached, could he step to one side and consider such claims? Or must he continue to bury them in his obligations to his work—as he now was doing?

Letting his being stranded in New York spoil his trip with Carole to see a house, letting JoAnn pile up enough rancor that she would flash out at him, risking all that their long friendship meant.

Why couldn't he, as of this minute, as of the time when this luncheon with Kottler was over, and the interviews—why couldn't he go to Robins with his report on the man, lay it on the wide desk, and say, "I'm taking three days off. I am stopping my work for that long to take care of an old debt."

Because he was in debt to Dr. Downes, he did feel an obligation to go there and seek to pay that debt—in some way. . . .

Of course Downes might be surprised to know that there was a debt. All right. That it might be a nebulous obligation made it seem, to Sam, all the more important to be cared for.

What would Robins say, or do, if Sam should go to him with such a declaration of independence? Well, he would probably shrug, wave his hand, and say, "Why not?"

And Sam would go, trailing, no doubt, a half-dozen strings of places to go, things to do, as side trips of that journey.

"So long as you're in Texas . . ."

Sam laughed, to himself, and said something to his luncheon guest about his feelings concerning processed cheese.

And then he returned to his ruminations. Was that the word? It would do. And what he next ruminated about, in direct succession to his thoughts about going to see Downes, was to ask himself if his job, as it increased in importance and responsibility, would give him time and mental peace to write other books. He had not done any work along that line for months, but the urge still was within him. He had even made notes on Robins and the college chaplain.

He would like to do the work he was doing, but he also would like to be a writer. Could he realize that personal aim? Or must it be lost in the size and demands of his professional job?

Robins—well, Robins' personal aim was the Ink. The man had prospered, survived. . . .

Could Sam, taking his place, or occupying it with Robins, make the Ink that important?

And if he could, must he give up all the things he now considered important, the Reuben sandwiches, his paper-stacked desk, the hearthstone of his home, and Carole's—and have in their place something he would consider worthwhile?

He must do some heavy thinking about that.

14

Later that day, Sam attended an executive consultation on Kottler, and at the meeting he discovered that he must go on a quick trip for the Ink.

He would, he planned, do his heavy, decisive thinking then.

He did some.

And he came back to the city on Friday night, early enough to call Carole, even to go to see her. Could he?

"It's snowing, Sam," she demurred.

"Don't you like me with snowflakes on my yellow curls?"

She laughed. "Where in the world did you go this time?" she asked.

"I'll tell you when I see you."

"I'll have things to tell *you*."

"Good. I'll mush right over."

He came to her door more quickly than she had thought possible. "Did you take a taxi?" she asked.

"Indeed not. I drove my own snowmobile."

"You didn't leave it in the street? That's a snow lane."

"I put it down in the garage."

"But, Sam—"

"All things are possible when a man is in love."

"Did the attendant buy that?"

"He said he'd seen me around."

She laughed, and shook her head. "I'm glad you think you are in love. . . ."

"I know I'm in love. Look, let's turn off the lamps, open the curtains and watch the snow come down on the roofs."

"I have something I want to show you, doctor."

He already was turning off lamps. But she insisted—she had pictures, she said. Of a house. "No, Sam, it really is one I think we could get, and like, and live in. Oh, darling, *darling!*"

Well, he wanted to make love, if she was all this ready. He looked at the pictures. Yes, it was a fine house, down among trees—there was a sharply gabled roof, half-timbers, diamond-paned windows. He turned off the lamps and sat beside her on the deep couch, and let her tell him about the house.

It had been built five years before. "So it's all settled, and everything—"

"What everything?"

"Oh, you know. All the little things a new house can turn up. A register that doesn't heat, a faucet that just will drip . . . But this house was custom-designed and built, the man is being transferred. He's a client of ours. . . ."

"I can't live in a coupon clipper's house!"

"Oh, you can, too. Will you look at it, Sam?"

"I'll look at it. I'll take an option on it. Next month I'll move into it with you, if you'll just stop talking about faucets, and let me kiss my girl."

He kissed her, his embrace urgent, his whispers pleading. Carole was sweet and loving. They could be married, she agreed, very soon. They could look at the house this week end, and buy it— Oh, that wouldn't take long.

She had the furniture of this apartment to start with. "And you have your writing table, Sam."

"That should do a lot for the parlor."

"The house has three bedrooms. One is to be your den, your office, a place for you to write."

"Mhmmmn. I haven't written a word in months."

"You will, when we're married. I'll see that you do."

"Yeah. You can take it up with Robins."

"Oh, Sam, we are *not* going to let that man prevent . . ."

"No. We are going to let him buy us a house. Where I can hole up and write and—"

She stirred. "Sam?" she asked.

He kissed her. "We'll buy the house," he said. "We'll be married. . . ."

"When?"

"When can you get the church?"

She laughed happily. "If things go well—you know—the house and your work—maybe early next month. I don't know if we should tell the Ink about it, or not. They'd find ways . . ."

"Do *you* know?" he said, stroking her arm. "Lately I've been thinking . . ." He told her about his ponderings. Or tried to. The room was warm and still. Beyond the windows the snow fell silently, its whiteness bringing a glow inside. The man's arms were strong, Carole was a woman in love, and happy. She wanted to talk about her wedding.

"At the church, Sam, but maybe only the Chaffines."

About her home. "The living room has a studio ceiling. I think, for those long windows, I'll use fiberglass curtains, in a soft green . . ."

She talked, and he said nothing—for so long that she began to notice his silence. She turned to look up at him. "You're thinking," she told him.

He laughed.

"But you *are!*" she accused. "You don't want a house, do you?"

"Oh, Carole . . ."

"Do you?"

He sighed. "Yes," he said. "I want a house. A home with you. But there are times when your house does seem to mean too much to you. More even than our marriage."

She was shocked. "It doesn't!" she cried. "It couldn't."

"But, Carole—"

"There was a time," she agreed, "when I doubted if I wanted it."

"A house?"

For a long minute she was silent. Then she said softly, "If I wanted *you*."

He frowned. "Carole?" he asked.

Her face brightened, and she touched his hand. "Oh, I decided that I did, Sam. I decided that I wanted you very much. Maybe too much."

"We were talking about a house."

"No, we weren't," she said quickly. "Not really. Or—it's all the same thing. Things. The house. Our marriage. You."

He was entirely confused. "Then," he began, "why—"

"Then," she said firmly, "you changed. Your career became the biggest thing in your life—"

He started to protest. "You come uncomfortably close to being right," he admitted. "But I hope I have realized that very thing in time. That's what I've been trying to tell you. I have to have my work, of course. My career. But I have to have you, too."

Her eyes lifted. "The house?" she asked softly.

"Yes. At least, what the house has come to mean to you." He kissed her. "And to me."

It was said, and now he was content to make love to his girl, and she let him. Until—

"I think you should go home, Sam."

"I like it here." He pulled her dress away from her throat and kissed the soft warm skin.

"Sam—"

"Let me stay, Carole." He did not lift his head.

"No. You can't."

Now he looked at her, his face so close, his eyes wide and dark. "I can," he told her. "We can be married—on Monday we'll pick up a license and get our tests. We can be married on Wednesday, all legal and proper. So tonight . . ."

"No, Sam. No."

"Carole . . ."

She was firm, though sorry, too. She said that she was sorry. And finally he put on his coat, grumbling and complaining about going out into the snow . . .

"It's stopped."

. . . and frustrated. "You know, Carole, a girl like you makes things easy for girls like Drozda."

"You can't blackmail me, Sam Fowler."

"You don't believe me? I speak the truth. You'd better face it."

She kissed his cheek. "I'll see you tomorrow, darling. Be careful."

He went down the hall, grumbling that he'd already been too damn careful. "A man should be a *man!*" he called back from the elevator. "And it would be real nice if you'd be a woman!" He disappeared.

The next day was sunny, with the snow beginning to melt. He drove Carole out to the house, and said he liked it. "But you talk too much about curtains," he assured her.

"Those things are important, Sam. Significant."

"Of what?"

"Sam . . ."

"How soon can we be married?"

"I'd think, maybe, in a month."

He took an option on the house, writing a check. He

wanted Carole to agree to meet him for lunch on Monday, to apply for a marriage license and get their medical tests. "You can give your boss notice. . . ."

She said they could talk about that again on Sunday.

"I'm not about to lose a thousand bucks. We'll take up that option and move into that house next month."

She smiled at him.

On Sunday, she agreed to meet him for lunch on Monday. "We've got this far before, and nothing has happened."

"It will this time. You tell your boss . . ."

Don asked Carole if she wanted to stop working.

"Yes," she said, "if I marry Sam."

Sam talked to Don more than he'd done to Carole about his situation and his self-questioning.

"You're in big, son, if you're slated to fill Robins' shoes," Don told him admiringly.

"I know how big it is. What I'm asking myself is, can I do that job, and have some of the other things I want?"

"Carole will help you."

"She will, but I want her to get something out of this, too. I want our life together to be as important as my work."

"A doctor's life, Sam . . ."

"I haven't taken a temperature in years."

"Now, look, Sam . . ."

"I am looking. That's what I've been doing, I tell you. I know all the arguments for my job. A hospital has to function well for the doctors to do their thing well. So that point is accepted. I know any job that involves trouble-shooting will make unexpected demands. I know Robins is breaking me in. He's said he was breaking me in to do the work he is doing. But, Don, if you know the man at all . . ."

"Only by reputation and by sight. But I do know that he is a big man, Sam."

"Yes, he is. Bigger than I'll ever be. I don't have his drive."

"You have your own kind of force. It isn't necessary that you copy Robins. His checked coats and bright green shirts would look ridiculous on you. So would his other external mannerisms and his work methods. What you'll be aiming at will be to accomplish the things he accomplishes. In your own way."

"But that's my hang-up. Can accomplishment result from my way? Can I have my home, my family, a time to write and be myself, and yet do what Robins wants me to do?"

"Have you asked him?"

Sam drew his eyebrows together in a frown. "No, I haven't."

"Isn't he a man you could talk to?"

"I don't really know. A time or two I've shown him—like that blasted fishing trip—then he came right out and told me he liked my ability to decide what I liked to do, and do it."

"Well, then . . ."

"But that was *fish*, Don!"

"I think the way you want to live your life could be almost as important to Dr. Robins."

That night Don told JoAnn that he thought Sam and Carole would make it this time. The boy was pretty serious. . . .

"I hope you're right. Carole thinks he's serious, too, and as starry-eyed as she is, it would just about kill her . . ."

"I believe you can wash my good shirt. He wants me to be best man."

Sam could not have been more serious, nor more sure that his plans would work out. But the next day he had to call off his luncheon date with Carole because there was a full-scale executive meeting. It had been scheduled for several days, but since he was out of town, he'd only found out about it when he reached his desk. Did she understand?

"Of course. I'll shop for drapery materials instead."

"Fiberglass, Carole?"

"A dull mossy green."

"I thought one made boats out of fiberglass."

"And curtains."

"All right, then. I'll call you tonight."

He did call her, but later that same night he took a plane for Chicago. He was away for ten days attending meetings, traveling—to San Francisco and Seattle, to Denver and St. Paul—across the country and halfway back, consulting, making his speeches.

"A hospital is not a factory."

"A hospital is not a hotel."

Just about the time he had determined to regulate the amount of time and energy he would give to the Ink, the pace of his job quickened and the claims upon him became greater than ever.

He returned to the city and had his usual Wednesday night dinner date with Carole. He also told her that he was leaving again the next day. He and Robins were to sit in on the planning of a new hospital.

"Do you have to go, Sam? If Robins is there?"

"I have to go. I know, and Robins knows, that I have never actually been a part of a hospital planning setup. In the job I'm doing, and hope to do, there will be a tremendous lot for me to learn."

"I suppose."

"I'm disappointed, too, sweetheart."

"How long . . . ?"

"I don't know about that, either. But I can tell you one thing which chirked me up. Robins is taking along the detailed administrative plans which I made for Sinai Hospital. Perhaps they will be used."

"That is good, Sam."

"It is very good."

It was good. Sam knew that it was. He was sorry about leaving Carole and the planning they would be doing—but if

222

she understood . . . He would call her often and get her to do the things needed. There was time still. . . .

Planning a big new hospital, he discovered, was exciting. Robins and Sam could confer with the board and the architect and solve all the problems on paper. Service, care, quiet, food—all the problems a hospital could know.

There were continuous meetings with the board, the staff, the housekeeper, the surgeons. Every detail must be thought of and ironed out. There was paper work, and more paper work. Sam kept a secretary busy, and himself. He slept when he could, but hardly ever for a full night. Ideas had a way of popping into his mind late at night or at four in the morning. He could thrash out some problem in the quiet of his bedroom, then bring it up, solved and planned, at a meeting on the next day. And the day after that. He worked out the use of conveyers with which to distribute supplies throughout the hospital complex. He took swift trips away to see things suggested by the architect, or some board member, as being effective in other hospitals. He went to talk to people. . . .

Robins was in the same swirl, but he was able to maintain his relaxed air. Sam filled in the crevices.

"We'll iron that out," Robins would assure a doctor.

Sam did the ironing.

He doubted if any other project would require more, even as much, pre-thinking as did the plans for a large hospital. There was so much detail, and every detail must be considered. From heat and air conditioning to the sorting of laundry. "It can be upsetting to a sick woman," Sam assured the architects, "to find her bedsheet stamped MORGUE."

The men laughed.

"It can happen," Sam assured them. He told of his laundry experience in Pennsylvania. "I know mix-ups don't need to happen," he declared.

"You get along well with the architects," Robins told him

when they returned to the hotel. "Do you have a full set of plans here?"

"Fuller, and more, plans than the architects do," Sam told him.

"I wanted to see what you had done, if anything, about the kosher food situation. This is to be a Jewish hospital, remember."

"Yes, and it expects to serve non-orthodox and non-Jewish in a proportion of three to one. I have that all worked out."

"The architect said you had. I'd like to see . . ."

Robins had "seen." Sam was sure that he had. But this was Robins' way to approach another question, another consideration. So, on a large table up in the suite, Sam unrolled the blueprints and the plans. He took off his coat, picked up a pencil, and used it to point out the areas as he discussed them. "I'm putting the orthodox patients into separate units, sir. A pavilion, if you like, of their own. Floor by floor, ward by ward. They will have their own kitchen and kitchen smells. The non-Jewish will be in these other areas, and can have their bacon and the aromas which are pleasant to them. I believe . . ."

"But that's segregation!" cried Robins. "You can't . . ."

"Why not?" Sam stood calmly looking at the boss.

"Well, it will be too damn expensive, for one thing. My good Lord, man, separate recovery rooms alone would add . . ."

"We don't need separate recovery rooms, sir, nor operating rooms, nor delivery rooms—"

"But you said . . ."

"I said the patients' rooms would be segregated, and they will be. As for the other services, how many times do you serve bacon in the recovery room? Or, for that matter, *gefilte* fish?"

He won. It was later that he realized he had stood up to Robins, and won.

Just then . . .

"The board has asked me," said Robins, "if you would consider coming here as administrator of this hospital."

Sam stared at him, rolling up the sheets of plans, sliding them into the tubes. "Me?" he asked.

"Yes. Beginning now. To supervise the building, manage the fund raising . . ."

Sam shook his head. "Not me. I happen to think the administrator should not have to take on hospital fund raising."

"Most of them do."

"Not this boy."

"Would you still like to be administrator here?"

"I could do it," Sam agreed. "Right now I just want to get all our plans and specifications down on paper, and then go back to my girl."

Dr. Robins nodded. "How soon . . . ?"

"As soon as possible. I—" He took out his wallet, found the little red and white calendar, looked at it, and stared. "Oh, my God," he said softly. "Oh—my—dear—God."

Robins took a step toward him. "Fowler?" he asked. "What's the matter?"

Sam looked up at him in anguish. "Everything is the matter!" he cried. *"Everything!"*

"You look sick."

"I am sick. I've blown my whole life to bits. I— Excuse me, sir. I have to telephone."

He turned and walked fast into his bedroom, closing the door behind him. He picked up the phone, and stopped to think where Carole would be at this hour, four in the afternoon. The time zone was the same. Indeed, he had been spending these days, these weeks, only three hundred miles away from her. But his time had been so filled, twenty hours a day, and every day, that he had forgotten . . . He had called her. Hadn't he? Yes, at least early in the project. But lately—not since he came back . . .

Four o'clock. He might catch her at the office, but he had

better wait until she could have reached the apartment. He had so much to say to her, so much he would say, and promise. . . .

He threw himself on the bed, his wrist lifted so that he could watch the slow crawl of his watch's minute hand.

To forget! The option had expired days ago! Their hoped-for wedding day . . . Why, by now Carole should have been his wife, they should be living in their home. If not that, in a larger suite in his hotel, or an apartment at Manor House until their own home . . . This was what day? Wednesday.

He laughed dryly. He should be having dinner with his wife-who-should-have-been.

In the hour he waited, Robins once knocked on his door. "Are you all right, Sam?" he asked.

"Yes," Sam barked. "I'm just waiting on a phone call."

"Shall I order dinner up here?"

Sam did not answer him.

At five, he made his first try.

"Your party does not answer, sir."

Sam said he would try again. He went over to the dresser, and to the closet. He would go home—as soon as he possibly could. He would pack now. He put his hand to his brow. Did he have laundry out? He could not remember. He could not remember anything! Except how to separate bedsheets in a hospital laundry, what color to paint the walls of the children's ward, and how to set the beds in orthopedics. He—

In fifteen minutes, he tried again, and this time Carole's voice came through, crystal-clear.

"Carole!" he cried. "It's Sam!"

"Yes."

Well, he could not blame her. He took a deep breath. "I looked at the calendar today," he said. "Carole, you cannot guess how sorry I am! What can I say to show you . . . ?"

"There is nothing to say, Sam. I don't want to talk about it at all."

226

"Look, Carole . . . I'm coming home."

"Is the job finished?"

"Not quite. But I'm coming home to talk to you."

"I tell you, I don't want to talk about it, Sam."

"It just—the time slipped away from me. I wish you had reminded me."

"I tried to call you, Sam. You were not at the hotel. I called your office. I thought Mrs. Drozda could tell me . . ."

Sam groaned. Mrs. Drozda had made the trip with him and Robins. She was down the hall in a suite of her own, with her typewriter. He—

"When you have finished the job and have come back," Carole was saying, "perhaps we can talk." She hung up.

Sam sat staring at the telephone. He had blown his whole life. No hospital, however fine, was worth that. No man, Robins or anyone, had a right to ask so much of another man.

Oh, God, oh, God! What would he *do?*

The sounds of the big hotel came to him, muted—hurrying feet, voices and laughter—dishes jingling—

He went to the closet and took out his topcoat. He could not face eating dinner with Robins, having to be polite to the man. He crossed the living room of the suite. Robins was not around. The roses were there, the books and the magazines. The big table with the rolls of plans and specifications.

He would go for a walk.

He did walk, for an hour, for two hours, ignoring the recognized dangers of the city streets at night, ignoring the cold and his hunger. Perhaps his torment showed in his face. He had never been so low in his life, nor so discouraged. He would go back and tell Robins what he could do with his lousy job! He would—

The whole sorry mess was his fault. He should have called Carole every night, no matter what the hour or his preoccupation with conveyer belts and lavatories. She had *told* him what the house—a house—meant to her!

He didn't know what she could think, or would think. The sound of her voice . . . She had been a stranger, talking to someone she did not like.

He stopped at a drugstore, asked for directions, and walked the necessary block to a corner where he waited for the bus.

He would return to the hotel, eat some dinner, no matter what, and tell Robins that he wanted to go back to his job at the Foundation, or be assigned to some job where the day had twenty-four hours. Eight hours to work, eight hours to sleep, eight hours for himself—and Carole.

15

He reached the hotel, and went up to the suite. Robins was reading the newspaper. "Have you had dinner, Sam?" he asked.

"No."

"Then I'll order."

"I'm not hungry."

Robins was talking to room service.

Sam went into his own room, he hung up his coat, changed his shoes—suddenly tired. He would have liked to take a warm bath and go to bed. He would have liked to call for a plane reservation and leave town. He would have liked . . .

He put on a clean shirt, a fresh tie, and came back to the living room of the suite. He would finish this job, then go home. . . .

He sat down and picked up his fork. He had no idea of what he was eating. He didn't care. He wished he were with Carole, making silly jokes about sheep chops, and—

"I'm sorry, sir," he said to Robins. "I'm afraid I wasn't listening."

"You're worried about something, Sam."

Sam glanced at him. "Yes, I am."

Robins nodded. "In this work we are doing," he said,

pouring wine into a glass, "we who do it cannot think of anything but the work and *do* the work. I mean, you must make a choice. . . ."

Sam picked up his water glass and drank from it, thinking of what he could say, and be diplomatic. . . .

Instead . . . He put the glass back on the table. Its sparkling side was etched with the monogram of the hotel. He leaned forward, and he spoke bluntly. "I have decided, Dr. Robins," he said, "that this work, this job, as we have been doing it, is not what I want to do."

"You are very good at it."

"I'm qualified. I have intelligence, and a strong body. But I do not—repeat, *do not*—want to work all the time, have no personal life. . . ."

Robins nodded. He leaned back in his chair, and gazed at Sam. "Something has happened," he said. He put up his hand. "I am not asking you to tell me, Sam. But I can see that something has happened. As for what you say you do, and do not, want to do, I'll agree that you need not work as we have been working this past month."

"As *I* have been working."

"Yes, as you have been working. This was a big project, and you have done well with it."

"I know it was important, sir. I've learned a lot. But this thing of —"

"I understand. You think you don't want to do the big jobs. And there are smaller ones, right within our organization. I offered you the one here, as administrator for this unbuilt hospital. I could take Curry out of Mt. Sinai and put you there."

In a quick flash, Sam could see himself at Sinai, inspecting the refrigerators, talking to the plumber, sitting on a bench overlooking the operating room, spending three hours at his desk on paper work—correspondence, records, the outline of a speech . . .

"You'd be good at any one of those jobs, so good that you probably could make an eight-hour day out of the one you chose. You could spend your evenings at home, or with your friends, at night sleep beside your wife."

Sam felt his face get hot. Robins could read him entirely too closely.

"Or," said Robins, picking up the round bone of the fresh ham steak which he had been eating, nibbling at it delicately, "you could do bedside doctoring. I've known you to speak nostalgically of doing that. Though, if you will remember, the hours are not too dependable there." He tossed the bone back to his plate, wiped his fingers briskly with his napkin, pushed his chair away from the table, and got to his feet.

"A man can always choose what he wants to do, Sam!" he cried, his voice rasping. "Look about you! Think of the medics who graduated with you. I happen to know a couple of them. There's Holt, a capable surgeon who is building up a class practice. He keeps fairly regular hours medically, but there is no limit to the time he has to spend on symphony and art museum boards, playing golf, smiling at the ladies. Then there's your friend, Chaffine. He's a good pediatrician. You could be Chaffine; he probably could do the work you do. But you chose—as a man does choose. You went into organization medicine. You did a good job for Harper; you, of your own will, came to us to do a bigger job. We wanted you, we needed you—or someone who could be trained to do the big ones. We decided that you were that one."

He walked to the window, looked out and down, then turned to face Sam again, taking out two matchbooks and holding them between his fingertips.

"Someone had to do the job you've been doing this past month, Sam. Someone has to do the big jobs. There is room at the top, as there is always room at the top. A crying need for the big man who can do the big job. Now I can guess at what the job has cost you this past month. I can guess because I know what it can cost.

"But someone, Sam, has to do the big jobs. Someone has to plan, to think, to run about the country, using his imagination, using his own creative ability, and finding other imaginations and creative abilities to use."

As Robins had found Sam, who had used his imagination, and his creative ability.

"A job like ours," Robins was saying, "requires many things of a man. Self-denial is one of those things, concentration is another, and both can be costly, if you figure the costs."

"A man has to figure the costs," said Sam, his voice croaking.

Robins went on talking, as if he had not spoken.

"You say you want fixed hours, a job that has an established routine. All right, but by now you know that in hospital, medical work, someone has to solve the overall problems that will give you other guys the continued security of a well-planned hospital, that will give you your homes, and families, and the PTA. For some years I have been providing that planning. I won't claim that my life is an example for any man to follow. But I have no apologies, Sam, for training you, and the other men in H.A., to do the work we are doing."

Sam stood up. "I know you are right," he said, his tone muffled. "There has been a job to do here. You seem to be doing it. As for me, I'm ready to call myself a failure."

"Not on the job, you're not," Robins told him. "You may —I suspect you may have flubbed your personal affairs. But if you're really good, as I think you are, you can handle both things."

Sam glanced at him. "My lip is split," he said wryly. "I'm going to bed!"

16

That night he wrote a letter to Carole; the next morning he rose early and set himself to finishing the job.

"Like killing snakes," Robins described his frenzied activity.

"I've promised to be at home by the end of the week."

"You could go, and come back if necessary."

"It won't be necessary."

His appointment book was written solid-black, every half hour accounted for, up to midnight. He slept six hours. He got Mrs. Drozda up at seven to take his dictation, to put his papers in order.

Saturday morning he flew home.

He dropped his bags at the hotel, went to the office for an hour. There, among his personal mail, he found an engraved invitation to the Harper Awards dinner. He laughed, and tossed it to one side.

At eleven, he appeared at Carole's door. "I'm not going to talk, or force you to talk," he said at once. "But I am hungry for a Reuben, and I want you to eat one with me."

She stepped back to admit him, her eyes wide and dark. He kissed her, but not as if he were pressing any claim. They went out for their sandwich; during the afternoon they drove downriver, and he suggested a movie for that evening. They talked about their friends. Sam told about the people he had come to know during the past month, he asked about the Chaffines. "Are we going out there tomorrow?"

It was almost like a first date; they carefully skirted any apologies and recriminations. They talked about interesting things. Carole wore a dress that was new to him, and she said he could use a haircut. "Unless you are trying for side-burns?"

"I am trying for a new personality," he admitted.

"There was nothing wrong with your old one."

He did not pursue the matter; he was not ready. And there was still a brittleness about Carole. . . . She was not wearing his ring. But he did not discuss that either.

Both of them had things to say, and would say them. But later.

"I'll come around early tomorrow," he said when he left her. "We can fill in an hour or two before going out to the Chaffines'."

She smiled at him, and closed the door.

On Sunday, he planned, he would get Carole to talk to him, to say all the things he knew anyway, but which she must have a chance to say. Perhaps then he could talk to her, and tell her of his own decisions. Maybe she thought she knew what he wanted to say to her. She did not.

So he planned. But at nine-thirty the next morning, the hotel desk called and asked him if he would see a Mr. Ginsburg.

Ginsburg? For a moment Sam could not place the name. Then—

"Yes!" he said. "Does he want to come up?"

Ginsburg did come up, his small, bright eyes eager to examine this place where "Doc" Fowler lived. Yes, he could take a cup of coffee. Had Doc been away?

"Did you try to reach me earlier?" Sam asked.

"Yeah. I even tried the office. You see, my mother sent me these clippings, and she thought maybe, as a doctor yourself, you could help the Downes'."

Sam turned to look sharply at the little man. "What's happened to the Downes'?" he asked.

Ginsburg held out the small sheaf of newspaper clippings. Sam took them over the the desk. Behind him, Ginsburg drank his coffee and watched Doc. Now and then Sam asked a question without turning around. He reached for his legal pad and began to organize what he had in hand.

Once the telephone rang. It was Carole. She was starting for church, she said. Would he like to come to the apartment as early as one o'clock, or one-thirty? "I'll make us a sandwich." Her voice still was that of a nice girl arranging a date with a possible man.

"I'll be glad to come," said Sam in the same sort of voice.

He resumed his scribbling on the pad, sifting through the clippings. The Downes' were in trouble, that seemed evident. Four years ago, it seemed, the old doctor had taken on a partner in his hospital and clinic. Two years ago he had become ill and had lost his leg. And, Sam supplied, he had not been able to attend to things in person.

Bad luck seemed to have compounded with bad management, and perhaps worse. There had been a fire—the old doctor, Ginsburg said, had paid through his nose.

Then there was a suit for malpractice, and another legal involvement concerning the hospital drug audit. Again, as owner, Dr. Downes was liable, and felt that he was. Sam questioned Ginsburg as to dates. The troubles had covered eighteen months.

Sam checked the details from the clippings. The fire, the new doctor, Dr. Downes' amputation, the lawsuit—and one brief paragraph which said that Miss Judy Downes had taken on the position of administrator of the hospital and clinic.

Sam stared at his sheet of yellow paper. Blue lines ran

across it, a red vertical line marked the left margin. His own handwriting . . .

"Maybe these things are not all what they seem to be," he said aloud to Ginsburg.

"A drug audit, Doc . . ."

"Yes, I know. But surely the old man was insured against malpractice suits."

"You'd think he would be. Only, he's got to be old. Judy would try, but she probably doesn't know about such things. My mother thinks the old man stands to lose everything he has."

The hospital would have to close down. . . .

Sam stood up. "Thanks for telling me, Ginsburg," he said, summoning an effort to be cordial. "I'll try to think of something I could do."

"Well, I hoped . . . I know your company gets hospitals out of trouble. I knew you used to be friends with the Downes', and you wrote that book about 'em."

"Yes. Thank you."

He walked Ginsburg to the elevator. He came back to his desk and looked at his notes. To make them he had folded back the sheet on which, last night, he had made what, during the past two years, he had learned to call a project sheet.

At the top of it he had stated the desired achievement. Below that he had made a detailed outline of what he would do about Carole and himself. And their life. There were various sections. 1, 2, 3—and so on. His plan all but filled his sheet of paper. 1—Carole and himself. 2. Job. Robins. (It had to be an important thing in relation to 1) 3. House. He took up his pencil and added a fourth category. 4. Downes.

Impatiently he waited for one o'clock, for one-fifteen. Above and before everything else, he must talk to Carole, really *talk* to her.

Again she met him with the gay, impersonal brightness of

236

a girl entertaining a young man with whom she might want to become better acquainted. Today that atmosphere might be the best one for Sam's purposes.

Carole was looking very pretty in a plaid pleated skirt and a sweater. She planned minute steak sandwiches, she said. Would Sam mind waiting that minute?

Couldn't he help?

Yes. Did he want his bread toasted? And would he select the condiments he would enjoy?

The fragrance of the steaks filled the air. The sandwiches were made—two for Sam, one for Carole.

"You've lost weight," she told him as he seated her at the small table.

"I've been working hard."

"I know. Planning a hospital."

"Yes. Doing things, and doing them over. Trying to think of everything, realizing that I'd forgotten more than I'd included."

"What sort of things?" She was making the man talk about his own interests. He would give her five minutes of that.

"Oh," he said, accepting his cup of coffee, "things like the routing of stretchers from emergency to ward, from ward to o.r. Plotting elevator use. Figuring a way to have enough electric circuits to prevent a total power loss." He bit into his sandwich.

"You must have a tremendous knowledge of hospitals," Carole said politely.

"This is a way to acquire that knowledge," Sam assured her. "I could work as a staff M.D. for fifty years and not learn as much about what a hospital is, does, and should be." He made a wry face. "Also about what a hospital isn't, doesn't, and shouldn't be."

She leaned toward him. "But not one of *your* hospitals, Sam."

He laughed. "Look," he said, "hospitals come pretty far down on my list of what I want to talk about to you."

She ate some of her sandwich, she drank some of her coffee. She looked up at him. Her dark eyes against her fair skin and hair always struck Sam with Carole's particular kind of beauty. "I suppose," she said, "today you want to talk about us."

He shook his head. "No," he said. "Today I have to talk about *me*, Carole."

She sat back, looking at him. She was puzzled.

"Look," said Sam. "What time do you want to go out to the Chaffines'?"

"Oh. Four would be soon enough."

"Mhmmmn. Well, can't we finish our lunch—the sandwiches are very good, incidentally. We'll wash up, and then sit comfortably and talk. I have a lot to say."

"Well . . ." she said uncertainly. "All right."

"About me," he repeated. "Last night I made a schedule of things to set straight about us, but this morning something has come up, Carole. I'll need your help."

"All right," she said again.

They finished their sandwiches and drank their coffee. Sam ate a tangerine. He carried the dishes to the kitchen. Carole washed the plates and cups and put them in the drainer. Sam folded the cloth and laid the napkins beside it.

Then he took Carole's apron, hung it over a chair, ignoring her frown of protest. She was not one to drape chairs with clothing. He led her to the couch, he opened the draperies so that they could see out, and he sat down beside her, not too close. He made no attempt to touch her. He wanted to touch her, but first they must talk. And with maximum concentration.

He meant to talk to her about Robins, about his plans.

. . .

But now he must talk to Carole about the Downes'. He was sure he had mentioned them both and Ashby Woods to her before. But he must tell her specifically now, because he meant to give money to the doctor and Judy. At least, he meant to do that. A percentage of his book royalties. He knew that he did not owe this to them, but his conscience said that they had a claim upon him.

He glanced at Carole. She was looking at him warily, curiously. He supposed she had been prepared to ward off any attempt he might make to resume his relationship with her, ready to forget that he had been away for six weeks, that he had lost the house on which she had been planning.

"I suppose you will want to know," he said slowly, and he heard the remoteness in his own voice, "what my plans are."

Carole folded a pleat of her skirt. "That would be nice," she said coldly.

He glanced at her. "I have been considering some," he assured her.

She said nothing.

"I thought, last night, that I knew what I wanted to do. This morning something came up—and I have been considering the plan of going back and starting over in my medical career."

She looked at him in alarm. "What do you mean by *back?*" she asked, her voice no longer cool.

"What it says. Back. Way back. To . . ." He leaned forward, his clasped hands between his knees. And he told her about Dr. Downes, how he had first come to the little town. He talked about the big house, and the hospital, about the work which Sam himself had done there for a year—and he told about Judy, tenderly describing the girl.

Carole listened to him, appalled. Had he looked at her, he would have seen that she was appalled. "You're in love with that girl!" she cried at last.

He sat smiling, not seeing the room, nor the view beyond the window. "I don't know," he said slowly. "If I ever was, I did nothing about it."

"But you are in love with her. You want to go back to her!"

Sam straightened, turned, and looked at Carole. "Yes," he said. "I do want to go back."

Her face was white. He still was not seeing her. To go back, to hold a patient's hand strongly, to feel the laboring, faltering pulse of an old man's heart. . . . "Perhaps," he mused, "I have already been 'back' many times. Writing my book—I lived there for the three years it took me to do it."

Carole remembered. That girl in the book. He had been in love with her. . . .

"Sometimes," Sam said reminiscently, "I think I owe everything I have and am to Ashby Woods." Though not Carole. He didn't owe her. . . .

"How much *do* you owe them?" she asked, her tone blunt. "And for what? Exactly, Sam. No dream abstractions . . ."

When he did not answer at once, she jogged his arm. "Sam!" she cried. "You've got to talk to me."

"I am talking to you, Carole."

"Only because I'm the one here. Not because I feature in what you are thinking."

"But you do feature. If I give money to the Downes', if I go back there . . ."

"And marry that girl instead of me."

She got up from the couch, her brown and orange plaid skirt swirling; she almost ran out of the room, and came back quickly. She held out her hand. In its palm was her engagement ring. Her hand trembled, and her voice broke when she tried to speak. Sam thought she meant to give him the ring. He was about as frightened as she appeared to be.

"Two years ago," Carole said, and gulped. "Two years ago

you gave me this ring. Didn't you mean it? Didn't you mean it at all?"

Sam sighed with relief. He stood up and drew her to him. He bent his head and kissed her warmly, then he took the ring from her hand and put it on her finger. "There," he said. "Keep it there. You'll wear the thing out, taking it off and on." She stirred in his arms, and he tightened them. "Of course I meant it when I gave you that ring. I said I loved you—I meant that, too."

She gulped again and rubbed her cheek against his coat sleeve. "I never know," she said sadly.

"Well, you should know. Whatever I do, wherever I am, Carole. I know it's been hard on you—but a man has to have his work, just as he has to have his girl—"

She straightened. "The trouble is, Sam, you've never decided which is the most important."

"Oh, yes, I have," he said quickly.

She leaned back to look up into his face, waiting eagerly for his answer.

"I've decided that a man has to have both, Carole. I do. Because I can't have one without the other. And if you are honest, *you* cannot. Me, and my work. They come in a package."

She freed herself and walked to the window. She stood thinking, turning the ring on her finger. Then she nodded and looked at him. "You're right," she said. "And—thank you for saying that to me."

He laughed, and put his arm around her shoulder. "I'm sorry you were upset," he said.

He knew that he didn't love Judy Downes. He hoped he could show Carole that he did not. He must show her, or lose her. "Let's sit down again," he said, "and talk."

"About that girl."

"About everything. And do you know?" His tone brightened. "Among my mail yesterday morning, I found an invitation to the Harper Awards dinner."

"But . . ."

"Yes, It was last Monday night. But we could have gone to it, Carole."

"And seen Lorraine. Honestly! The women in your life!"

"Pooh. There's only one woman in my life. Lorraine knows that, if you don't. We could have gone to that dinner, me pretty as a picture in my ten-year-old Tux . . ."

"You could have rented a new one. . . ."

"I could have. And you could have worn that shiny white dress I like, the long one. . . ."

"It's pale yellow."

"Looks white, the way I remember it. We would have gone—there would have been a crowd. A glittering assemblage. Chandeliers, flowers, and stuff."

"And Lorraine."

"Yes, she would have glittered, too. I don't remember. Does she wear hats to those bashes? If she does, her hat would certainly have glittered."

Carole laughed, feeling comfortable again, and sure of Sam.

"She would have greeted us graciously," he continued.

"And seated us behind a post."

"Oh, now really!"

"If you took me with you, it would have been behind a post, actually or figuratively."

"All right. And we would have craned our necks to see her give one of her awards to the same Dr. Hauser I was plugging for when I left the Foundation."

"Big of her."

"She'd expect me to think so. When I went up to thank her, she would have said something feminine like, 'You didn't think I would do this, did you, Sam?' And then she might have asked me if I was grateful."

Carole turned on the couch to look at him. "And what would you have said?"

"Oh, something terribly witty and cutting. Like, 'I am sure Dr. Hauser is grateful.'" He smiled at the girl beside him.

And a tear ran down her cheek.

"Carole!" he cried, fishing for the spare, folded, clean handkerchief he always carried in his hip pocket.

She sniffled into it. "I know," she said, "that it is wrong for me to be jealous, Sam. I was jealous of Lorraine. I was jealous of your work, and that certainly is wrong. And I'm just going to believe it would be wrong for me to be jealous of this girl. . . ."

"Of *Judy?*" he asked, unbelieving.

She nodded.

He comforted her. "If there is any *wrong* in all of this," he said, "it would have to be the wrong I'd do you by marrying you, and holding you to the sort of life I am going to live. I think I should not ask that of you, Carole."

She wiped her eyes again, and looked closely into his face. "But you can't do that to me, Sam Fowler!" she said earnestly. "Fifteen minutes after you put my ring back on my finger . . . Look. I am going to be different. I am not going to care how hard you work on your job, how long you stay away. . . ."

"Because you'll go with me."

"Because I'll go with you," she agreed. "And I won't care about secretaries and other women."

"Because you'll be right there, ahead of them."

"You're teasing me."

"I wouldn't do a thing like that."

"But I'm serious. You are right. You do owe things to those people in Texas. Downes? Even if you loved that girl, Judy—it was years ago. And if you go down there now, I'll go with you. As your wife, Sam Fowler! As your *wife!*"

He laughed at her, and hugged her, and laughed again. "You're wonderful," he said.

"And someday you'll write a book about *me,* won't you?"

His laughter died away. He kissed her. "All my heroines are you, Carole," he told her.

She snuggled against him. "I'm so happy," she confessed. "I'll believe even a corny thing like that."

"I'll write that book," he promised. "And we'll have your house, too. Not as a symbol, my darling, but a house—a home—where we'll live together. It will be good, that house."

The hands of the clock moved steadily, and eventually she became aware of them. "Are we doing all your talking?" she asked dreamily.

"Enough. Enough."

"You're right, you know, Sam."

"Always."

"*Listen* to me. I'm going to say that you're right, that you must do the right thing by those people. Pay them some of the book money, go back there—whatever it takes."

"And you will go with me? The wind tears across those prairies, Carole. There's dust, blizzards in the winter—"

"Whatever it takes," she agreed. "Do you think you could, or would want to, pick up your Dr. Downes' work, and do it?"

Sam sat up straight, startled that she was ready to agree even to that. But he could do it. He had a quick vision of himself as a one-man clinic. "I'd love it," he said. "And certainly I could do it. Not only that. I could do it, and be excited about the doing of it."

"If that's what you want, Sam. . . ."

"No," he said slowly, "what I want is the job that is hard on you."

She lifted his hand and kissed it. "You're an honest man, Sam Fowler. And I love you."

244

"I don't have to do that job, IF I do it—"

"Of course you're going to do your job with Robins!"

"I started to say that I wouldn't have to do it the way he does it. I wouldn't have to be Robins, or even try to be."

"No," she agreed, and waited.

"It is good work, and work I believe in, Carole. But I could do it my way. . . ."

"Would that be what Robins wants?"

Sam glanced at her and frowned. "I hope so," he said. "It's what he would get." He stood up. "And yes, it is what he would take. I'll do it, sweetheart, and have the other things I want, too. I think I can manage that. I hope so, because someone has to do the big jobs." He heard the echo of Robins' voice, and ignored it. "Someone has to be the man on top."

"And you'll be that big man," Carole assured him. "Because you are really big, Sam. Bigger than Robins, you know."

He laughed and looked at his watch. "Don't tell him. Look, I suppose we have to go out to the Chaffines'."

"Don't you want to?"

"Do you?"

She smiled and shook her head. "They expect us. But, Sam —" Swiftly there was a rosy color in her cheeks, and her eyes were shining. "Let's come home early."

A happy man, he watched her. "If that's what you want," he said deeply.

"It is. And tonight, Sam—you may stay here if you want."

He strode to her then, and took her into his arms. "Carole?" he asked.

She clung to him. "Oh, I have missed you, Sam!" she cried. "I have missed you so dreadfully. I determined that never again . . ."

He kissed her. He kissed her hard. "I won't stay tonight," he whispered. "But tomorrow . . ."

She laughed excitedly "You've said all that before. License, blood tests—give up my job—"

"I know I've said it before. Twice before. But this time . . ."

"Unless Robins . . ."

"This time," he promised, "Robins will have to wait. He will have to wait. Some things are important. Like you and me, fiberglass curtains . . ."

"And we're going to have them, aren't we, Sam?"

"We'll have them all," he promised. "We'll have them all."